I0763431

CHASING KANE

By Warren Allen

First Edition

Printed in the United States of America

Published by Allen Literary Works, LLC

ISBN: 978-0-9962394-3-1

Library of Congress Control Number: 2018964463

For more information, visit:

www.iamwarrenallen.com

Editors: Tricia Scott, Char J. Patterson, and Emma Liddle

Cover Design by Matthew Morran

CONTENTS

DEDICATION

How do you address a queen? A true question of great thought. Do you bow at her majestic presence? Do you honor her royalty when she enters a room? Do you give tribute to her splendor when she is near? Or do you speak kindly of her existence? Again I ask, how you do address a Queen? Surely, her kingdom can answer that, for you see a queen's reception is found in the response of her people. There are two extraordinary queens that I dedicate this book to, as I am their people and they are mine.

My Grandmother, Rutha Mae Allen "Mema," and my Great Great Aunt, Dorothy Bennett; although they have gone on to be with the LORD, I still speak kindly and boldly of their existence. Two lives well spent, full of love well received. So how do you address a queen? You address her by giving her the love she deserves, and the respect she's earned. I honor you both now and forever, two queens whose reigns still continue. For I know that you merely traded your earthly crowns, for heavenly ones.
Until we see each other again…love you always,
Warren

CHAPTER 1

HARBOR STONE

Edge City has always been and still remains a very dangerous place for newcomers to find themselves. Its allure and beauty are two-sided. On one hand, it offers the fulfillment of unspoken fantasies; on the other, a cruel and unforgiving fist lies in the shadows to deliver a mighty blow to those who come to its streets ill-prepared. Indeed, it is a city that doesn't suffer fools lightly, although it's not all bad. When navigated correctly, it can offer untold riches and the obtainment of any goals that a person may deem worthy to pursue. Yes, it is a city of dichotomy and offers no apologies for it.

However, it's not the only city in the world that deals in absolutes. No, there *is* another city whose streets can be just as unforgiving, and its underlying nature as cold as a thousand winters. A city whose dark alleys are to be circumvented wisely but slyly enough so that you don't cause any offense. This is a city that forces its inhabitants to play by its rules, regardless if they find them fair or not. This is a city that owes no one, and yet makes promises to everyone. It promises to stay the same if you do. It promises to give you more if you give it more. Sometimes the promises are empty; nevertheless, they're promises just the same. After all, this is the city where Kane Edwards was born, this is *Harbor Stone.*

"OK!!!! OK!!!"

"Please don't drop me!....Oh *God*...Please don't!! I'm begging you, just give me more time!" The man desperately hollered.

It was cold outside that night, and the air had a certain sharpness to it that helped magnify sound. In this case, the sound being magnified was the bellowing yelps coming from a man who had made too many mistakes. The man's name was Ben Larson and his cries were no doubt heard by someone; however, not by anyone who would lend assistance. People in this city knew all too well the sounds of a desperate man. They also knew that anyone screaming at this hour probably wouldn't make it through the night. So there was no need to get the police involved.

The man was hanging upside down over a ledge, about twelve stories up. As he hung there, he would fidget constantly but not too much for fear of being dropped. It was impressive he hadn't passed out by now. It was less than a minute ago that he watched the two quarters that were in his right pocket silently fall out. They almost seemed to float to the ground as they flipped slowly through the night's air, disappearing out of his sight as they descended into darkness. All of this was made possible by the beastly behemoth that was holding Mr. Larson over the ledge by one of his ankles. The beast had a name, Marco, but more importantly, he had a master whose orders he obeyed without question. Marco held the man's ankle with a grip that would rival an anaconda. He squeezed it so hard that he heard the sound of the man's ankle break only moments earlier.

"Agh!...Ok…please...please..I'll pay…I'll pay it…I swear!!!" cried the man.

Marco stood there like a tomblike hulk, awaiting further instructions. His face was still, void of any emotion as he watched the man squirm. His eyes were nothing more than windows into a heartless desert, immune to all the intense violence they had witnessed over the years. The city had bred him to be cold, his ears were numb to the desperate cries of a dying man. He had seen this scene play out too many times to feel anything for the poor soul that found itself in his deadly path. His reputation was one that need not be uttered by the lips of men; it lived in the fear of their unspoken thoughts. After all, he was an enforcer for the most dangerous crime family in the city.

"I'm sorry…just don't let me fall!" the man continued to sob.

Marco paid no attention to what he was saying because there was another voice far more prevalent than this whining one. As he stood there, that other voice he was waiting for suddenly emerged from the rooftop's shadows behind him.

"You know Ben, I was pretty good at math in school."

A small flame flickered in the darkness from the cigarette lighter this mystery man was holding. He had already finished his cigarette and enjoyed playing with the lighter. It helped pass the time in heavy moments such as this. He took several steps forward, the moonlight illuminating his visage with each step to reveal his identity. Truthfully, there was no mystery to the man, since all parties present knew who he was. His name was Rico Coloso, heir to a very infamous throne. His last name struck fear in the hearts of many, not necessarily because of him but because of his father; Nero.

"Something about this just isn't adding up" continued Rico. By now, Rico was standing next to Marco, peering over the ledge as he watched Ben continue to beg for his life. Some would say that Rico was too young for this line of work; he was just shy of thirty. But he didn't mind it and enjoyed being in this position. In fact he craved it.

"Mr. Coloso, please! I'm sorry, I won't do it again! I swear!" hollered Ben in a desperate tone of voice.

"Yeah but see that's the thing Ben. It's like I told you, something's just not adding up," said Rico.

He was young but had an old soul. He had a way of sifting through lies to get to the truth of the matter. A trait he undoubtedly picked up from his wise father.

"You knew what would happen if you didn't pay up," said Rico

"And you *definitely* knew, Ben. So then why would you do this?" asked Rico.

As Rico asked the question he glanced over at Marco as if he was waiting for Marco to help make sense of the situation by somehow offering up an answer on Ben's behalf. As Ben's unfortunate luck would have it, Marco stood silently. Only staring intently at Ben, he too awaited what the possible outcome might be. At this point, Ben couldn't muster up a response, only gasps and tears.

"Ok, let's go over this again; shall we? You pay us money to protect you from the other so-called gangs around this city. And guess what we do in return for that money?" Rico rhetorically asked."You guessed it, we protect you!" he sarcastically exclaimed.

Rico continued to stare over the edge of the rooftop watching Ben squirm.

Ben replied, "Nobody had been bothering me in months."

"I thought…"

But before he could finish, Rico cut him off,"Nah, stop lying Ben!" he exclaimed, much like a disapproving parent. "You stopped paying because you felt like it," he said. "You got fed up with forking over money every month to us, so you said to yourself, 'Screw it! I ain't paying them thugs!' "That about sums it up?"

Ben could only stutter in response "I…I..I..I"

"Yeah, that sums it up." stated Rico, answering his own question.

"Well let me say this before I allow that concrete down there to rush up and greet you."

"NO!!!!" "PLEASE!!!" wailed Ben.

Rico put his hand up to deflect the unpleasant sound-waves coming from a soon to be deadman.

"Slow up, just let me finish," Rico said, with a rascally smirk."What I was going to say before you interrupted me was, the problem with your mode of thinking is, you're stupid." Rico bluntly stated.

"And when stupid people have ideas, Ben, their ideas tend to be stupid too. But tell you what, it's getting late and I'm kind of tired. So how about we do this. I'll let you live, that way you can pay us back the money you owe us and I'll forget this whole thing ever happened."

"Yes!" "Please! Please Mr. Coloso! Thank you!" hollered Ben. His words almost lost in translation with all of his continuous sobbing.

"You don't have to call me Mr. Coloso. You can save that for my father," replied Rico nonchalantly. "But he'd never meet with a runt like you, so you don't have to worry about that, either. Just call me Mr. Rico."

He nodded at Marco, granting permission to allow Ben Larson to live to see another day. Marco then pulled Ben up and over the ledge with complete ease, showing no signs of physical fatigue despite holding a man who probably weighed close to two hundred pounds with one hand. Once Ben was safely back on the rooftop, Marco finally let go, dropping Ben almost directly on his head. Ben's head thumped on the ground as he continued to sob over what was almost the end of his life. For a moment, Rico stared at him as Ben laid on the ground trying to muster up the strength to push himself to his feet. Rico stood over him dressed in an all-black tailor made suit. His hair was neatly combed back as if it had been trained over the years to lay obediently on his head. His neatly trimmed beard completed his tailored look as it wasn't too thick to suggest long-time lumberjack, but thick enough to make him look slightly more endowed with sophistication. He was a distinguished-looking man, and judging from his appearance no one could guess his lethal methods.

He shook his head and scuttled toward the rooftop service door. It was the same door that Marco violently dragged Ben through about ten minutes ago before holding him over that ledge. Ben was still on the ground with Marco standing over him. Rico stopped for a moment to look back. When he did this Marco quickly pulled Ben to his feet, his hands roughly grabbing Ben's body. As he hoisted him up, Ben screamed,"Agghhh!"

His ankle was broken due to the gorilla like strength that Marco possessed while he was holding him in the air. Now that Ben was standing upright his body reminded him of the damage that had been done once he put his weight on his ankle. Rico stared at Ben almost playfully for a moment before turning into a harsh gaze.

"Do you know why I'm dressed in all black tonight?" asked Rico.

As he posed the question, Marco held onto Ben, his titan like frame towering over him from behind. Marco was no mere mortal. He was the equivalent of a wild beast trapped in the casing of a man's body, waiting to be released. He quietly welcomed moments of violence, for they signified momentary releases of his true nature.

Rico, answering his own question, replied,"Because I was ready for your funeral tonight Ben. And I could be ready for your funeral at a moment's notice. Remember that."

There was a dark sincerity to his words. They left no room for doubt. Not allowing Ben to reply, Rico nodded his head at Marco, giving him another signal. His physical gestures didn't need to be translated for Marco. He was fluent in the Coloso family's unspoken dialect. Marco moved with almost lightning speed and with astounding brute force, he grabbed Ben's left arm and snapped it violently.

Ben let out his loudest scream of the night. "Ahhhhhh!" His body went limp from pain. Marco loosened his grip and allowed him to slide slowly out of his arms, down to the ground. Rico smirked, still playing with the lighter in his hand, flipping the top open and closing it with his thumb. As Marco got closer to him they looked at each other in silence, for a moment. Then the beast spoke.

"Your father would be impressed," said Macro. The depth of his voice was intimidating, but it had a mellowness to it that balanced it out.

"Well, let us hope that you are right, dear Marco," replied Rico.

He continued to watch as Ben rocked from side to side on the ground holding his arm in pain. Rico glanced up at the moon; it appeared to stare back at him as if it were a witness to the violence that had taken place to-night. Truth be told, the moon had seen its fair share of violence through-out Harbor Stone's existence. It never once told any of the city's transgres-sions; indeed, it kept silent over the decades. With that sort of track record in place, there was no need to go back on its loyalty now.

CHAPTER 2

KING NERO

It was just a few minutes past noon and the sun was out, but it didn't seem to be in full effect. It was as if it had decided to relax and allow its gentle rays to do all the work, at least for the time being. There was an estate located about thirty minutes outside of Harbor Stone. In fact, this was the estate of the King of Harbor Stone himself. This man earned his reputation through a hefty price of spilt blood throughout the last few decades. The tale of his legend was still very much alive in the streets of Harbor Stone. This man was none other than Nero Coloso, ruling king of the Coloso Family. Although there was another term that summed up his urbanite monarchy: The Don.

The smell of red grapes wafted through the air in an alluring manner. Behind the Coloso mansion, which held the strong resemblance to an old castle, was a mid-sized vineyard. Nero was a man of old habits and old pleasures, probably because they served him well over the years. Although today was not the day for a stroll down memory lane with The Don. No, there was a report to be given and things to be accountable for.

This afternoon, Rico would have to come face to face with his father and tell him of his late-night deeds. Rico walked with hesitant stride through the vineyard, his $500 loafers moving cautiously as they trampled on miscellaneous twigs and crushed leaves. Not too far behind him was his appointed guardian, Marco.

As the two journeyed forward, they could see their destination ahead seated at a long wooden table placed elegantly in an immaculate garden just outside the vineyard. It was surely a sight to behold. There were fresh flowers all around that displayed a beautifully orchestrated symphony of colors. The shrubs and bushes that surrounded them were neatly trimmed. The Don's preference for order was evident in his finely manicured garden. He had an unmistakable air about him. Even his presence had presence. He had the poise of a regal lion that had seen its fair share of battle. His head was laden with grey hair, some strands lighter than others, which made it appear as a grey and silver marble. His eyebrows were still dark with minimal grey strains. His beard was more of the same pattern, with some of its original piano black hair toward the bottom. This was physical evidence that the old king was once a younger one. But the most striking feature on his face was his eyes. They were brown and rich with deep history, given the sort of life he led. His eyes had already borne witness to enough events to last him three lifetimes. There was a story to be told written across his eyes in the ink of memories, a darker history. The kind of history that didn't need to be spoken aloud and was better left in the deep recesses of his mind, never to be heard of again.

He was still strong though. His sixty plus years of living had not taken an ounce from his spirit. He was still a fighter, only now his wisdom took prevalence over his actions, instead of his emotions. There he was seated like an old king enjoying some of his leisure time, which was made possible from the years of immense hustle he endured while constructing his empire. While he waited, he was in the middle of enjoying a fine meal along with a bottle of wine from his own vineyard. As Rico walked out from between the bushes along the pathway of a freshly cut lawn, he watched his father seated at the head of the table enjoying a fine steak. One of the servers stood a few feet away, close enough to be summoned when needed, but far enough to stay ignorant of unpleasant topics that could arise in a conversation with the Don.

"Father," said Rico, his voice calm but yearning for approval.

Nero, still chewing a bite of his steak, took a sip of wine. Rico briefly glanced at Marco, looking for some unspoken form of assurance. Although none was given, Marco's eyes stayed locked on Nero. This was evidence of the unspoken truth that when it came to having a conversation with the Don, it was every man for himself. Rico leaned in closer this time before he spoke again.

"Father," he repeated.

Nero cleared his throat and made eye contact with his son.

"You have something you want to tell me?" Nero asked, his voice sounding like a time- worn veteran.

"Yes sir," answered Rico.

However, before he could respond, his father interjected with another question."What happened with that man, Mr. Larson?" he asked. He neatly wiped his mouth with his napkin and placed it on the table. His attention was now solely on Rico.

"Marco and I paid him a visit as you ordered," said Rico.

"And was the outcome how I wanted?" Nero asked, still staring directly at Rico.

Rico smirked before answering the question, "Oh yeah. You should have seen it. Marco had his little ass hanging over that roof..." Nero suddenly interrupted his son,"Watch your mouth," he said sharply.

His voice was more than enough to correct any misguided behavior that somehow made its way into his presence. Rico then straightened up his posture and followed with a serious look on his face.

"Yes sir, my apologies" said Rico. He managed to look away for a brief moment, this time not at Marco but at the butler that was off to the side. He was dressed in all white with a short sleeved polo shirt that was neatly tucked in at the waist. The butler didn't make eye contact and continued to look straight ahead, steering clear of matters that didn't concern him. Rico quickly looked back at his father to make sure he made no further offenses.

"The message was made loud and clear to him," he said. "He won't miss another payment, we broke a few bones to make sure of that."

Nero turned his head toward Marco, as if he already knew what Rico meant when he said "*we*." "You broke bones Marco?" he asked.

Marco responded quickly and accurately like a soldier addressing a commanding officer.

"Yes sir, Don Coloso," he said.

Nero nodded his head and looked back at Rico. "It sounds like you did what you needed to do," he said. His complete approval went unspoken but it was a good sign that he didn't voice any *disapproval.* There was a brief silence in the air, before Rico presented a question of his own.

"Hey, uh, have you thought about our last conversation much any?" Rico asked, inching a few steps closer toward the table, quietly observing as his father now resumed his gourmet meal.

Nero took another bite before responding."Have I thought about our last conversation," he said, repeating the question in a manner that suggested he may have been slightly irritated that it was asked in the first place. "Yes Riccardo, I have," Nero said sharply, his voice slicing through the air quickly to get to the ears of its intended target. "My answer remains the same as it was the last time you presented your request. A simple error in this business can get you killed. Choices can result in life or death, not only for you but for others. Tell me again why do you want what you're asking for?"

"I've been doing this for a while now and…" started Rico, but was swiftly cut off by the Don.

"No son, you haven't been doing *this* for a while. You've barely stepped foot into this world," stated Nero. "You've watched from a distance for most of your life and only recently came into this dangerous fold," Nero further commented. He shook his head slightly and ran his fingertips across his forehead as if to put a stop to an annoying itch. Although it was more so annoyance from the present conversation they were having. "I've got secrets older than you!" declared Nero. His words weighed heavily in the air as they were spoken. "So don't tell me you've been doing *this* for a while. Because believe me when I tell you son; that you don't even know what *this* is!"

His words were like that of an old dragon spewing wisdom to some wayward knight that thought he might defy the odds and slay the ancient beast. Disappointingly, there was no such luck for the fictitious knight, nor was it for Rico in that moment. It was clear Rico wanted to be elevated to a higher position in the family business. It was also clear the Don was hesitant. The air was still, not a word uttered after the Don had spoken. For a brief moment, Nero glanced over to Marco; however, Marco dared not say a word. Marco was very familiar with moments like these, which always commanded silence, unless the Don addressed him.

Rico, still immersed in the moment, slightly folded his bottom lip under his top one. "I apologize, Dad. I meant no offense," he said, his words covered in remorse for his previous verbal actions. "I just want you to know that I *can* do this."

Rico stood there, staring at his father. He wasn't one to let other people see him sweat when faced with a situation. However, it didn't take an expert to see Rico had begun to perspire, more noticeably on the outside and maybe even internally as well. Nero took another sip of his homemade wine, the sun's rays beautifully dancing off the clear glass. The brief display of organic elegance provided a lovely visual to the current uncomfortable situation. Nero swallowed a sip of wine, and then glided his tongue across his teeth.

"You want to show me something?" he asked.

"Yes," Rico replied.

"Then show me something," stated Nero.

Rico had been around his father long enough to catch his drift. Nero's words carried weight. He nodded his head in agreement to the underlying challenge that was presented before him. Nothing else was said in the moment; there wasn't much to say. The Don had spoken and that was the end of the matter. There was no negotiating, no whining, no objection. The only thing left to do was leave the old king in peace before someone found themselves in a position they may not be able to come back from. Rico tilted his head up as he turned to walk away, looking in the sky. Perhaps he wanted to take a mental moment of escape from the pressing reality that he found himself in. Marco stayed put for a second and allowed Rico to walk past him before he followed suit. The walk back was a pretty lengthy one. To get back to the car, they would have to cross the vineyard and then go around the estate. However, the long walk wasn't an issue this time around. It was good for Rico to get more fresh air and allow himself to think about his next move. He walked through the vineyard at a fairly brisk pace, his frustration translating itself through his legs as he walked harshly over the ground. Only two steps behind him, Marco followed with no compelling emotion steering his actions. After all, the Don's uncertainty had nothing to do with him. Even if it did, Marco was always one who liked to govern his emotions. In his line of work, sometimes emotions could end up getting you killed. They walked in silence for about three minutes, then Rico came to an abrupt halt. He paused staring at the ground, swirling his tongue over his bottom front teeth. He fidgeted with his hands for a moment before putting them on his hips. He still wasn't facing Marco, only looking up in the sky. After another moment, he decided to give words a try.

"I don't know what it is," he said, his voice low and riddled with irritation.

Marco looked at him, not uttering a word. He stood there allowing the angry prince of a violent kingdom to say his peace.

"Or how I'm going to do it, but I will *prove* to him that I can do this!"

snapped Rico.

His words came quickly, as if they couldn't wait any longer to be released into the atmosphere. However, now that they were out, there was still one thing Rico had to do. Make them manifest.

CHAPTER 3

A WARRIOR'S BIRTH

A few hours outside of the sprawling city of Harbor Stone awaited a slightly different world. It offered less trouble with a drastically slower pace. Here, a person could be a little less leery of things that lurked over their shoulders, or if necessary, stay hidden long enough to devise a plan of attack. However, eight months had gone by for such a plan to be formulated, and still no plan had been made. It had been eight months, approaching nine, since the names of Jonathan Cross and Rachel Monroe were spoken in connection with another name; Kane Edwards.

In this small town of Olberton, Jonathan and Rachel were deemed safe. No one knew who they were, and frankly, it was a strong possibility no one would even care. Nevertheless, that was a chance neither one of them would take. So for the sake of complete anonymity, new names were given to protect old identities. *Carl* and *Elizabeth* were the ones living in Olberton now, not Jonathan and Rachel.

There was an old junkyard in town, and inside it was an old boxing gym that had long since seen its glory days. This junkyard and gym were owned by an even older man named Daniel Culgary. Mr. Culgary had lived in Olberton his whole life. He was a quiet yet hard working man who kept to himself. Most people who knew him would speak highly of Mr. Culgary, and the ones who didn't probably did something stupid to unleash his wrath upon them. Either way, he was a man to be respected. A few months ago, he met this young couple who looked like they could use a solid hand up in life as opposed to a hand out, as Mr. Culgary would say. So he gave

Jonathan (or Carl, as he knew him), a job cleaning up around the gym. It didn't pay much, but it was enough to keep money in Jonathan's pockets and food in his and Rachel's stomachs.

In his younger days, Mr. Culgary used to be a boxer, and his love for the sport never faded over the years. Jonathan soon figured this out and saw a way he could use this to his advantage. So in addition to paying Jonathan, Mr. Culgary agreed to have his grandson, Henry, spar with Jonathan and teach him how to box. All of this took place under Mr. Culgary's watchful supervision of course. So for the past several months, almost without fail, Jonathan would run through boxing drills and spar with Henry, Mr. Culgary's grandson.

Today was no exception to the grueling regimen. Inside the old Culgary gym was the aroma of fresh sweat mixed with hard work. The gym was filled with rich history. Old flyers from past fights were splattered across the bone white walls. The equipment was only a few years old, due to Henry training in the gym under his father and grandfather's tutelage. The floor was old hardwood that was in much need of a touch up and repair. Inside the gym there were two boxing rings, but only one was ever really used. Jonathan and Henry always sparred in the right ring or as Mr. Culgary would call it "the right fight" since it was on the right side.

It was 3:00 p.m., which meant Jonathan and Henry were hard at work and well into their routine. Jonathan was pretty light on his feet and kept them planted just enough to stand firm when he threw a punch, but light enough when he needed to get out of the way. He was already sweating heavily. His face looked as if he had been dunked underwater with a blanket of sweat covering the majority of his gray sleeveless shirt. The proof of his hard training showed through the transformation of his physique. His arms were more defined due to endless push-ups, pull-ups, and shadow boxing sessions that he had willingly endured. He was better for it, which is what he wanted. Part of it was mental for him, due to both the mental and physical beatings he sustained back in Edge City. It pushed him to be a fighter in both a literal and metaphorical sense. He wanted to sharpen his skills as a warrior, so to speak, and he felt like boxing allowed him to do just that.

Jonathan shifted his upper body quickly to the left as he dodged a straight right jab delivered by Henry. Henry outweighed Jonathan by a solid 15 pounds of muscle, so it was always in Jonathan's best interest to miss anything coming from Henry's direction, although that wasn't always possible given the fact that Henry was an experienced fighter. Henry was doing a good deed by taking the diligent time required to train Jonathan. After Henry's failed jab, Jonathan's thoughts were on full alert, bringing forth the remembrance of countless drills he endured in this very ring. Jonathan shuffled quickly to the right, appearing to glide in that direction. He didn't want Henry to fire off another shot, so he attempted to keep him busy by throwing a jab of his own. Over the course of the last several months, Jonathan also discovered he was naturally quick with his hands. So he put his speed to work; he threw two left jabs in rapid succession. While slightly stepping forward with his left foot with each jab, Henry kept his guard up, showing his disciplined nature. At this point, Jonathan was closer to Henry, so he went in for a hard body shot with his right fist, turning all his weight and channeling it into to a mighty missile. Success! He caught Henry wide open, and a deep thud resounded as Jonathan's black boxing glove rushed to greet Henry's midsection. The sound of the thud alone was enough to let both boxers know that a solid hit had landed.

Although he landed a good punch, Jonathan had been laid out enough times by Henry before to not allow even a hint of cockiness make its way into his thoughts. In this sense, experience was indeed a greater teacher because sure enough, after Jonathan landed that lovely body shot, Henry came back with a punch of his own. Although it was to no avail since Jonathan had gracefully managed to dodge that as well. It was a good thing too, given the fact that from time to time Henry liked to spar with no helmet gear, and today happened to be one of those days, which meant Jonathan wasn't wearing any headgear either. Henry took a step forward with his guard firmly up. He was well built, like a mid-sized tank. His back looked like it was carved out of marble, his muscles appeared permanently defined. As he approached Jonathan, he had a stern look on his face, focused on his intended target. The look suggested he wanted to inflict some serious bodily harm to Jonathan. Perhaps Henry wasn't too pleased about the shot Jonathan so elegantly landed only a few jabs ago. As Henry sized up his opponent, sweat rolled down Jonathan's forehead. Light streams made their way down his face, with a few drops getting close to his eyes. He blinked to clear his vision; he needed his eyes' full attention at the moment. Any obstructed view of his adversary or even the simple act of blinking too long could result in him getting his lights knocked all the way out. Having a man of Henry's physical caliber delivering a hard hit to the face wasn't a pleasant feeling.

However, Jonathan was all too familiar with that feeling, and the pain that accompanied it. Henry once landed a hard jab right below Jonathan's nose that caused his lip to split open. It was so bad Jonathan tasted the coppery tinge of his blood for a week straight. He was in no mood to have something like that happen again. So his guard was up; this time he wanted to be a little more on the offensive side instead of letting Henry come after him. He went for a two punch combo; he led with a stiff left jab and followed it up with a right hook. However, his attempts were to no avail. Henry's guard was strong as it was quick. He managed to dodge the left jab and covered himself with his right arm for the hook. As Jonathan's glove landed on Henry's right arm, he could feel Henry's muscular definition through his gloves. He was definitely not a man to be taken lightly; he was all business in the ring. He then reminded Jonathan of that very fact as he pivoted to the right and let off an assault of sudden blows. Henry was

Jonathan's superior, both physically and in level of experience, so the fights were never evenly matched. Jonathan suddenly found his back against the ropes of the ring. Henry connected with a hard body shot of his own, sinking heavily into Jonathan's side. Jonathan winced at the pain that was brought forth by one of Henry's blows. As he stood there with his back against the ropes, his mind was speaking to his body, telling him that he needed to move and do it fast. Having his back against the ropes didn't put him in a good position.

Jonathan kept his hands up tightly in front of him, doing his best to shield himself from *"Hurricane Henry."* He paid close attention to how Henry was throwing his punches; he counted four seconds since he last threw one. Although Henry was experienced, Jonathan had begun to gain a certain level of knowledge about the ring himself. He knew that when Henry went on a myriad binge of throwing punches, he would at some point tire himself out. He knew that this was one of those times. Henry had exerted a nice amount of his energy throwing those types of blows and was getting tired. This was his time to turn the tide of the fight. Jonathan had to go for it.

Henry paused for another three seconds, enough time for Jonathan to get off the ropes. Jonathan side stepped to the right and quickly lunged forward, putting him right next to Henry. Henry turned to face him, as Jonathan let off a left and right hook, both blows colliding with Henry's face. It was a good maneuver that seemed to be paying off for him. Henry's back was now facing the ropes, but he wasn't touching it just yet. From this position, Jonathan could not only see his opponent, he also had a good view of the front door. From the current angle he was facing, the door appeared to be next to Henry's head, since it was behind him in the distance. For once, Jonathan might actually take the win in a sparring session with Henry. Normally it was the other way around and would usually end with Henry providing Jonathan with some sage advice on how to do better next time.

It would seem that Henry's words didn't fall on deaf ears and today Jonathan would use his earned wisdom to produce a winning combination. As he steadily controlled his breathing, he continued to throw out good shots. That was until an unexpected distraction made its way into Jonathan's view. All of a sudden, Jonathan noticed a bright white light coming from the front door. The light was so bright that at first glance, one might have thought an angel was about to enter the room. Jonathan wondered about this celestial light suddenly piercing the doorway. He managed to split his focus for a second, giving the brunt of his attention to the 230-pound situation that stood before him. However, he also gave the doorway a much deserved second look. The radiant light was also accompanied by a faint sound that managed to make its way to Jonathan's ears. It was the sound of the door opening. As Jonathan advanced, Henry managed to throw a left jab that connected, but probably not the way he had intended. It reminded Jonathan of Henry's presence and that the fight wasn't over.

Still glancing over, Jonathan saw a shadow taking form in the light until it became familiar in shape. The shape was the form of a man and that man was Mr. Culgary. No doubt he heard that his grandson and good ol' *Carl* were in the ring giving each other the business. Mr. Culgary's presence wasn't new. He loved boxing, so anytime he got the opportunity to see his favorite pastime in action, he reveled at the chance. Given the fact that Mr. Culgary liked to attend the sparring sessions, Jonathan wasn't thrown off guard by this unannounced entry. It was the person who walked in the door after him who proved to be a distraction.

In Jonathan's eyes, she was the essence of beauty personified in one body. That body belonged to none other than the woman he loved. The woman who had agreed to leave her once exciting life behind to support him. To show him she too loved him the way he loved her. To show him she trusted him in a way that she hadn't trusted a man before. This woman was none other than Rachel Monroe. Her eyes were just as beautiful as her face, and they made contact with Jonathan's as soon as she walked into the room. Unfortunately, Jonathan's eyes weren't paying attention to the task at hand, and his face paid the price. He immediately felt the strong thrust of a powerful uppercut connect with his chin. The hit was swift, clean and went unnoticed until its presence was felt. The force of the hit wasn't enough to land him on his back, but it sent his head staring straight up at the ceiling for a few moments before he could bring it back down and process what just happened. By the time he brought his head back down, Henry was already off the ropes. This wasn't good. Up until a few seconds ago, Jonathan was controlling the fight, and it appeared he was going to take the win. Now, with Rachel in the room, the tide of the fight was taking an unwelcome turn.

Henry was back on the offensive and coming to reclaim his authority in the ring. He landed a successful right jab at Jonathan's expense. Jonathan planted his feet and bit down on his mouth guard hard. He couldn't lose his head in the moment. He had to stay calm or else things could get worse. Jonathan took half a step forward. It was more of a personal choice than boxing strategy. He no longer wanted to feel like the victim in his life. He had enough of that back in Edge City. He was different now; more of his inner warrior now lived on the outside these days and refused to stay hidden.

Jonathan threw a right hook, however it was unsuccessful as Henry ducked. Jonathan couldn't get discouraged even though things weren't exactly how he wanted them at the moment. He stayed in his stance, ready for another opportunity to strike. He may have been ready, but he was impatient as well, as he quickly threw a right jab. However, his attempt was interrupted as Henry lunged a punch of his own. Luckily, Jonathan was ready. He quickly eluded the oncoming hit by dropping down low. As Jonathan looked up from his crouched position, he saw a neatly gift-wrapped present: Henry's unguarded chin. Jonathan sprang forth, his fist erupting from his side like molten lava tearing its way through the top of a volcano. His glove met the bottom of Henry's chin with an unapologetic fury that refused to be ignored. Henry's mouth guard flew out of his mouth covered in saliva as it twirled in the air. He took a few steps back with a surprised yet angry look residing on his face. They both stood a few inches apart like two gladiators in the Roman Colosseum. Instead of a thunderous applause from an adoring crowd, they heard another sound: the resounding claps of Mr. Culgary as he stood to the side of the ring with a wide grin plastered across his face.

"Now *that's* what I'm talking bout!" hollered Mr. Culgary. His voice carried and there was a certain depth to his natural country twang.

He had a certain sense of familiarity about him, like the old retired coach who always gave the neighborhood kids good old-fashion wisdom and sound advice. He was a man of average build and wore glasses because he refused to wear contacts. A few wrinkles had managed to make their presence known on his face without making him look too much like an old man. He was dressed in a ruby red short sleeve shirt with gray sweatpants and a worn down pair of old sneakers that never made noise when he walked. Years of good use gave the shoes a sort of natural silencer. They came in handy at times, because Mr. Culgary could enter a room and people wouldn't notice he was there until he said something.

"I see you Carl! Good job, son!" said Mr. Culgary with a loud tone. He gave Jonathan a thumbs up as he continued his bright-eyed smile.

Jonathan was still getting used to people calling him by another name. He tried to take a deep breath, as he was still winded from the blow for blow bout. He nodded his head at Mr. Culgary, which was his way of saying thank you for the compliment that was just given.

"Aye Henry, he's getting better ain't he!?" asked Mr. Culgary. Henry said nothing. He only shook his head in agreement as he looked at Jonathan as if he wanted to go another round to settle the score. To him, that would mean the fight ending with Jonathan on his back.

"Well damn, what's the problem? Both y'all boys on hush mouth this afternoon?" Mr. Culgary jokingly asked. What….y'all trade a couple of licks and ya can't speak, what's the deal?"

Jonathan figured he'd be the one to speak up first before Mr. Culgary lost his jovial mood and things really got out of hand. "Oh I can still talk, just a little winded," he replied. "Your grandson's a pretty tough guy, Mr. Culgary." He looked over again at Henry, who seemed to have calmed down over the last few seconds. That was a good thing, because Jonathan knew good and well Henry could seriously hurt him if he wanted to.

Although the male bonding was enjoyable, Jonathan was very much aware of the only lady in the room. Now that he wasn't involved in a toe-to-toe sparring session, he could take the necessary moment to look at Rachel. She was as beautiful as always, her hair wrapped in a ponytail with one bang softly draped over the left side of her face. Although this time her beauty didn't seem as welcoming as it normally was. Inside the allure of her normally pleasant and inviting visage, there was another emotion that seeped through at the moment, and that emotion was frustration. Jonathan knew it would be a good idea to see what was wrong. He didn't like to give her the opportunity to let something sit and fester; that technique never seemed to end well for him.

"Well what do you think Ms. Elizabeth?" asked Mr. Culgary. "How you think your boy Carl over there fared against my Henry?" His eyes were still wide from all of the excitement.

Rachel placed her hands on her hips before she said a word. She looked at Jonathan as she spoke, not once taking her eyes off of him. "I think *Carl* should come down from there so I can talk to him about something," she replied.

Her voice was still soft as it was pleasant, but the other two men weren't as versed in Rachel's personality as well as Jonathan. After all, how could they be? They knew her as Elizabeth, and they were none the wiser to her past.

The fact that they didn't know the grim details of Jonathan and Rachel's previous lives was a good thing. The town of Olberton was a far cry from the menacing streets of Edge City. There was no need to bring that kind of evil to such an unassuming place. Nevertheless, Jonathan still had the memories of a life he was not completely rid of. If he was being honest, it wasn't that Jonathan didn't want his old life back. To the contrary, that was exactly what he wanted. The only difference was he wanted to have the life he had before the words Kane and Edwards were even a part of his vocabulary. He even wanted Edge City, just minus the megalopolis tyrant that violently turned his world upside down.

He knew Rachel wanted that, too. Her mere presence served as a silent reminder to the both of them about where they came from. Two living bodies of physical evidence of a once exciting existence, forced to interact with one another under false pretenses. They may have left Edge City, but they still had their problems, and today Rachel's face served as a reminder to that cold fact.

By this time, Mr. Culgary had climbed into the ring so he could help the guys get their gloves off. He started with Jonathan first, no doubt showing some unspoken favoritism to the *winner* of the friendly sparring session. Jonathan stood there, in a state halfway between anxiety and pride. He was happy. For the first time he seemed to have gotten the better of Henry. However, the short lived victory was interrupted by the uneasy gaze of the woman who had his heart. Jonathan took in deep breaths, his body still recovering from the intense workout it was forced to endure. He wondered what Rachel was thinking as he looked at her. She stared back at him in a way that made him feel as if he had done something wrong, although to his immediate recollection, he couldn't think of any offense he might have made against her to receive such a look. Once Mr. Culgary was done getting his gloves off, Jonathan broke eye contact with Rachel long enough to show Henry the proper respect by giving him a warrior's embrace. Henry hugged Jonathan, suggesting he was pleased with the way Jonathan handled himself in the ring.

Although that would have been enough for Jonathan, Henry also wanted to speak his mind. "You done well kid," he said, his voice dull. His voice was not the type to be remembered or even appreciated in a conversation, although Henry was memorable more for his size rather than his speech.

"Well, I had a good teacher," replied Jonathan, his voice competing with the air that wanted to get in his lungs after being a little winded. "Next time I'll let you win."

Henry smirked and gave him a playful punch in the arm before he headed toward the other end of the ring to get his gym bag nestled in the corner. At this point, Jonathan's attention was back on Rachel, although hers wasn't on him. She looked off into the distance, her face dipped in beauty but plagued by an unspoken grief.

What could she be mad about? Jonathan wondered as he made his way over to her. Before he stepped out of the ring, he leaned against the ropes. He figured he would test the waters before he jumped into the deep end of the pool.

"Hey gorgeous!" he said.

Rachel looked at him, her face void of a friendly smile."Hey," she simply replied.

Jonathan hopped out of the ring by maneuvering his way over the ropes. His feet made a slight thud as he landed on the gym floor. "Whats going on?" he asked as he walked over to her. He figured this wasn't the time to try and move in for a hug or a kiss. Not to mention she probably wouldn't appreciate the fact that he was dripping with sweat and didn't have the most pleasant aroma.

"I need to talk to you," said Rachel, in a worrisome tone.

Jonathan didn't like to hear Rachel sound uncomfortable, or in any form of distress for that matter. He turned around to see if Mr. Culgary and Henry were close enough to hear their conversation. They were busy no doubt talking about the match, or maybe some personal family matters.

"What's wrong?" he asked.

Rachel stared at him for a moment that seemed to last too long in Jonathan's eyes. "Do you even have to ask me that question?" she asked with a snare. "Look around *Carl*. This isn't exactly what I pictured for myself! Being a fugitive for a crime I didn't commit and living in the shadows is *not* ok with me! And it shouldn't be ok with you either!" Her voice had begun to rise.

Jonathan put his hand up in a signal to try and calm her down. He turned his head to see if her rant was being heard by a third party. To his surprise, Mr. Culgary was actually looking in their direction. Jonathan wondered if he heard what was going on, but he tried not to stare. He didn't want it to look obvious that he didn't want their conversation overheard. It wasn't so much that he didn't want them to see Rachel upset with him, but he wanted to make sure their secret wasn't on the verge of being exposed. The last thing Jonathan needed was federal agents busting into his room tonight because they were tipped off by some Dudley-do-right citizen.

"Look Rachel, I know this isn't ideal, believe me I do," he said, attempting to defuse the bomb that was about to detonate."You know that neither one of us planned to be in this situation."

Rachel might've heard him but it didn't look like she was actually trying to listen. "Ok, but what are you doing to fix this, Jonathan?!" she snapped.

Jonathan hoped no one overheard her referring to him by his real name. He turned around again. Luckily Henry and Mr. Culgary now seemed to be deep in conversation themselves.

"You told me we would come here to lay low and while we were here you were supposed to be coming up with a plan to get our lives back, not in here trying to be the next heavyweight champ!" she continued, as she pointed at the boxing ring, her tirade not showing any sign of slowing down. "We've been here over eight months!" She lowered her voice down a decimal level. Perhaps she realized that she too didn't want their untold truth to see the light of day in the town of Olberton. "It's been almost a year…a year and I don't feel like we're any closer to getting our lives back. I mean, can you honestly tell me you've come up with a plan?" Her eyes were sternly fixed on Jonathan, awaiting answers to her barrage of questions. However, before he could come up with an answer, Rachel added: "You said you needed time…well you've had plenty of it."

In her defense, Jonathan knew everything she was saying was true. It had been long enough for him to come up with something, anything that might even offer the smallest inclination of hope. Their brief stint in Olberton turned into an extended stay. At first it was ok, since it offered them anonymity in their current surroundings. Now it was time to leave the nest. Truth be told, a proper game plan was well overdue and he knew it.

"Look, I told you that I'd come up with something…and I will," he tried to assure her. He placed his hands on her arms in an attempt to console her and let her know his promises would be fulfilled. He wasn't fearful about moving forward. If anything, he was guilty of over analyzing the situation. He knew his next move had to be the *right* move. Now it was beyond clear to him a move had to be made. They could not hide out in Olberton forever.

"I can't continue living like this," said Rachel, the anger now subsiding in her voice, desperation making its way into the equation.

"And you won't have to," replied Jonathan. His words were direct and because he loved her, he couldn't let her life end in ruins, especially over something that at its core had nothing to do with her. She got caught in the crosshairs of the wrong man. That wasn't her fault, and Jonathan could not and would not allow her to suffer for it. "I meant what I told you Rachel, we'll make this right." He leaned in and gave her a kiss on the cheek and whispered in her ear, "I love you."

As he spoke these words, a tear rolled down Rachel's face. She wiped her eyes as if she were trying to dismiss her own vulnerability. However, that wasn't necessary since in his eyes. He'd be there for her because he loved her. He could tell she was beginning to calm down, and he knew she just needed to vent. He couldn't blame her. She had been through an ocean of turmoil with him and had a right to go off for a moment. She was owed some patience and understanding.

"Let's talk tonight. I know we've both been working as our new selves and haven't had a chance to relax," Jonathan said. "We should do something tomorrow night. Just the two of us."

Then that's when Jonathan was shown a sight that he longed to see: a smile on Rachel's face. "Goodness, you're forever the romantic aren't you?" she sarcastically asked.

Jonathan smiled back at her in response to her question. "Yeah, and let's be honest, you love me for it."

The laughter coming from Rachel's lips was like a heavenly symphony gracing its celestial sounds on Jonathan's ears. It proved to be more than enough for Jonathan. Given the times they were in, he welcomed the presence of spontaneous joy. It reminded him that life was still good and there were still many amazing things it had to offer. It showed him all was not lost and his life wasn't over.

He watched Rachel as she made her peaceful exit from the gym. It was ironic she was leaving a place designed for battle. She was a fighter as well, even though she may not have always acknowledged it. As Jonathan stood there and watched her walk out, he couldn't help but think he needed to hurry up and figure out his next move, for her sake and for his. As the contemplative thoughts rattled in his mind, he felt a hand touch his shoulder. He turned his head slightly to the right to see who it was that made a sudden entrance inside his personal space. It was none other than Mr. Culgary, who stood there for a moment and watched Rachel continue her elegant exit.

"Let me give you a piece of advice, son," he said."Actions are better than words."

A slight frown came upon Jonathan's face as he was trying to figure out what Mr. Culgary meant by that.

"Look, now I didn't hear what you two were talking about, but I could tell from her reaction, she's ready to eat whatever it is you've been trying to feed her. Whatever thing you said you'd do, it's time to do it," Mr. Culgary continued.

Jonathan's facial expression was that of a young man soaking in the unsolicited wisdom of a more seasoned man in the game of life. He gave deep thought to what Mr. Culgary was saying. The small-town old timer hit the nail right on the head. Jonathan's ears were now locked onto the words that were coming forth from Mr. Culgary's mouth. He listened intently as he made sure not one word of what Mr. Culgary was saying hit the ground. His time in Edge City matured him in ways that he wouldn't have imagined, nor would he have asked for it in the first place. He knew Mr. Culgary was right, even though the guy didn't know the particulars of the conversation.

"She wants to see action son, plain and simple!" said Mr. Culgary, with a wide grin plastered on his face. He smiled as if he was pleased with himself, like he knew for certain the advice he gave would completely change things for *Carl*. "Hell son, I know you got it in ya now. I've seen you fight in that ring, so I know you know how to fight in life. I've never seen you give up in there," Mr. Culgary, lifted his hand and pointed to the ring behind his back, with his thumb. "I'll admit, a couple times I thought maybe you had a death wish, tempting fate with Henry like that. But the more I watched you, the more I saw that you weren't crazy, just determined. And let me tell you, a determined man is a powerful thing."

By this time, Henry was making his way to the front door of the gym and was about to pass them. This served as a cue to Mr. Culgary to wrap up their conversation. Jonathan had his hands on his hips, giving everything he had just heard the credence it deserved.

"I hear you Mr. C," he said, "It's just that I don't really know where to start." He knew that was a problem, he just didn't want to admit that to Rachel.

"Oh don't you worry about that, kid. It'll come to you," replied Mr. Culgary. As he said this, he reached out and put his left hand on Jonathan's shoulder again. "You just make sure that you get serious about *getting* serious, which I know you will, because you and I both know that you love that girl."

By the time Mr. Culgary had finished talking, Henry had now made his way up to the two of them. Mr. Culgary ended the conversation by patting Jonathan on the shoulder. Jonathan said nothing as he watched his sparring partner and Mr. Culgary exit the gym. That little pep talk was good for him and it proved to be something he needed to hear. It spoke to both him and the depth of the situation at hand. He had been refined by the fires of trials and experience, yet he came out a better man for it. Due to that, it would make this next part of Jonathan's journey a lot easier. He now knew what it was time to do.

It was time to act.

CHAPTER 4

THE FORGING FIRES

The day was coming to a close. The sky had begun to darken from the sun's gradual disappearance. This town was a far cry from the megalopolis war zone that Jonathan had become accustomed to. Indeed, he was put through the forging fires of trials and tribulations. The proof of the flames showed themselves through the *heat* that steamed from Jonathan's very being. Even though he might not have wanted to go through that particular process, he knew he had grown from it. He had been battle-tested and had the scars to prove it. Although his growth was evident, it didn't mean he was any closer to devising a plan to defeat the criminal mastermind responsible for orchestrating his recent pain.

His earlier conversation with Rachel jolted him a little. His initial mission was still true. They were laying low long enough to come up with their next move. However, in the process of planning, it seemed he and Rachel became marooned in their current environment. In truth, Jonathan had to admit he enjoyed the feeling of being settled for a moment and not having to look over his shoulder every two to three seconds. Even though he knew the *settled* feeling was artificial, it still provided him with real time: the time needed to sift through the possible routes he could take to get the two of them back to where they wanted to be in life.

But along the way, he found himself *preparing* more than planning. He prepped himself for the next wave of war because in the back of his mind, he knew Kane wouldn't go down without a serious fight. The man was too smart and too seasoned in tactical warfare. Jonathan now knew from brutal experience a man like that couldn't be handled lightly. The unspoken but ever present fact was that Jonathan was out-matched when it came to Mr. Edwards. Jonathan thought he had him before, but that proved to be a costly miscalculation. It ended with him and Rachel being exiled from what he once thought was a dream come true. However, the dream he thought he was living was nothing more than an illusion that only caused pain he was more than eager to be rid of.

This pain affected more than just him. It also caused Rachel to literally give up everything to be with him. Jonathan would find himself thinking about what could've happened that day he showed up with a gun in his hand at Mr. Edward's home. Rachel could have gotten out of the car and stayed, perhaps trying to work things out with the police (although the better angle for her would have been to appeal to Mr. Edwards' mercy in some way, which Rachel would have figured out a way to do). If she had done that, she wouldn't be on the run now. A simple wave of the hand or a written check from Kane Edwards, and her problems could have been over before they even started.

Jonathan was thankful for her presence, but at the same time he couldn't help but think she might have been better off staying in Edge City. At least that way she wouldn't have had to lose everything she worked for. Jonathan knew he wasn't the one who took Rachel's life from her, but that didn't mean he didn't feel responsible for her pain. It wasn't an ideal situation. However, if his time in Edge City taught him anything, he at least knew how to handle stressful situations without losing his head. In fact, his behavior toward Rachel earlier was a testament to his newfound sense of zen. He knew she was upset, but he tried to keep her calm. After all, he understood where she was coming from. These thoughts circled around in Jonathan's mind as he made his way toward his room.

He managed to find a place to stay at an old Extended Stay motel; the locals called it *"The Passer."* This was because most people who stayed there were drifters, runaways, basically people who were just passing through. Jonathan fit the bill, since he knew he wasn't planning on staying there for the rest of his life. Although, since he had been in town over eight months, he and Rachel were now in the running for being the longest guests to ever stay there. Due to her initial frustration of being forced to live in a town that you couldn't even locate on a map, she had opted for her own room. It was perhaps her way of venting. Though separate, she wasn't far from Jonathan at all. In fact, she was right next door. The manager of the motel gave them a conjoined room, and they were only separated by a door in the middle of both rooms that opened from either side. It was truly a jack-and-jill setup. Each room was its own small apartment equipped with a bed, tv, closet, dressers, and one bathroom. It was more than enough for them. Jonathan was just grateful they didn't have to sleep on the street. Things weren't what they used to be for them, but it wasn't as bad as it could've been, either. In fact, even though Jonathan enjoyed walking, good ol' Mr. Culgary was nice enough to let them use one of his old pickup trucks. It reminded Jonathan of Winterville; even Mr. Culgary's pick up truck reminded him of *Old Betty*, except this truck was kept up better than *Old Betty*. It had a fresh coat of royal blue paint that faded to navy blue toward the bottom edges. Also, Jonathan had to admit, the town of Olberton was a lot nicer than Winterville.

All these things added up to being a melting pot for Jonathan's emotions. He was in a place that was unfamiliar yet it was still familiar. He was free from the grasp of Kane Edwards, but he could still feel the residual effects of his villainous touch, which was why he had to get his life back. He may have been out of sight but he wasn't out of the fight. Rachel and Mr. Culgary were right: it was time to act.

He walked up the stairs to his room, the faint breeze of the evening providing a comfort for his body. It was as if the wind innately knew that at the moment Jonathan just needed some reassurance. He was tired from his bout with Henry. When he got inside, he planned on taking a warm shower. As he made his way toward his room, he had to pass Rachel's door first. He stopped right in front of it for a moment; the door itself was a pale gray, almost absent of a distinct hue. He took a step toward the door and lifted his left hand as if he were about to knock, but paused in mid air. He wasn't worried as to whether or not she was still upset with him. He knew she would be ok. His thoughts focused on the idea that maybe he should make some headway in the whole *stop Mr. Edwards so they can get their life back* plan. He also needed this break for himself. So, he lowered his hand back to his side and walked a few steps toward his door.

As he entered the room, a thick invisible cloud of heat wrapped its way around his body. The air had a heaviness to it due to the warm temperature that occupied the room. Jonathan could feel his mouth getting dry just from walking in the room. He closed the door behind him, frowning as he gave thought as to why the room was so hot. Then it dawned on him that he left the heat on due to the previous night's frigid air. The room was quiet as he looked around, accompanied by the mundane furnishings of a cheap motel. Jonathan left the place neat. His life had been cluttered enough as it was. He didn't need the burden of physical evidence to add to it. He cut off the heat as he walked over to the bed and threw down his stuff. He sat on the edge of the bed, pausing for a moment while staring off into space.

Except it wasn't exactly space he was staring off into. It was the recesses of his mind. His unspoken thoughts seemed to replay on a loop, still mulling over the events of today and contemplating the actions of tomorrow. Some thoughts came fast while others were slow, but they came nonetheless; all offering their unique opinion on what Jonathan should do next. He would have to silence them first before picking a viable candidate to possibly act upon.

However, before he would go any further with formulating a plan of attack, he needed to detox for a moment. He figured a shower would help do the trick, so he got up and went into the bathroom. He stayed in there long enough to let the healing powers of a warm shower settle in his body. Once he was finished, he came back out and to put on his clothes. There was a small desk in the corner he used as his little workstation. As he sat at the desk, he got quiet for a moment to see if he could hear Rachel moving around in the next room. He couldn't help but think of her. Truth be told, Jonathan never really stopped thinking about Rachel. Even when she wasn't in his presence; *her* presence was still felt. She had that invisible effect on him. She took more residence in Jonathan's private thoughts probably more than she realized.

The room was still as he leaned in the direction of the door, in hopes he would get some audible evidence of her activity in the next room. However, as he listened he heard nothing; only the sound of pure silence. Ironically, this was a sound that was eerily familiar to Jonathan. It's void was recognizable. It reminded him of hard nights in the city, so there were no pleasantries in the deafness.

Since he didn't hear anything, there was no need for him to continue his unsuccessful eavesdropping session. He turned on his laptop and watched the screen as it lit up. While it took a few moments to turn on, he slid back in his seat and felt a sense of anxiety creeping forth slowly out of thin air. That feeling almost acted as a live entity with its unwelcome hands stretching across Jonathan's back, trying to make its way into his mind. Though it seemed the emotionally intrusive hands were put to a pause, Jonathan noticed the login screen came up. He leaned in to type his password; the keys on the keyboard clicking with each stroke of his fingers. Perhaps this simple act of minute distraction was enough to take his mind off any unpleasant feelings that may have been trying to rear their ugly heads.

He logged onto the internet and pulled up one of the popular search engine sites. He then stopped for a moment to collect himself then rubbed his hands as if he were about to go a few more rounds in the ring. He lowered his hands and let them hover over the keyboard for a moment. He typed his name in to see what the rest of the world, or at least the digital world, had to say about him. To his surprise, there wasn't an article with his name at the top of the list. Even though he wasn't in the best of situations, perhaps it wasn't as bad as he thought. As he scrolled down the page, that mode of thinking quickly came to a halt when he saw an online article with his mug plastered next to it. He clicked the link and read the title *"Manhunt continues for missing intern."*

Jonathan skimmed through the article, already aware of its lies. He knew he had been framed for money laundering, attempted murder and theft. His mind immediately went back to that violent day where he witnessed the bulky henchmen Percy come ripping through his condo door. He remembered that day all too vividly. That was the day death tried to pay Jonathan a visit. Luckily for him, he was able to close the door on death before it entered the room. He was grateful he managed to grab Percy's gun and fire a few rounds into the hired muscle. Although it was traumatic, Jonathan was thankful all lives were spared that day, even Percy's. He knew he did what he had to do, but at least this way he didn't have to add murderer to his criminal resume. He wasn't ready for the type of warfare that required the taking of another man's life.

He clicked the back button, and this time he typed in Rachel's name. He found more of the same. There was another article that talked about them both and listed Rachel as an accomplice to Jonathan's elaborate scheme. The slight silver lining in the cloud was that at least Rachel wasn't the main focus of any of the articles. She was always the plus one, the guest to the corrupt party, but never the headliner. Things were just as bad for her as they were for him, but at least this was something that seemed to soften the hard blow. Jonathan was sure Rachel wouldn't feel the same way, and this wasn't something he would bother bringing to her attention.

He sat there for a second and just looked at the screen. He shook his head almost in disbelief that this was all real. That he was really on the run, that he had really been set up, that he really was in a cheap motel living in Winterville 2.0 under a different name. It was enough to make most people crack, but Jonathan found out the hard way that he wasn't like most people. He discovered he could endure and overcome. He vowed that this situation would be no different for him because deep down, he knew he would get through this. He didn't know what, who, when, where, why or even how. All he knew was that his story was not going to end here. He couldn't let that happen; he refused to. Besides, if he had learned anything from the pow-wow he had earlier with Rachel, it was that he had someone else to think about other than himself. There were other pieces to this equation that had to be considered.

Not to mention, there was another name that Jonathan had to look up. To be honest, it was the reason he got on the computer in the first place. He knew what needed to be done next. His fingers again hovered over the keyboard, waiting for his mind to give the go ahead. As he began to type, he watched the name manifest before his eyes. He stared at the screen, giving way to that unbearable silence that re-entered the room. This time the name on the screen that was spelled out was one that he wouldn't mind never speaking of again: Kane Edwards.

He pressed the enter key and anticipated the computer's results. Immediately, the screen was bombarded with information on the subject at hand; Mr. Edwards. There was enough juicy gossip on the tycoon of Edge City to fill an encyclopedia. Without warning, Jonathan felt the hands of anxiety resume their way up his back. It was as if those uneasy feelings were lying in wait this entire time. The air in the room suddenly turned cold, as if winter itself decided to pay Jonathan a visit without warning. Surely, the iceman had cometh and it appeared as if he were there to stay.

Jonathan didn't expect to feel this way, however if he were being honest with himself, his mind wasn't too surprised at the onslaught of emotions. After all, he was looking at the man who had all but destroyed his life. He caused Jonathan the kind of pain that one doesn't know existed until they find themselves face to face with its unforgiving punishment. He scrolled some more and clicked on an image of Mr. Edwards. There he was, live in the digital flesh, being represented by thousands upon thousands of pixels in that single image. The pixels formed a pattern to make the visage of a madman come to life. Jonathan continued to stare at the screen. By this time, his heart rate was up and his teeth were grinding. His body tried to cope with the emotions that flooded him. Jonathan wanted to just turn the computer off and walk away. However, he refused to take the easy route in this moment. He decided to test his own resolve as he forced himself to look at the picture of someone he once feared. He stared until the hands of anxiety withered and loosened their evil grip on him, his breathing slowed down and his heart rate returned to normal.

He was calming down; the mighty waves of his emotions began to settle. They faded quietly back into their respective places deep within his psychique, until he felt nothing. For the moment, he was a blank canvas awaiting the brush strokes of a master painter. The emptiness proved to be nothing more than the eye of the storm. Soon he found himself at the mercy of yet another emotion; anger. His mind played back moments in time that he experienced in Edge City. Back to the first time he met Mr. Edwards that night at the museum, then again on that dreadful afternoon where he found himself face to face with the man pointing a gun directly in his face.

After Jonathan passed his self-inflicted test of endurance, he clicked back to the rest of the links for other articles. When he hit the back button, his eyes had gotten a glimpse of another headline that he wasn't too fond of but also was not surprised by. It read "Business mogul wins election." Although Jonathan and Rachel's lives were put to an abrupt halt, that wasn't the case for Mr. Edwards. During their impromptu hiatus, Jonathan and Rachel missed the current political news that Mr. Edwards had become Mayor Edwards sometime in the last eight months.

A stern look of disapproval took residence on Jonathan's face as he read the headline again, hoping that his eyes had played a trick on him. However, this was no trick. It seemed Mr. Edwards had been elevated to a new seat of power, with undoubtedly new levels of authority to match. Jonathan knew what this meant: Mr. Edwards had gotten stronger.

"Kane," said Jonathan, under his breath, speaking the name of his enemy aloud, as if this were a mild form of a war cry. Previously, this sort of revelation would have been disheartening to Jonathan, however this time he wasn't afraid of the adversary that stood before him. He knew it would be another journey, another fight, which was yet another reason that made its way on an ever piling list of reasons why Jonathan needed a plan of attack.

As he thought about it for a moment, his mind couldn't help but drift to another thought. He thought about those that had been affected by all of this madness. Besides Rachel, there was another person who came to mind; his mother. He wondered how she was coping with the reality of her son being a fugitive. He knew it was beyond painful for her, but he also knew his mother would stand on the memory of her son and the kind of person she knew he was. He knew she would never believe the lies that had been fed to her. In his defense, Jonathan called his mother on several different occasions. She just didn't know it was him. He called her a couple of times over the past few months. He would dial from an unknown number to see if she would answer. When she did answer, he wouldn't speak. He just listened to her say hello and ask who it was. Her mother's intuition seemed to kick in and she would say Jonathan's name in hopes of it being him on the other end of the line. For some odd reason, he couldn't bring himself to speak to her whenever she would answer. Perhaps he was still carrying the shame and guilt of being in the situation in the first place.

With all this newfound revelation he had received in the last few minutes, it forced feelings of nostalgia and his yearning for the life he once knew to return back to him. He thought it would be appropriate for him to call her and perhaps speak this time. He owed her that. He grabbed the cheap cell phone he purchased a while back at one of the local stores. He knew the number by heart as he dialed, thinking of what he would say as his fingers hit each button. He dialed the number and waited for a moment. He then heard the phone began to ring. Part of him didn't want her to answer the phone because he knew this conversation wouldn't be easy. Nevertheless, he stayed on the line, and then he heard her pick up the phone.

"Hello?" she said, her voice sounding worn down, void from the normal joy that once filled her vocal cords. This alone caused a deep sense of grief to come upon Jonathan because he knew the source of her sorrow.

"Hello?" she said again, her voice still in a dull monotone. Then, "Look if this is another reporter, I told you guys before, my son didn't…"

Her pre-rant was cut short as Jonathan interjected."Mom," he said.

A short silence came between them on the phone.

"Johnny?!" she hollered, her voice almost piercing Jonathan's ears from the decibel levels of her scream."Johnny is that you?!!"

"Yeah Mom, it's me," he said, as he ran his hand over his head. He was angry at the fact that she too had to endure her own level of suffering. What made it even worse was that she had nothing to do with what went on in Edge City. Her pain was a casualty of an unnecessary war, and Jonathan knew it wasn't right for her to have to pay that penalty. Jonathan sat there as he heard the wailing cries of a mournful mother on the other end of the phone. It hit him hard, and he could all but feel her pain as she continued to sob. There was no way for him to truly know the magnitude of what she felt because he had no point of reference of what having a child felt like. All he could do in the moment was to try and meet her where she was, saturated in her own grief. However, Jonathan now had a gift in his possession that he could present to her that would push past the heaping mountains of her pain and penetrate her heart. He had the gift of hope and relief wrapped in his voice from the simple fact that he was alive and well; this alone would prove to be joyous news.

"My GOD!! Where have you been?!" she hollered, her voice still shaky from the shock.

Jonathan could hear the confusion in her voice. He too was experiencing his own internal struggle at the moment. He felt like a giant burden had been lifted from the outer casing of his heart, but he still held on to a dose of guilt for going so long without talking to her. Before Jonathan could respond to the expected question that was posed, his mother spoke again.

"I didn't know if you were alive!" she hollered.

"Oh *GOD* thank you!!! Thank you!"

As she gave praise to the Almighty for answering her prayers, she came to herself and presented Jonathan with yet another question: "Where the hell are you?"

At this point, tears were smoothly pushing their way past Jonathan's tear ducts while making their way down to his mouth and conforming to the curves of his lips. He could actually taste the salty bitterness of his own pain, a physical reminder of some of the feelings that he had internally, now organically making their way to the surface so that they could be recognized and dealt with.

"I'm sorry Mom. I'm so sorry," he said with guilt and remorse, grabbing his vocal cords and stroking them like strings on a guitar. "Believe me, I never meant any of this to happen. And Mom, you gotta believe me when I tell you, I didn't do any of the stuff that the police say I did!" He kept explaining further, trying to plead his case, hoping his mother had not succumbed to the lies the media and police had no doubt been feeding her over the last several months.

The phone was silent for a moment as neither one of them spoke a word. Jonathan could hear her breathing on the other end.

"I know you didn't, Jonathan," Mrs. Cross said in between intervals of her sniffling from the outpour of tears she had released only seconds earlier.

Jonathan was relieved to hear these words coming from the lips of the woman who had known him his entire life. It gave him a certain level of reassurance knowing his own flesh and blood was still on his side. Although he was beyond pleased to hear this, he also couldn't help but wonder in the back of his mind what made her so sure the police weren't wrong. However, he was given grace because the answer to his unspoken question was given to him.

"Because I know my son," she said, allowing both confidence and ease to finally take their place in the conversation. "But what I don't know, is what in the *hell* is going on?! What happened over there Johnny?" She asked the first question in a myriad of others.

Jonathan took a moment and looked at the other door, the one Rachel was on the other side of. He took a deep breath, allowing the oxygen in the room to give him some of the required strength he needed to have the necessary conversation the moment called for. He would have to tell her everything, and he did. Everything from the moment he placed his foot on the solid concrete of that metropolitan jungle, to breaking into the Mayor's house, everything. Even the part about him having to shoot another man, which was an important part to cover to explain the whole attempted murder thing. Jonathan laid it all out there on the table for her to see, so she could be the judge for herself. He took his time stopping to answer her questions, which were frequent in nature, almost after his every sentence. Naturally, she was angry that her son was now a wanted man, labeled as something he wasn't, a criminal. He almost went as far as to tell her where he was, but for her own safety he didn't. Besides, that way if the police showed up again asking her if she knew where he was, she wouldn't have to lie. This part didn't go over well with Mrs. Cross, but the situation was complicated.

It was good and much needed for the both of them. Tears were shared, loads lightened, and hearts comforted. There was a certain level of healing that took place in their conversation, something they were both grateful for. By the time they finished talking, Mrs. Cross was still on the emotional side, and who could blame her? However, she was miles away from the low state she was in before Jonathan called her, and he brightened her entire world. At first, she didn't want to get off the phone with him, but eventually she did.

By the time he finally hung up the phone, Jonathan was relieved. However, there was something more important to him than relief that now swam in the base of his belly like a shark pacing its prey. Now he became motivated. He was motivated to get it all back and then some. He had already been put through the fire once. He'd seen combat on the front lines. Yes, Jonathan had tasted the harshness of battle. He had not forgotten its lessons or its devastating blows. In fact, all these things made him stronger. As he sat there in his chair, he knew he was ready for whatever would come next. A warrior had been unleashed in him and he was ready for war.

CHAPTER 5

THE REBEL FISH

The smell of cheap beer and greasy burgers merged together as one to reveal themselves as an appetizing scent. The colorful aromas danced on the outer rims of both Rachel and Jonathan's nostrils, while seducing their taste buds in the process. It was a long overdue night of leisure for the both of them. A *taste* of normalcy in the midst of lies, false identities, and coverups. It was an evening that Jonathan had both offered and promised in the same breath to Rachel the day before. He was glad she graciously took him up on his offer. They allowed themselves to experience the pleasures of a normal, young couple.

The truth was, Jonathan didn't feel like they were in much of a relationship lately and for the sake of argument, he definitely felt there was a difference between them. She was the Bonnie to his newly found Clyde. A power couple in a different sense of the word, they were stronger together, a unified front that refused to be broken. However, their recent closeness appeared to be formed out of necessity instead of heartfelt romance, or at least in Jonathan's eyes.

He knew he still loved Rachel, and honestly he knew Rachel loved him too, but it was his unspoken thoughts that sometimes made him unsure. He just wasn't feeling the love lately, which really had all to do with them both being on the run, not to mention the fact they were using false identities in a town that they knew nothing about. It was a helpful tidbit that the same town knew nothing about them, which was the way they both wanted it. So there the two of them sat, across from one another like a teenage couple sharing a milkshake after their first date. In all honesty, that was the type of innocence Jonathan yearned to return to, and he knew Rachel's sentiments weren't too far from his own. Jonathan stared at Rachel, marveling at her inner beauty and raw courage she displayed just by still being in his life. It also didn't hurt the equation that he still found her breathtaking in a physical sense as well. She was 360° gorgeous. To him, she looked good from any angle and at any emotional level.

She was in the middle of her meal as Jonathan took a moment to soak in his present surroundings. A half eaten bacon cheeseburger sat on her plate. She normally didn't eat bacon but she had grown fond of it in their new found residency. She said she liked the way the restaurant cooked theirs. It had a caramelized taste to it. It was a good place for food, a regular mom and pop type diner called "The Rebel Fish." Ironically, the diner didn't serve a single ounce of seafood, not even the run of the mill popcorn shrimp dinner, so why the place was so inappropriately named was anyone's guess. However, Jonathan was sure there was some explanation and backstory to the history of the title that most of the older locals were probably aware of. Its secret would elude him since he didn't make it his mission to uncover such a trivial fact.

He had already finished most of his burger and was making his way through the last few bites of chili cheese fries. He needed a break from the strict boxer diet Henry told him to adopt. So tonight was a far step outside of the things they had uncomfortably begun to get used to.

"I love you," he told her, wanting to give her the world she deserved in just those three words.

Rachel was chewing a mouthful of the bacon cheeseburger she so adored as she playfully squinted her eyes and pushed her food to one side of her mouth. While her left cheek was full of burger and fries, she responded.

"I wuv you too!" she said, before coughing from the mouthful of food.

They both laughed in unison, Rachel covering her mouth as she giggled. It was a peaceful moment on that youthful Friday night. To say they were in rare form wouldn't really be true, because in all actuality this was their true form. Their jovial ways had been repressed due to the mounds of troublesome turmoil they endured. However, tonight, they released the weight of the world along with their false names and stripped the lies that had been told. They allowed themselves to have their own time. It was a nice and very much needed change of pace. They appreciated every second of the moment and took nothing for granted.

So there they sat in a comfortable booth nestled in the back corner of the diner, the red leather seats adding to the allure of the whole small-town feel. Seeing Rachel like this was good for Jonathan, he *needed* this. He needed to see that she was still alive, that the harsh reality of their current circumstances hadn't robbed her of her spirit, that her true nature had not been defiled by the deeds of an evil man. Jonathan was always aware of how he felt inside, but for obvious reasons he didn't have the same access to Rachel's inner thoughts the way he had access to his own. So the current outward display of merriment did them both a world of good.

Jonathan wanted to hold on to this night as he looked into Rachel's eyes, thinking about how their life could be like this all the time. He knew he could make her happy and she had already done that a million times over for him. This was but a mere glimpse into the future that he yearned to share with her, but he was also aware of another crucial tidbit of information. In order for them to enjoy their lives again the way they wanted, and the way they deserved to, they would have to clear their names and deal with the past of Edge City and everything that came with it. This thought made Jonathan shift his focus. As he sat there in his seat looking at Rachel, a flash of last night's conversation played in front of him. He remembered the cathartic talk he and his mother shared. He remembered the rush of motivation he felt surging through his veins that night. The power of its electrical current still rang between Jonathan's ears. With all of this swirling around in his head, he knew he needed to let Rachel know about what happened. He needed to tell her he finally spoke to his mother, but more importantly, he needed to tell her it was time to act.

Rachel sat there drinking the last few ounces of her orange soda. Part of Jonathan hated to interrupt the night with bringing up news that would cause both of them to think about Edge City and its rippling after-effects. Although it wasn't all bad, he knew he would have to eventually mention it.

"Hey listen. I want to tell you something," he said, slightly shifting in his seat as he spoke." Lowering his voice, he leaned in and said, "I spoke to my mother last night."

This newfound information got Rachel's attention, but not in a good way. She lifted her head from the glass and looked him in the eyes. "You did what?"

"Rachel, I haven't talked to her since we left the city," responded Jonathan, hoping to cool down the fire before it started."I owed her that."

Rachel paused before she said anything. The look on her face suggested that she was giving brief thought to what Jonathan had just uttered."Yeah, I know," she said, her voice sympathetic and nurturing. "What did she say? I mean, goodness, is she all right?" Not really giving Jonathan time to answer her first question.

"Well yeah, I mean as good as she can be for a woman talking to her fugitive son," replied Jonathan.

"Right." Rachel nodded her head in agreement with the same sarcasm that plagued Jonathan's previous response.

"I told her what she needed to know, which honestly, was just about everything," said Jonathan.

"Well not *everything* everything right?" asked Rachel, as a semi-frown swept its way across her face.

Due to her response, Jonathan was confused. "What do you mean?"

"I mean, did you tell her where we are?" Rachel asked in a concerned tone of voice.

Jonathan was irritated at her question. He didn't want the innocence of the night to escape their midst while they were having a good time."No, Rachel I didn't tell her that. Look, just hold on a second. All I'm saying is I talked to her. She had the right to know that her son isn't the criminal they're saying I am." His voice was becoming sharper as a result of the frustration wrapping around his vocal cords. He wasn't angry at Rachel, but the emotional thought of all he endured had a way of resurfacing at times like this. Rachel reached across the table and put her hand on his. "I get it," she said. "But trust me, she knows that, Jonathan. Anyone who talks to you longer than five minutes knows you're not a bad person."

Hearing those words come from Rachel's lips was soothing music to Jonathan's ears. It gave him strength hearing her speak from her heart like that.

"Thanks" he said, as he gazed upon her beautiful face. He grabbed her hand as it rested on his. "Look, I was thinking about last night. You're right. It's time. It's time to get out of here. We've been here long enough. We can't stay here forever, and we won't. I don't have all the answers but we'll find a way to prove our innocence."

After Jonathan finished speaking, they just looked at each other for a moment, neither one of them having the right words to say next. This in itself was rare, or at least on Rachel's side, she was normally never low on verbiage. Instead of them forcing it, they let the evening play out. They didn't have it all figured out that night. They just needed to be together and have some peace.

After they finished their meal, the two of them made their way toward the door arm in arm. When they walked outside, the night's cool air met them where they stood and greeted them with sounds of what the small town's nightlife offered. Their car was parked across the street in what happened to be a joint parking lot for a few of the shops nearby, including the diner. The moon was out in full effect, its nightly rays illuminating the streets that laid before it. Rachel held onto Jonathan's arm as they walked and talked through the street, appearing like a typical couple on a Friday night. It wasn't until they got closer to the parking lot that Jonathan noticed something he hadn't seen since he first laid eyes on Rachel: another beautiful, young woman.

CHAPTER 6

MEN OF THE MOMENT

Truthfully, it wasn't like there weren't other women out there. It's just that Jonathan's eyes were always fixed on one. Yet this time he couldn't help but notice this particular woman. He didn't get a good look at her because she was in the midst of two men who didn't seem to be getting along. In fact, they were arguing; about what was yet to be seen, but Jonathan recognized the looks in both of their eyes. He knew those eyes all too well. He had seen them before. In fact, he had even had those same eyes lodged in his own head at times. The kind of eyes where fires of rage burn behind the pupils. The kind of eyes that only see hatred and bloodshed. The kind of eyes that knew no reason or logic, only hate.

The man closest to the young woman was slightly shorter than the other guy. He was of average build. He had the look of a young lumberjack. He wore an old red baseball cap that had surely seen better days than the current one. He had a scruffy beard with long hair flowing past his ears. His shirt was wool plaid made up of red and black blocks, which he paired with ripped, worn-down jeans tucked snugly inside his mountain boots. The guy the lumberjack was squaring off with had a completely different look. His clothes were more modern. He wore a black leather jacket with what looked to be designer jeans from what Jonathan could see. Things were already heated between the two of them and escalating fast. By this time, Rachel also noticed the storm that was brewing.

"Reminds me of my college days," she commented as she looked on.

Jonathan said nothing as he kept his eyes steady on the whole situation and headed in the trio's direction. As he looked, his eyes also couldn't help but notice the pretty face that was at the center of it all. She tried to lodge herself in the middle of the two men, but the lumberjack moved her aside so he could have a good view of his intended target. Apparently that move turned out to be a bad one because the guy in the leather jacket lunged at the lumberjack and hit him in the face, hard. Jonathan could hear the sound of the man's knuckles collide with the lumberjack's face and it didn't sound pretty. He was sure the guy just lost a couple of his front teeth. The lumberjack stumbled back a little bit, putting both his hands up to his nose, probably to stop the bleeding that was gushing out of his nose at this point. Unfortunately, the guy in the black jacket didn't stop there. He immediately followed with a surprise push, then an NFL-style tackle to the midsection that sent the lumberjack falling like a stack of chopped wood. The young woman, who was probably the object of both men's affections, screamed at the guy in the black jacket.

"Let him go, Derrick!"

Well, at least one of the guys now had a name: Derrick. By now, Derrick had the lumberjack down on the ground. He had him pinned like one of those MMA fighters Jonathan had seen on TV. That's when Derrick started to unleash his fist of fury and let the lumberjack really have it, with three steady blows to the face.

Jonathan had seen more than enough when he watched the poor guy get his head knocked back on the hard pavement as good ol Derrick dished out a harsh punishment for pulling the short stick in the who-would-win-the-parking-lot-brawl-contest. He knew he had to step in, and quickly, before things went too far south for either party.

"Stay here," he told Rachel, with a certain firmness coming over his voice.

A look came across Rachel's face that suggested she was about to speak, but she didn't say anything. If she had spoken, she probably would have told Jonathan to be careful, or maybe to not even get involved, but neither comment would have swayed him. He was tired of watching people getting beat up on, especially himself. That newfound courage seeped through his actions and even his words at times. He dashed toward Derrick with a strong sense of urgency. Jonathan could hear the sound of his shoes brushing against the pavement as he hurled toward Derrick, his eyes locked solely on his intended target. Before he knew it, Jonathan was upon them both.

By now Derrick looked up, seeing a moving body swiftly approaching him. Jonathan grabbed him by the jacket and slung him off of the lumberjack. He glanced back for a moment to check the guy out as he lay there, sprawled out on the cold and unforgiving black concrete of the parking lot. Blood was all over his nose and mouth. He had taken a couple of hard hits. But this wasn't the time to play doctor for the guy. That would have to wait. Right now, Jonathan had someone else he had to focus on: this Derrick guy who was now standing to his feet with a mean look plastered across his face.

Now that he and Jonathan were standing face to face, Jonathan was able to get a good look at the guy. They were about the same height, except he looked like he was fresh out of a modeling ad, with slicked back hair parted in a perfectly crease down the side. He looked more like a pretty boy than a backstreet brawler, but then again, Jonathan knew all too well that looks could most definitely be deceiving. Jonathan saw the guy had a slight scar above his left eye that separated his eyebrow with a bald line going through it. Most of all, Jonathan could see his eyes, those fiery eyes that spoke hate and wanted to inflict damage onto someone. Jonathan knew those eyes as he identified them earlier when he watched from a distance. There was something else Jonathan knew, he knew he wasn't the same man he used to be. He was stronger than before, both physically and mentally; he was more of a fighter now. He had seen enough monsters to know the difference between a real one and an animal that merely *thinks* it's a monster.

Jonathan had tangled with beasts before, so he knew he could handle the man that stood before him. He had been groomed in the art of war and now stood as a warrior, so this encounter would be over quickly. Jonathan would surely snuff out the flames of those fiery eyes that found themselves lodged in this Derrick guy's head and Jonathan would do so with aggression if the situation called for it.

"Who the hell are you?!" shouted Derrick.

He didn't give Jonathan any time to respond as he darted toward him. However, Jonathan wasn't going to answer him anyway. Derrick came at him all wrong. Jonathan could tell by the guy's stance he didn't know what he was doing. As he lunged at Jonathan, it was like time slowed down a little, enough for Jonathan to get a full picture of the scene unfolding before him. He could see the left punch that this guy was going to throw from about a mile away. His left shoulder was arched back, winding up and then there was the obvious sign of his left fist steadily rising. His form was all wrong. He was swinging too wide and he left himself wide open for the immediate taking. This proved to be a horrible mistake for Derrick, as Jonathan would surely capitalize on it. As time stood still, Jonathan could taste the air as he felt the sensation of his senses almost in some heightened state. In the moment, he was truly in tune with his surroundings. He even noticed Rachel from afar, as she made her way nervously toward the commotion.

Although he noticed Rachel, that didn't mean he was going to make the same mistake he did with Henry back in the gym. This time, he would focus on the matter truly at hand and pay attention to his opponent. Jonathan put his hands up and let his muscle memory do the rest of the work. His hands tightened quickly, assuming the position they had become accustomed to by folding into war-ready fists. After this was done, Jonathan's left forearm rose to meet the incoming blow. Jonathan's defense proved itself to be strong as he successfully blocked the punch. He then immediately followed up with several of his own as he decided to unleash a combination. He first countered quickly with a right hook, followed immediately by a hard body shot with his left. Jonathan could feel the guy's rib cage alongside the top of his knuckles. The sound of his fist made a deep thud as it hit its intended target combined with the yelp of pain made by his opponent. All of these things told Jonathan he made good contact. Jonathan wasn't quite finished just yet, as he noticed Derrick stagger back a few steps. He stepped forward, moving in fluid movement with his opponent, not giving him time to recover. He then followed up with an explosive uppercut. Jonathan could hear the sound of the guy's teeth clanging together; only the impact would determine if missing teeth would be the result. Unfortunately for Derrick, this wasn't the end of the fight. Jonathan hit him with one last punch. This time, it was a stiff right jab landing firmly in Derrick's mouth as he lowered his head from the uppercut he was forced to endure only seconds earlier.

Derrick went down like a ton of bricks. His battered body and crushed ego sprawled out onto the pavement. Now the fight was over, although by Jonathan's standards he wouldn't have called it a fight, mainly because the whole thing was over before it really even got started. Jonathan stood there for a moment as the unchallenged victor of the parking lot boxing round. He stared down at his less than worthy opponent, but not in an arrogant way. It was partly due to the fact that Jonathan had learned not to underestimate people. He kept his wits and focus about him, especially in moments like these.

Jonathan glanced back at the lumberjack, just to see if the guy managed to make it back on his feet. He was on his knees, lightly touching his face with his left hand. He then extended his hand so he could check how badly he was bleeding. Jonathan had seen bloodied faces before, so in comparison, he had definitely seen much worse. Although, Mr. Lumberjack probably wouldn't want to hear something like that right about now. The next sound Jonathan heard was the sound of high heels clicking on the pavement. He knew it was Rachel walking, but before he looked up, he glanced at Derrick, who was still flat on his back, rocking back and forth. It looked like he was attempting to escape the pain Jonathan caused him.

Even though the clacking of Rachel's heels could be heard approaching, there was still an uncomfortable silence that blanketed the air. It was the silence that existed after an argument between two people, or that moment when someone has reached the end of a rageful rant. In this case, it had been a violent encounter between three men, although ironically violence was used to stop violence. Regardless, it didn't make it any less awkward. Thoughts were now doing their usual, swirling around in Jonathan's mind. He stopped to think about the aftermath of his actions. He looked behind him, quickly glancing back over the scenery. It was late and the streetlights were talking to the air with their luminescent bulbs burning bright. Jonathan wondered if perhaps someone else witnessed the parking lot brawl and if so, how much time did he have before the police showed up?

Those few questions would have to wait to be speculated on, well before they could even be answered. The first thing Jonathan needed to do was to check and see if the young lady was alright. At this point, she wasn't standing too far from Jonathan, only a few feet away. Due to his close proximity, he was now able to get a good look at her and see what all the fuss was about. It didn't take a genius to do this social math. There were three people standing outside of a bar. Two of the three were men, and they were in some sort of argument. This left one person, who was the mystery woman. It was more than likely they were fighting over her. She wore slim fitting dark jeans that were fashionably torn in the front to show off her legs, which were nice to look at. She wore a black bomber jacket with a tight white shirt underneath that had black and red lips on it. Her hair was in a ponytail, a sandy dark brown one with gold highlights throughout. Since her hair was pulled back and her full face was revealed, she had the looks of a supermodel, with sharp brown eyes that undoubtedly sent men into a craze. Given the fact that two men had just fought over her, it wasn't hard to believe. As Jonathan silently admired her beauty, he noticed two sparkling glimmers coming from both her ears. They were diamond earrings. Jonathan had tasted some of the finer things in life back in Edge City, so he knew real diamonds when he saw them. He hadn't been in Olberton long, but by the looks of her, he could tell this woman wasn't from around here, either. After his assessment, he finally spoke to her.

"Are you alright?" asked Jonathan.

She didn't respond immediately. She appeared to enjoy the awkward silence. Jonathan watched her closely as he noticed her eyes studying him with seductive intent. "Yes," she answered in a whisper.

Her voice was light and refreshing. But there was something that he felt was slightly off about their brief exchange. She didn't seem to be too shaken up at all of the recent activity. She was surprisingly calm and didn't even bother to look at the lumberjack or Derrick. Before Jonathan could speculate on any of this, Rachel approached him, breaking his concentration on the mystery woman.

"Goodness Jon…*Carl,*" said Rachel as she corrected herself mid-sentence. The look on her face suggested that she hoped the mystery woman didn't hear her slight verbal misstep. "You alright?" she asked, concern overcoming her voice.

Before Jonathan could answer her question, Rachel interjected and answered it herself.

"Of course you're fine. You're not the one on the ground bleeding," she said.

It was good to see Rachel using some sarcasm in the situation. That let him know she wasn't furious with him. Plus, given the fact that they were having such a wonderful evening until now, he didn't want to spoil their night, as crazy as that seemed.

"Yeah, I'm good," said Jonathan, as he was cooling down from the adrenaline rush he was experiencing. Rachel reached out and hugged him, squeezing him tightly. Jonathan squeezed her back as he held her for a brief moment. He noticed the woman was staring at him as he held onto Rachel. He knew something was off with this whole scenario. This woman was acting almost as if she didn't care about what happened to the guys that were fighting over her just a few minutes ago. As he loosened his grip on Rachel, she too turned to ask if the lady was ok. However, before the mystery woman could answer, the parking lot started to get a lot brighter. The source of the light was coming from behind him. Jonathan turned around and placed his right hand in front of his face in an attempt to keep the light from shining directly into his eyes. Jonathan got enough of a glimpse to see what the bright light was. In fact, the source of the light was split in two. They were headlights from a car. Jonathan calmly placed his left hand on Rachel's arm in a protective fashion. As usual, his mind started to calculate what was going on, or what could possibly be going on. Perhaps someone *did* see them after all and decided to give the police a call. This wasn't good in the slightest. Neither Jonathan nor Rachel could afford to have any more run-ins with the police, not even for a simple parking ticket. Even though Jonathan was smart enough to have fake ID's made for his and Rachel's alternate identities, he didn't have enough confidence in them to endure the probing of an official police officer.

The car which Jonathan could now see was an SUV, and it was getting closer. It approached, then came to a complete stop. Jonathan and Rachel were in the direct path of the luminous rays coming from the headlights. Jonathan lowered his head in an attempt to keep the lights out of this eyes; they were too blinding to look directly into. Rachel stayed where she was, and she moved her hand down to Jonathan's as he was holding her arm. He then grabbed her hand instead of her arm. The car was now parked, and the few seconds that went by felt like several minutes of anxious anticipation to see who would come out of the vehicle.

As Jonathan was still processing the whole situation, he happened to notice what he didn't see. What he didn't see were flashing blue and red lights, which would of been on by now if this was a police car. Perhaps this wasn't what Jonathan thought it was, and if it wasn't, then who was in the car? It seemed that the unspoken question was about to be answered as both the passenger and driver side doors opened simultaneously. Jonathan was close enough to see the SUV was black, as the two doors remained open. Jonathan's eyes stayed glued on the driver side door, to see who was coming out.

His concentration was broken when he saw a large-bodied frame step out from the passenger side. The headlights were distorting his vision so he could only see the large silhouette of the person. Jonathan may not have been able to make out the face, but he could tell it was a very large and muscular man that was moving in the shadows of the night. He looked like a bodybuilder from where Jonathan was standing and that's when he thought of someone...could it be? The last time he saw a frame that size, it belonged to Percy, Mr. Edward's muscle-bound henchman. Was it possible he had found them? The mere thought alone sent Jonathan into defense mode as he now pulled Rachel directly behind him, snatching her quickly from the grasp of perceived danger. The hidden figure moved in the darkness, his movements cloaked in secrecy. Due to this, Jonathan was unable to see exactly what the man was doing.

As he tried to piece this puzzle together, another variable presented itself. Jonathan noticed a man step out of the driver side. His image was a mere silhouette as well, which put Jonathan at ease because it ruled out this mystery accomplice being Adrian, due to his frame. So perhaps it wasn't the two dealers of death that he thought it was. Yet that still didn't answer the question of who *these* two were.

The large man on the passenger side door lifted his right arm while he closed the door with his left. Then Jonathan heard an all too familiar sound that sent memories that were better left dead, rushing back to his mind. It was the sound of a gun being cocked. The man had just pointed a gun at him. None of this made sense. Perhaps it really was some henchman from Mr. Edwards that managed to track them down. The night began to replay before Jonathan's eyes as he thought about how he didn't want to die like this. Jonathan took a deep breath doing his best to remain calm and in control of himself. As he did this, he felt Rachel clench onto his shirt balling it into knots with each of her hands.

The man on the driver side closed the door and stepped forward into the light, revealing his face. Jonathan looked at the man. He was well-groomed and young; by the look of him, he was older than Jonathan, but still young. He was dressed in a suit that didn't look cheap, and it was obvious that this man wasn't from Olberton, either. Jonathan had no idea who he was, but then again, why would he? Jonathan was definitely unfamiliar with this man's face, and even more unfamiliar with the world this man came from. Jonathan had never even heard of the name *Coloso*, so there was no way of knowing that the man who stood before him was *Rico Coloso.* Nor was he familiar with the name of the violent deliverer of pain and death named Marco, who revealed his face along with the large chrome-plated pistol he held firmly in his hand.

Jonathan knew nothing of Rico and Marco from Harbor Stone City or why in the world he suddenly found himself in their crosshairs. But there was someone else in their midst who recognized both of these men, and for the sake of the lives of everyone in the parking lot that night, this person's voice would soon be heard.

CHAPTER 7

THE HIDDEN TRUTH OF A LIE

"Well well well. What on earth do we have here?" asked Rico, in an arrogant yet jovial tone of voice. He took a few steps forward with unwavering confidence presenting itself in his every step. He stood there basking in the awkwardness of the night's crazy turn of events. It was as if he was the gatekeeper for the evening, holding all the keys and knowing all the answers. Even if he did know all the answers, it would be ironic that the first thing to come out of his mouth was a question. He took a few more steps toward Jonathan, staring him directly in the eyes while doing so.

Jonathan was standing in front of Rachel, shielding her from any oncoming danger that may present itself. Right now, it looked like the danger was standing before him wearing a tailored suit and had some sort of guardian beast with him. He hadn't seen a man the size of Marco since his last encounter with Percy. He could see the viciousness in Marco's eyes as he too took a few steps forward. To Jonathan, their identities were still hidden, and they were moving in for what looked like an intended kill. The question still hid in the darkness of the night, hovering above them all.

The question was simple, but it still needed to be presented. *"Why?"* was the appropriate question. It was valid, however seeing as to how Jonathan had a gun pointed in his face, he didn't have time to ask. Then by a stroke of questionable luck or maybe even divine intervention, something happened. A woman's voice came forth behind Jonathan, flowing past his ears. Initially, he didn't turn his head, and instead kept his focus on the two men in front of him. By now he knew every ebb and flow of Rachel's voice no matter what emotional state she might have been in, so he knew that wasn't her. The voice belonged to the mystery woman who Jonathan so graciously fought for only a few minutes ago. It wasn't without a raw sense of irony that made him think that if he hadn't tried to be the hero, perhaps he wouldn't be looking down the wrong end of a gun's barrel right now. Nevertheless, he was eager to know what this lady had to offer to the situation as he listened closely.

"What the hell, Rico?" she snapped, her voice filled with agitation toward the new found assailant. *Rico,* Jonathan thought to himself, quickly searching his brain's database for any memory of a man with that name that he might have possibly come into contact with before. He was definitely drawing a blank on any possible leads. He stayed quiet as he continued to listen for any other forms of valuable information. He then heard the sound of the woman's heels clicking as she walked on the parking lot's worn and cracked concrete. Her heels made a slight but sharp pop with each step that she took.

"You wanna tell your boy to put the cooler away?" she asserted. By now she had moved toward Jonathan's right side. She came close enough for him to get another look at her face. He wondered what she meant by "cooler." She said the phrase with such ease and underlying confidence. It was no doubt an understood term from wherever the three of these people came from. Honestly though, it wasn't too hard for Jonathan to put two and two together. He took one look at the hulking behemoth with the gun in his hand and figured out that she was in fact referring to the gun. He continued to get a good look at the woman. He looked directly at her face to see what silent story her facial expressions might tell. Judging from the context clues of their currently one-sided conversation, he could easily gather that the mystery woman and *Rico* knew each other. As he continued to look at her face, it was clear her eyes were doing more of the talking than her mouth. There seemed to be a certain level of familiarity between her and this Rico guy. Perhaps he was another one of her suitors who didn't appreciate the cat and mouse game. Jonathan would have to wait and allow the situation to play itself out and see exactly how the pieces to this bizarre puzzle fit together.

"Did he send you here?" the woman asked, her arms now firmly folded across her chest.

Jonathan continued to stand planted in front of Rachel because her safety was his main focus right now. He felt her tight grip still clinging onto the back of his shirt. He knew she was scared which was why he needed to stand strong at the moment since there was no room for weakness in the streets. Jonathan wasn't just pretending or putting on a strong face. There was a part of him now where fear no longer existed. Situations like this brought out that once dormant animal in him. There was now a certain readiness that pulsated in Jonathan's veins pumping life into that inner warrior that lay in wait, ready to step into battle with full force. As he stood outwardly still yet inwardly ready, he wondered who was she referring to when she asked if a man had sent Rico. Yet again, this was not the moment to ask questions, Jonathan knew he would have to let some answers come to him, if they were to be revealed.

"How did you even know I was here?" she asked, her frustration steadily becoming more apparent as her tone sharpened. It was beyond obvious the woman didn't fear for her life, as her safety seemed to be assured in her eyes while she stood there staring at Rico. It was as if she knew he wouldn't hurt her under any circumstances. Jonathan knew that for this lady to act this way, there must have been some strong history between her and this Rico guy to give her this level of certainty and confidence.

"Answer me, Rico!" shouted the woman, her body language in militant unison with her tone, both clearly demanding that her question be answered.

Rico remained calm and collected as a small smirk came across his face. The whole scenario was a bit odd, truth be told, to the point where it baffled Jonathan that no one else either heard or saw what was going on. Jonathan kept his head still while his eyes swiveled as much as they could. He was trying to look around to see if there was anyone watching what was going on, some sort of witness to this parking lot madness that seemed to be running rampant at this point. Rico still hadn't answered the question just yet. He glanced up in the air and rubbed his mouth before responding. Then he finally graced everyone with the gift of his long awaited response.

"No, little one. Papa doesn't know you're here," answered Rico, his voice sounding smooth with the thickness of what sounded like the truth overlaying his response.

Jonathan felt a slight twinge in the back of this throat as a result of what he just heard. *What did he just say?* he wondered, the question echoing deeply in the recesses of his mind. *Did he say Papa? Were they related? Was this woman his sister? Also more importantly at this point, who the hell was this woman?*

With each passing second, Jonathan felt that old familiar feeling that he hadn't experienced since he left Edge City. It was the suffocating feeling of some invisible force pulling him into a situation he had nothing to do with. The feeling of being at the mercy of drama that belonged to someone else. It wasn't something that he wanted to experience ever again. This was the sort of thing that caused him a world of pain the last time he came in contact with this type of dilemma. Jonathan stood there, angry inside. He could almost feel his intestines warming up from the heat of his unspoken wrath. He couldn't allow this sort of thing to control his life yet again.

He again tried to replay the night in his mind, retracing his steps. He wondered how he could go from enjoying a much needed peaceful evening with Rachel to having a gun pointed at his face. It didn't take long for him to locate the point at which the evening took a bad turn. It was when Jonathan tried to be a good Samaritan and break up a fight he had nothing to do with. This was not what he wanted. He was just trying to prevent some guy from being beaten to a pulp in parking lot.

Perhaps some part of Jonathan identified with the feeling of taking a beating and being left with nothing but the icy embrace of the ground to offer some wayward form of comfort. He just wanted to help someone else from becoming a victim like he once was. However, he had no way of predicting the future, so he wasn't going to punish himself for too long. The last thing he needed to do now was fall into the trap of despair and blaming himself. He wasn't going to take this, not again. He looked at the giant henchman pointing the gun. He couldn't help but see flashbacks of his tussle with Percy back in Edge City. He barely survived that fight, so he wasn't in much of a rush to try and go toe-to-toe with a man who looked like he could bench press the truck he got out of. His mind calculated his possible routes of success: he couldn't charge Rico because big man would put a hole in Jonathan's head before he got to him; however, the mystery woman who now stood to his left was just slightly out of arm's length. Judging from their conversation, this woman meant something to Rico, so surely if Jonathan took her hostage he would have no choice but to let them go.

This wasn't the friendliest plan that Jonathan could come up with, however it wasn't the friendliest of moments that he found himself in, either. It also went against his nature. He would never harm a lady, although for now he just needed it to look like he would. He made up in his mind he was going to make his move, and he knew he would have to be quick. Fortunately, Jonathan trusted his newfound body and his skills to get the job done. He took a slight breath, then prepped himself for the task at hand and any possible aftermath.

He then heard a cough and a deep grunt, the sounds of a man clearing his throat. Jonathan turned his attention to the right, slightly behind Rico. It was the lumberjack finally back on his feet. The guy looked upset, which was something that was completely understandable. Jonathan could also see a hint of embarrassment as it nestled itself in the corners of the man's eyes. The lumberjack's awakening got everyone's attention, everyone, that is, but the big man as he stayed focused on Jonathan with his gun aimed steady. Jonathan still didn't know who these people were, but he could at least tell one thing; they weren't common street thugs. Rico and the big man were definitely trained. It was clear they'd done this kind of thing before. This also made Jonathan rethink his idea about grabbing the girl. For now, he could only watch and pray that things didn't get any worse.

Rico slightly turned his body to get a better look at the lumberjack as he stood. He looked him up and down, eyeing over the poor sap who looked like he had seen better days, although the look in Rico's eyes suggested more disgust than pity. He shook his head, a brazen physical display of his disapproval of the mystery woman's choice in men.

"You know Aaliyah, you should be thanking me," said Rico, his voice filled with pride. "Because if Papa *did* know what was going on, I guarantee you this little encounter would have turned into a bloodbath."

As he spoke these deathly words, he had a demented look plastered on his face, as if he preferred the latter option. It was clear to Jonathan that this man wasn't in the mood for games and it was also clear that he had just given up more valuable information. First, the mystery woman had finally been identified: her name was *Aaliyah*. Second, he cleared up any confusion about how these two knew each other; they were definitely brother and sister. They seemed to be a troubled family to say the least. If the children were like this, then Jonathan certainly didn't want to meet their parents or any other relative for that matter. All he wanted to do now was get himself and Rachel out of that parking lot unharmed and alive.

What an evening this turned out to be; that was the invisible banner that continued to flash across Jonathan's mind. He almost got sick at the thought that this sort of trouble could dare find him in a place like Olberton. Perhaps trouble was looking for him and refused to be ignored. Jonathan still dealt with that tiny thought he managed to silence earlier. The thought that said perhaps he should have stayed out of the whole lover's quarrel thing when he saw the guys arguing. It just wasn't right that he found himself at this level of trouble in a town that couldn't even seem to spell trouble.

"So now what?" Aaliyah asked Rico, her arms still firmly crossed and her left leg out slightly in front of the rest of her body. She tapped her foot for a moment, as if in an attempt to pass the time before Rico was about to answer her question, but before Rico could say anything, the good ol lumberjack finally decided to join the party.

"Hey babe, what the hell is going?" said the lumberjack. It was clear his skull was still rattled from the punches he ate about ten minutes ago. He was obviously having some trouble completing his sentences. As the lumberjack took a few staggering steps with blood making its way down his nose and over his mouth, he made eye contact with Jonathan. When their eyes met, the man looked at Jonathan as if he knew him. Jonathan could see the inner churning of the lumberjack's mind trying to come up with the answer to who Jonathan was. He had the half-beaten look of *hey, don't I know you?* lodged in his bloodied face. Surely this wasn't the case, because Jonathan had never met the man before tonight. So there was no way he could know who he was, although Jonathan still prayed this wasn't the case. After all, no one else in this town recognized him or Rachel. Could it be that this guy knew who he really was? Or maybe that was just the only expression that his face could muster up at the moment, given it's recent trauma. This was a good possibility until the lumberjack began to point at Jonathan.

"Hey man....don't...don't..I know you...you're on TV?" the man mumbled.

Given the fact that everyone was in a pretty close proximity of each other, they all heard what he said. Jonathan could sense the curiosity and confusion come amongst them all like a storm front wind appearing out of nowhere. Rico and Aaliyah both took a moment to look at Jonathan, both of them half-entertained with the rambling of a man that may or may not have had a concussion at this point.

"No," said Jonathan, his voice blanketed with a false calmness that he purposefully wanted to exude. It was an attempt to throw the dogs off his trail. The last thing Jonathan wanted was for this apparent psycho family to know his true identity.

"What the hell is he talking about?" asked Rico, in an almost dismissing tone."You know, you should be proud of yourself," he said to Aaliyah, as he nodded his head in the lumberjack's direction. He appeared to be further making fun of her as well as her latest romantic decisions. It was beyond ironic at this point, that one of the very people Jonathan was trying to help earlier was now seemingly about to cause him unwanted harm. He now found himself wanting to knock the guy out.

"Yeah, you're that guy…from Edge…City" the lumberjack said, still sounding a bit awkward as he paused between words. It was odd, and a bit unfair that it seemed to be playing out like this as no one cut the guy off from talking. Jonathan couldn't really do it, or if he did he would have to do it in an organic way that didn't seem too obvious. He couldn't make it look like he was purposefully cutting the guy off from revealing important information. At the same time, he didn't want this half-beaten fool to run his mouth. Unfortunately, the fool's mouth did indeed run.

"Yeah, I've seen you…you tried to kill….that guy…that business dude…Edwards Kane," said the lumberjack.

As those dreaded words left the lumberjack's mouth, Jonathan felt the rage of a hundred suns engulf his very being. He wanted to snap the guy's neck for running his mouth. He tried to remain cool as he looked at Rico's face then turned his attention to Marco. Jonathan wondered if he was in the clear, perhaps since the lumberjack said Mr. Edward's name backwards. Maybe, just maybe, they wouldn't recognize it. Better yet, maybe they didn't even know who Kane Edwards was. After all, this was a small town. Jonathan knew that was a long shot because for starters, it was made clear Rico and Aaliyah definitely weren't from Olberton, so there was no telling what they knew and didn't know. Jonathan could only hope for the best as he awaited some form of reaction from the dangerous trio.

Rico's face changed, in an uneasy and very noticeable way. He stared at Jonathan for what seemed like a long time, but was actually no more than a minute. Rico bit his bottom lip as he looked deep in thought for a moment, before turning his gaze to his sister. Aaliyah too looked at Jonathan, but only for a few seconds, her beautiful face making a slight frown as she looked him over, studying him from head to toe. It was while Aaliyah was studying Jonathan for the moment that he got a chance to study her as well. Her eyes were an astonishing hazel color; they had a mesmerizing quality to them. No doubt they had melted the hearts of many men that stood before their seductive gaze. Although this was far from the appropriate moment to check the girl out, his eyes still found the time to do so. Above her captivating eyes laid her perfectly trimmed eyebrows that looked as if they were drawn on her face by some famous renaissance artist. She was a true marvel to behold, which was probably how she managed to have two men duking it out over her in a small-town parking lot. Her beauty was as dangerous as it was apparent. While Jonathan's silent lust was running its course, he noticed Aaliyah's eyes beginning to wander.

Aaliyah briefly turned her attention from Jonathan to Rachel. Jonathan noticed her eyes looked slightly past his shoulder. Jonathan didn't quite know what to make of the group's uneasy silence. In fact, he was still trying to figure out in the back of his mind, how no one was seeing what was going on in the middle of this parking lot. It's not like they were hidden. Tonight's events had been played out in the open for any and everyone to see, if anyone was looking, which was now very clear that no one was. All it would take was for an unlucky soul to come traipsing out of the bar and rest their eyes on the guns-drawn drama that was taking place. However, no such luck seemed to be present tonight. There was no outside party coming to the rescue. It was almost uncanny how such a predicament managed to ensnare Jonathan like this. He thought he was long gone from problems such as these. After all, that was the whole point of he and Rachel hiding out in a town like Olberton. It was to stay miles away from things that even remotely looked like what was happening tonight. Jonathan's desire to lunge across the pavement and violently beat the remaining consciousness out of the idiotic Mr. Lumberjack was mounting by the second. If he had stopped to think about it, there was an underlying gross irony to the whole thing. It was due to the fact that Jonathan found himself wanting to inflict bodily harm on a man he was defending about ten minutes earlier.

"Let's go Marco, and let these fine people continue the rest of their evening in peace," said Rico, his tone sounding upbeat in a surprisingly genuine way.

In that second, there was yet another piece of information revealed to Jonathan. It appeared the beast had a name after all: Marco. Jonathan watched as the barrel of the gun he was staring into began to slowly but surely lower its way back to Marco's side. Once there, it disappeared into an unseen holster that Jonathan assumed was on the man's waist.

What just happened? Why were they leaving? Were they really leaving? Was this some sort of trick? These were the questions that found themselves swirling around the pool of Jonathan's thoughts. There they were and there, is where they would have to remain. There was no way Jonathan was about to verbalize any of the thoughts that were currently presenting themselves to his conscious mind. Truth be told, the answers were irrelevant at this point because Jonathan's desired outcome was manifesting; the deadly trio was leaving. This meant he and Rachel would get out of the night alive and well, living to see another day. Marco kept strict eye contact with Jonathan as he stepped back into the truck. He left the door open, as some sort of underlying precaution, a just-in-case type of move. Jonathan didn't care about that. He was just glad the gun was now out of his face.

"My deepest apologies for the inconvenience folks," said Rico, his tone not sounding as genuine as it did before.

Jonathan noticed that sort of thing, but yet again, that was a detail that was of little consequence to him. As long as Rico got back in that car, Jonathan was fine. He felt Rachel try to move from behind him. She was probably trying to get a better look at what was happening. Jonathan firmly kept her in position with his right arm. This was for Rachel's own safety; until the coast was clear, he wasn't taking any chances. Jonathan kept his mouth shut and stayed alert to Rico's every facial tic and bodily move as he made his way back to the driver side door. Although as Rico was walking, he didn't stop directly in front of the driver side door; he took about a half step past it as he reached for the passenger door next to it. He pulled it opened,turned around and looked at Aaliyah.

"Your chariot awaits, little princess" he said.

Jonathan slightly turned his head to see how Aaliyah would respond. She was quiet at first, her arms still folded. She looked over at Jonathan one last time, their eyes met in that awkward moment. There was something revealing in the way she looked at him. Jonathan couldn't quite put his finger on what it was, but it was almost as if she could tell he had been *looking* at her before. Looking in a way they both know he shouldn't have been looking. However, she said nothing as she turned her attention back to Rico before she reluctantly marched her way to the car. The lumberjack, still nursing his wounds spoke. "But baby, wait." he said, his swollen mouth making his words sound comical.

Aaliyah said nothing as the battered man watched her walk by. She simply allowed her sharp heels to do all the talking, as the clicked against the concrete. The slight echo of their noise rose to the air, serving as a reminder to the poor soul that thought she was his, that she was leaving and unlikely coming his way again. She stepped inside the car with Rico, closing the door behind her.

Rico and Jonathan locked eyes as Rico put his hand on top of the driver's side door before entering. The two of them seemed to have an unspoken conversation, one that suggested this wouldn't be the last time that they saw each other. Rico closed the door and Marco followed suit. The truck slowly backed out of the parking lot, its headlights still shining bright as it pulled onto the street and drove off into the night.

Rachel finally moved from behind Jonathan, and he turned around to see if she was ok. Her eyes were slightly red and irritated from the silent tears she had been crying. He placed his hands on her shoulders as he looked at her in the face. She began to sob, almost at an uncontrollable level.

"What the hell was that?!" she shouted.

Jonathan placed his hand behind her head and pulled her into his chest. He then put his arms around her to reassure her that he was there and they were ok. "That was our cue to leave," he said. He listened to the sound of his own voice as if he too were awaiting his own answer to her question. He gently stroked his hand over her head, and kissed her on the forehead.

As he stood there holding her in the parking lot, he noticed an older gentleman make his way out of the bar. The old man had a surprised look on his face as he studied the scene before him, one guy laying on the ground with his nose bleeding, another man standing up with blood covering a large portion of his face, while Jonathan was still holding Rachel as she cried in his arms.

"Hey y'all alright out here?" asked the man with a bewildered, yet concerned look over his face.

Jonathan looked up at the man and said, "Yeah…we were just leaving."

CHAPTER 8

THE KNOCK AND THE OFFER

Tensions were still high from the unexpected events of last night. Jonathan thought it would be best if he and Rachel kept a low profile and stayed out of sight for the day. It was a few minutes past three when Jonathan looked at the clock. They had been held up in their hotel rooms since they got in last night; they didn't even leave for food. To remedy that, Jonathan ordered Garry's Pizza an hour ago to ensure he and Rachel wouldn't have to go anywhere for any reason. After last night, an uneasy level of precaution occupied his mode of thinking. He couldn't take any chances since that idiotic loud-mouth lumberjack spilled the beans about their connection to Mr. Edwards. Jonathan could tell something changed after that revelation was put in the atmosphere. Although, it still didn't make sense that Rico and his heavily built watchdog would just let them leave in peace. Jonathan tried to stay calm for his sake as well as Rachel's. He knew she was shaken up after last night, even though she wouldn't admit it.

She was concerned. Hell, they both were for that matter. There was no telling what could happen now. Jonathan had spent most of the morning praying that a SWAT team wouldn't come busting down their door with guns drawn. For all he knew, that could still be a very real possibility. It was like a silent alarm had been tripped. He knew they couldn't stay there any longer. Alas, their time in Olberton, had come to an end, an abrupt end at that. Yet again, a dose of irony gone wrong made its way into Jonathan's life. Just last night, he and Rachel briefly discussed leaving town and getting their lives back. Now it seemed like they would be leaving, although not on their own terms, nor in the calm manner that they pictured. Jonathan watched as Rachel sat on the edge of her bed, still chewing on a slice of pepperoni pizza. He could see the grease from the slice of pizza on her plate from where he was sitting. She was in somewhat of a trance, blankly staring at the TV screen, watching a rerun of an old game show.

Jonathan didn't want to have to tell her that they were yet again on the run, that they would have to uproot and probably change their identities again. He went down the invisible list of things they would have to begrudgingly repeat in order to start over. He then felt something, almost like a subtle change in the air, but it wasn't really a change that was taking place in the air. It was something taking place inside of him. He felt a strong sense of stubbornness wrap itself around his heart. He could feel it branching off like a vein now, making its way toward his mind. He couldn't do all of that again. He couldn't put Rachel through all of that again. He refused to. He was tired of running and hiding under the covering of the customary shadows to keep them out of trouble. They had already given up too much to have the life they were currently living. No, if they were going to leave, they wouldn't go to another no-name rock to hide under. They would leave to return to the place they left. They would be going to get what was taken from them. At this point, anything less than that would be wrong and unfair to the both of them.

So Jonathan quieted those thoughts as he made his way over to Rachel. He sat next to her on the edge of the bed. She looked at him as he stared back at her. They had an unspoken moment of communication. Her eyes told her pain, and his look of compassion spoke as a testament to his love for her and let her know he was there for her. He would be whatever she needed to get through this, because Jonathan was determined they would most definitely get through this. He would be the waves that carried her ship safely to shore in this storm they found themselves in.

He put his right arm around her and pulled her close. "It's going to be alright," he said, secretly trying to convince himself as well.

Rachel took a moment before responding, the air was soft as they both sat in silence for a moment. Jonathan wondered what she would say and didn't know how to fully respond to her initial silence.

"Can you really say that though, Jonathan?" she asked, with frustration and concern both blasting from her voice. As she said this, she slightly adjusted herself inside his arm, so she could get a better look at him. "Look, I mean I just don't know…"

As Rachel was speaking, Jonathan finished the rest of her sentence for her. "You don't know how much more of this you can take," he said.

Again, Rachel was quiet, allowing her facial expressions to do most of the talking. She felt exhausted, and Jonathan couldn't blame her; in fact, he too was tired of the way things had been. They both needed a way out, they were in desperate need of a break.

"I miss my life," said Rachel, her voice beginning to sound shaky. Jonathan could almost feel the desperation coming through her every breath as he noticed her bottom lip began to quiver. She was getting emotional again, her tears were imminent. Jonathan knew Rachel was feeling vulnerable at the moment, and again, he couldn't fault her in any way. This proved to be a stressful time for the both of them. Sometimes it felt like the weight of the world was on both of their shoulders. Jonathan knew there was only so much that their metaphorical shoulders could bear before they snapped.

"It's not over Rachel," said Jonathan as he looked her in the eyes.

"I hope you're right," Rachel gently replied, her voice carrying the burden of her discomfort. She stared back, still looking like she needed to be further convinced as well as reassured that things would return to how they were before she ever heard the name Jonathan Cross. She didn't say it, but Jonathan could see it like some foreign object, embedded in the emerald fields of her eyes. He wondered: *was she still all the way with him?* In all honesty, that was more than a fair question to ask. After all, it's not like the two of them were married, there was no sort of undying covenant made between them. Did she still offer up that sense of pure loyalty she once lovingly offered him on a silver platter? Was she still all in with him?

It was odd to even call these things into question, especially since they had a good conversation last night, obviously referring to the part before the two of them were held at gunpoint. Jonathan continued to look at her as he softly rubbed his hand on the side of her face, cherishing the gift of her presence, silently acknowledging the fact that he didn't want to lose her, nor could he even minutely entertain the thought of her not being in his life. He felt like she was owed her restitution for everything that had happened to her. Jonathan didn't want the pain of the current circumstances to negatively affect their future together. He knew he would have to come up with something, and do it fast. The answer to their dilemma was long overdue, and it was time to deliver.

As Jonathan was about to speak, there came an unexpected knock at the door. The sound of some unidentifiable fist pounding against the old hotel door was a startling one. Jonathan's whole head turned to attention as he stared at the door. Rachel, too, had a bewildered look plastered across her face. Given the fact that neither one of them were expecting company any time soon. They both looked at one another as yet another knock at the door echoed throughout the room. Jonathan paid attention to what wasn't said, he didn't hear anyone identify themselves as a police officer, so from that standpoint that was a good sign. Although as he continued to plow through his thought process, assessing the situation, it dawned on him that just because it wasn't a cop, didn't mean they were in the clear. After all, last night's little adventure was a testament to the fact there were worse things that could happen than the police catching up to them. With this in mind, Jonathan arose slowly from the edge of the bed, putting one finger to his mouth, signaling to Rachel to be quiet. He stood there, alert and ready to handle any threat that might arise. He could feel the tiny hairs stand at attention on the back of his neck. Jonathan looked at the door only for a second, before he directed his attention to the other door that connected he and Rachel's room. He was thinking quickly and moving even quicker on his feet as he made a dash to the connecting door. Once he got there, he gripped his hand firmly around the door knob. He remembered that sometimes the door knob would squeak when he would turn it slowly. To avoid this, he turned it quickly and with force so that it wouldn't make too much noise. Jonathan could almost feel Rachel's eyes burning a hole in his back. It didn't take rocket science to know she was watching him and probably wondering what in the hell he was doing. Rachel didn't know he kept a loaded glock in his room. He learned the hard way to be prepared, so now he always tried to make sure he was ready for an unexpected situation such as this.

Jonathan stood a few steps past the doorway looking directly at his closet, which was where he kept the gun. As he began to move toward the closet, he heard another knock at the door. The fact that there was still no voice to backup the unidentified knocks was a problem for him; a problem he intended to let his gun solve if the situation called for that sort of response. But given the history of recent events, Jonathan couldn't be too careful at this point. He had to make sure he and Rachel would live to see another day. He wasn't about to go through what he went through last night. He couldn't let the two of them be side-swiped on that level again. He felt he had learned too much about survival to be handled like that. It was an insult to his very growth to take a hit the way he did last night. Although this time around, Jonathan made a vow with himself that he would be the one doing the hitting.

He opened the closet door with haste as he moved with precision in the shade of the closet's darkness. He had no time to turn on the closet light. He felt for the small leather bag that the gun was in on the floor. His hand operated more on pure muscle memory from reaching for it in his earlier "practice runs" in case he ever needed it like he did now. As he reached his hand inside the bag, he heard another knock at the door, except this time it was louder and harder. He could tell by the cold hard thuds coming from the door that it was a man's fist doing all the pounding. As Jonathan gripped the gun firmly in his hand he made sure the safety was off. He also listened out for the possible chance that this time someone may identify themselves after the loud knocks; unfortunately he heard no such thing. Jonathan dashed quickly inside Rachel's room. He moved so quickly he could feel the air brush past his face. In his hastiness, he managed to catch a glimpse of Rachel's face. She looked concerned and burdened. He couldn't keep letting her go through this kind of stuff. There had to be an end somewhere soon because Jonathan couldn't lose Rachel to all this madness, he just couldn't.

He readied himself as he approached the door; finally he spoke out.

"Who is it?" he asked, although it came out as more of a demand than a question.

As he laid his body up against the door, Jonathan couldn't help but think back to when he was in similar situations in Edge City. Especially when someone knocked at the door and he couldn't see who it was because he had no peep hole. Well, the same annoying fact rang loud and clear today because their hotel rooms didn't have peep holes either, which really made no sense, when Jonathan stopped to think about it. However, the fact that he had a gun in his hand made him feel a little more at ease. Those thoughts were nothing more than an unwanted trip down memory lane for Jonathan. Right now he was more focused on who was on the other side of those knocks he was hearing. To say the next sound that Jonathan heard was a surprise would be a gross understatement.

"Uh, hey it's Aaliyah, the girl from last night," she said.

Jonathan squeezed the handle of the gun with an even tighter grip as he glanced at Rachel with a confused look blanketing his face. As he locked eyes with the woman he loved, he could see she was shocked as well to hear the voice of a woman that had been the cause of their recent discomfort. She shook her head in disbelief as well as disapproval.

"No!" she mouthed at Jonathan, her face contorted in an angry expression. It was clear she wanted nothing more to do with this woman, or what she had to offer. Jonathan knew deep down Rachel was right, but his curiosity sat in the corner of his mind like an eager child waiting for someone to play with it. He knew what he should do, but for some odd reason that wasn't the choice he found himself making.

"What the hell do you want?!" he snapped, his voice strong and solid as he belted out his next oxymoron of a demanding question.

"Hey, listen, I can imagine you're upset. I just wanted to apologize," Aaliyah said.

Her voice had a beautiful calmness as it seeped through the door and walked into Jonathan's eardrums. He wondered why he was even entertaining her conversation. Part of him wanted to just ignore her altogether, but for some reason he couldn't pull himself to do so.

"Look, if you would just open the door, I'd really like to apologize," she said.

Rachel, not being moved at what she was currently hearing, stood to her feet.

"No. Her ass can apologize through the door!" she snapped, this time speaking at a more audible level. Jonathan, took a breath through his nose as he thought about what was going on. He put one hand up to Rachel as a sign to relax. He didn't say anything for a moment, then he holstered his gun, and reached for the door.

"Jonathan what are you doing?!" Rachel asked.

Truth be told, Jonathan didn't fully know why he was opening the door. By all accounts, it made no sense for him to do such a thing, other than the odd feeling of being drawn to do so. It was almost as if this woman had some sort of magical pull on him through just the use of her words, although this was something Jonathan himself didn't seem to be fully aware of. Perhaps this was the power that she wielded over the two poor souls from the night before.

Jonathan felt his hand touch the cold lock on the doorknob as he unlocked the door, still trying to understand what exactly it was that he was doing. As he opened the door, he felt a slight touch of the day's breeze come dancing through the doorway, before it revealed the dangerous beauty that stood before him. There she was, in all her perilous glory. Jonathan looked at her. There was something that was forbidden yet alluring about her. She had a presence about her that was unusual, something Jonathan hadn't yet been exposed to. He couldn't quite put his finger on it, but it was akin to seeing a rare nocturnal creature walking around in broad daylight. Something about her didn't fit, but that seemed to be the very thing that was appealing.

She was a beautiful enigma, a puzzle that looked as if it needed to be solved. Anyone could tell she took pride in her personal appearance. She was wearing a deep blue dress that hugged her body tight enough to reveal her curves. Her legs were toned, enough for people to see she probably went to the gym regularly, but not overly built. Her heels were high and black as onyx. As Jonathan looked at her face, her hazel eyes were burning bright under the light of the day's sun. Her hair was loose, yet styled. It flowed freely and wildly like the unforgiving currents of a wild river. Her lips were coated with a bright red lipstick, probably to compliment the sweet nectar from her words that allowed her to get what she wanted. Her features were majestic yet slightly intimidating to the average man. It was like she was manifested from raw beauty. There was nothing ordinary about her in the slightest. Perhaps this is secretly why Jonathan opened the door. However, even he didn't have the answer to that unspoken question. Jonathan shook the lust off his eyes as he pulled himself together long enough to ask her a question.

"What do you want?" he asked, still unsure as to why he was even entertaining her presence by talking to her.

"Well, we just wanted to come talk to you for a moment," Aaliyah answered, her eyes still trying to work their mesmerizing magic as she stared at Jonathan.

Jonathan couldn't see Rachel's face since she was standing behind him, but if he had, he would have seen the look of disgust as well as confusion as to why Aaliyah said the word "we." Fortunately, Rachel wasn't the only one who noticed Aaliyah's confusing grammar. Jonathan arrived at the obvious conclusion to what she said, replaying the scenario before him, reminding him back to the loud thuds at the door from her knocking a few moments ago. He began to realize her soft hands were incapable of making those kind of sounds. Those were the sounds of a bigger fist that belonged to a bigger being, or should he say, a bigger man. Jonathan reached for his gun that he tucked away on his hip with his right hand, while he tried to slam the door with his left as quickly as he could. His mind shouted she wasn't by herself and that she must have her villainous brother and his demented bodyguard with her! Although, he didn't react as fast as he felt, and he saw the giant hand that was responsible for the knocking he heard earlier as it pushed on the door from around the left corner. Time seemed to be slow for a moment, as he pulled his gun out hoping to have it fully drawn in the next second. Jonathan's eyes then shifted to the right corner of the door as he saw the glare from a gun come peering out of the corner at lighting speed.

For the next two seconds there was nothing, only a moment of silence for the stupidity that lead to yet another gun standoff. *Why the hell did Jonathan open up that door?* This was the psychological phrase that seemed to be mentally linked to both his and Rachel's mind at the same time. The answer to that would have to be found on another day. For now, everyone's attention was on the pressing matter at hand. Jonathan had his gun pointed just past Aaliyah's face at his intended target that stood behind her, Rico. There he was again, only this time he wasn't wearing a suit. He seemed to be gracing everyone with his less than formal attire. Jonathan could see that he was wearing one of those designer-ripped shirts that probably cost him north of $200. Obviously, this was far from Jonathan's main focus. He was more concerned about Rico's gun that was aimed directly at his head. Jonathan wouldn't call himself a gun aficionado by any means, but he did know that he picked up a thing or two from his days in the city, and he was pretty sure the gun Rico was holding was a chrome plated desert eagle. Not only would that put a hole in Jonathan's head, it would probably blow it clean off if Rico pulled the trigger. Jonathan felt his left arm getting slightly tired as he still tried to push it closed, but he was wasting his time. The door wasn't moving, not when the behemoth known as Marco was pushing it the other way. At this point, Marco stepped out in full view from behind the corner, revealing his enormous frame.

"Jonathan Cross!" exclaimed Rico, his voice sounding oddly enthusiastic given the deadly circumstances. "Man I gotta tell you, I'm excited as all get out to talk to you buddy!" Rico had a wide-eyed smile rolling across his face.

Jonathan stood there with his gun drawn, along with the feeling of utter agitation that this mad man knew his true identity. Just on that fact alone, he wanted to pull the trigger, but he knew he couldn't.

"And that lady you have with you is none other than the lovely Rachel Monroe, I presume," said Rico. His vocal cords were still filled with excitement, but he managed to dial it back a few notches this time.

Jonathan found himself in a bit of a bind. There wasn't really any room for him to deny who he was. What was the point really? Thanks to the lumberjack from last night, they already knew the truth. There was no denying it now. He and Rachel were both exposed. They were in the wind so to speak, with no way of covering up now. Knowing all of this, Jonathan didn't have much to say but the obvious question.

"What do you want?!"shouted Jonathan, his voice increasingly becoming filled with the toxic mix of rage and frustration. His emotions were shown through the expression forming upon his face. He didn't like to feel vulnerable; it reminded him of those darker days he spent back in the city. It wasn't the type of feeling he liked to revisit. Before Rico responded, he looked around, quickly to his left and right, to see if anyone was around.

"Well, tell you what, how about we take this conversation inside?" he asked.

To say that letting these lunatics in was the last thing Jonathan wanted to do, would be a gross understatement. He didn't want them breathing the same air as him, let alone sharing a room with them. Even though he felt a large disdain for complying with that option, his common sense reminded him he was yet again looking down the barrel of a gun. To be honest, the desert eagle took the option out of the equation. There wasn't too much Jonathan could do short of squeezing the trigger that his finger was currently resting on. He knew that a bloodbath wasn't much of an option either; but he was sure neither him nor Rachel would survive if he pulled that trigger. The stinging truth hurt as Jonathan processed his assessment of the situation; he was going to have to allow them to come in. Jonathan took a second to halfway turn his head so he could glance back at Rachel. She stood there, silently not allowing her outrage to be verbally revealed. That tactic may have worked for the other parties in the room that didn't know Rachel the way that Jonathan did, but he knew she was angry. Her body itself gave away its hidden emotion. She was more like an open book to Jonathan at times. He had studied her long enough to know things about her without her having to speak a word.

Jonathan wasn't pleased about the idea of them coming in and closing the door behind them, though it was a very reassuring thought to have his hand around a gun of his own, just in case he needed to use it. He held onto its authority in the palm of his hand as he took one step back. Surprisingly, as he moved he could hear the sound of Rachel's feet move as well. She was moving closer toward him in order to get behind him. That simple act proved she was still with him.

Jonathan kept his eyes on the trio that stood before him. He felt a lot better this time around versus their last encounter. Aaliyah was the first to step in of the group, and she swayed to the left of the door as she came in, eyeing Jonathan up and down like a lioness stalking her prey. She said nothing as she looked him over, only stood there in silence as if she was awaiting for an opportunity to strike. Rico was the next to follow suit; he too still had his gun aimed at Jonathan. There was a stillness to Rico as he walked in the room. A certain calmness and swagger that suggested he had been in situations like this before, and a little standoff was nothing new to him. Jonathan could see there was no sign of hidden aggression tucked away in Rico's eyes.

Jonathan didn't quite fully understand what Rico's intentions were at this point. He had gotten better at studying people but he wasn't a master at it. With this in mind, he watched Rico and something was telling him he wasn't really there for a fight. Besides, Rico said he was excited about talking to Jonathan. Plus it had been his experience that whenever someone wants to kill someone, they generally weren't excited to talk to them, though all of this reasoning didn't change the fact that Rico still had a gun pointed directly at Jonathan, so unfortunately he would have to wait and see how this thing played out. Last, but definitely not least, to enter the room was the big bull himself…Marco. He came in the room with a hushed aggression, waiting to speak if Rico gave him the order. He closed the door behind his massive frame as he stood there towering over everyone else in the room.

"Now, how about we have a more civil conversation Mr. Cross and put the guns away?" said Rico, his voice sounding reassuring as if he wouldn't go back on his word.

On the other hand, Jonathan wasn't much for playing the fool today as he kept his gun steadily aimed right between Rico's eyes. "I'll keep mine out for now, until you say something that convinces me to do otherwise" He replied in a snarky tone.

Rico stood there for a moment, with the slight sign of a smirk appearing to form from the right corner of his mouth. He seemed as if he were giving thought to Jonathan's artful words, perhaps thinking about a few himself to serve as a retort. As Jonathan kept his sights on Rico, he did something Jonathan wasn't expecting him to do. He began to put his gun down.

"Fine, we'll do it your way," he replied, with a certain bit of hesitance conveyed in his voice. He gave a nod to Marco, giving him the silent order to stand down. Marco said nothing; as usual, his silence spoke as his agreement. Also, the fact that Marco hadn't tried to rip Jonathan's arm off yet was another indication that he was compliant with the orders. Jonathan, on the other hand, still didn't take their presence nor the situation lightly as he continued to keep his gun firmly drawn on his intended target.

"Ok. Ok," said Rico, as he held his gun in his right hand. He then extended his arm in Aaliyah's direction; yet again another silent signal that he assumed would be acted upon. His assumptions proved to be true as Aaliyah reached for the gun and put it in her medium sized handbag that she was carrying. It was funny: until now, Jonathan hadn't noticed she had a handbag. It was probably because his thoughts as well as his eyes were on other things when he first saw her standing in the doorway. He didn't dwell on the small details long, as he directed his attention back to Rico.

"I think this would be a good point for you to start talking," said Jonathan. His pulse was steady. He could feel Marco's eyes studying him from a short distance as he stood across the room. Jonathan was angry and agitated, but fear was absent from the emotional soirée he was experiencing at the moment. He didn't have time for fear. It was useless and he couldn't afford to have any useless behavior in his survival arsenal. He could see Rico was about to talk, and he was hoping it would be something good. Jonathan was secretly in need of some sort of good news, and by good he meant anything that didn't end with him being killed or in handcuffs.

"Relax Mr. Cross, we're not here for trouble," said Rico."I think you and I can both agree you had enough of that last night." As he spoke, he turned his head slightly in the direction of his sister Aaliyah. Although Jonathan didn't know any of these people, he was starting to get the picture that trouble liked to follow Aaliyah. Perhaps trouble loved to live among their whole family for all Jonathan knew.

"I understand you don't know us and we probably shouldn't have come in guns blazing," said Rico. His facial expressions acknowledged the words that were coming out of his mouth, and he appeared somewhat remorseful.

"So allow me to remedy that and properly introduce myself. My name is Rico Coloso," he proudly stated, with a strong sense of conviction being wrapped around such a tiny statement. He then turned and pointed his hand toward Aaliyah. "And this annoying beauty is my little sister, Aaliyah" said Rico, minus some of the bravado he spoke with when he introduced himself.

Aaliyah made no sort of motion when Rico pointed to her, nor did she speak, she only made eye contact with Jonathan. She hadn't even looked in Rachel's direction since she entered the room. However, Aaliyah's slight gaff in manners didn't go unnoticed as Rachel took it upon herself to stare intently at Aaliyah. Perhaps she sensed something about her that the men didn't; maybe it was a tinge of a woman's intuition. Whatever the reason, Rachel was watching Aaliyah in a manner that silently suggested that she wouldn't take her eyes off of her anytime soon. Meanwhile, Rico continued his introductions,

"And you no doubt have noticed my *guardia del corpo,"* he said.

"Let me guess, he's your bodyguard?" said Jonathan, with slight sarcasm in his voice with just a swirl of annoyance to compliment the vocal mixture.

"Ahh, you speak a little Italian, Mr. Cross?" asked Rico, in a semi-jovial tone.

"No, I just recognize the hired muscle when I see it," Jonathan slyly retorted.

He kept a stern look on his face, as his gun was still drawn. He began to think to himself that for the sake of keeping the atmosphere at a certain level of peace, perhaps he should lower his weapon; after all no one had given him cause to use it so far. He then slowly lowered his gun without making a big spectacle about it. Yet, he still didn't know what these people were capable of, so he couldn't let his guard completely down and run the risk of something happening to Rachel or himself. He was done with being in a vulnerable position. That posture no longer sat well with him. In his previous experiences, being in that position brought him nothing but pain. With this in mind, he was in no mood to be caught off guard again; this time around there was just too much at stake.

"Well, you seem to be a man who pays attention," replied Rico."That's good because I want you to listen to what I'm about to say. Because if I'm right you're going to like what I have to say...I know who you are and I know you're an *innocent* man."

Jonathan's eyes slightly brightened, in a way he couldn't completely conceal. He wasn't trying to completely break his poker face, however he was unable to fix the look of hope that floated up to the surface of his eyes. It had been a long time since Jonathan had heard the word innocent in conjunction with his own name, especially since it was coming from lips that weren't his own, Rachel's or Mrs. Cross's for that matter. If Rico didn't have Jonathan's attention before, he certainly had it now. Was there some way this slick man knew something about what happened almost a year ago in Edge City? Jonathan silently pondered on this for a moment in the back of his mind with only his private consciousness to converse with. Though his inward conversation only lasted but a moment before he turned it into an outward one.

"Wha...What do you mean?" Jonathan asked, stuttering in his question from the shock and intrigue by Rico's statement.

"I did my research on you, Jonathan Cross, and your whole little situation with a certain

Kane Edwards" Rico, answered. "I know about the charges the police have against you and what they're saying you did. But I also know something else…" Rico eluded in a mysterious manner.

"Yeah, and what's that?" asked Jonathan.

"I know that no small-town, country bumpkin from a place called Winterville is going to have the stones to steal from a man like Kane Edwards," Rico retorted with a tinge of aggression in his voice. "Not only that, but I read they got you pegged for attempted murder, like a big dawg!" His joy was wrapped in an obvious case of sarcasm.

"And believe you me, I know a killer when I see one Mr. Cross. I grew up around them." Rico's facial expression synced up with his serious tone as he spoke those words. "I can look at you and tell you're not a killer. A survivor yes, but a killer…no." continued Rico.

His words rang true as they saturated the air with honesty. After all, Jonathan wasn't really a killer nor did he want to be one. Sure, he shot Percy, but that was completely in self-defense. Had he not shot Percy, Jonathan wouldn't be breathing today. His body would probably be at the bottom of some lake by now or buried deep in some woods where no one would find him. Jonathan thought about what Rico was saying. He could tell Rico was observant. There was a certain level of command Rico seemed to possess, and there was a distinct air about him that told its own story. Jonathan could tell Rico wasn't pretending to be something he's not. He was the real deal of what he was portraying. This in itself was interesting enough to gain Jonathan's attention. Although, he still needed answers.

"You still haven't answered my question." Jonathan looked around the room once more, observing the trio that stood before him. "What do you want?" he asked, his voice allowing his inward frustration to come out sounding aggressive as well as annoyed.

Rico smirked as he mumbled under his breath "The enemy of my enemy…"

Not fully hearing what Rico had just said, Jonathan spoke again, "What was that?"

"Since I know you're not as bad as the police say you are, I think it would be fair to say that some of the things they're saying about you aren't true", said Rico.

"None of it's true!" Jonathan snapped.

"You were set up, by Kane, I presume," replied Rico, his voice calm as he spoke the truth.

"You presume right," Jonathan said, still not fully understanding where all of this was going.

"Kane Edwards has made a lot of enemies over the years, during his rise to power," said Rico.

"Yeah, tell me something I don't know," quipped Jonathan.

"What you don't know is that one of those enemies is my father, Nero Coloso," Rico answered, his demeanor slightly changing as he mentioned his father's name.

"One could say there's a serious case of bad blood between the two of them. It's obvious you have an axe to grind against Edwards; as does my family." He took a few steps toward Jonathan in a slow manner, in a way that suggested he didn't want to startle him. While Rico walked forward,

Jonathan kept a good grip on his gun just in case he suddenly needed to use it. At this point, Rico was face to face with Jonathan; they looked at each other directly in the eyes, silently studying one another. While Jonathan looked in Rico's eyes, he saw something that looked familiar, only he hadn't seen it in another man's eyes, only his own. Jonathan saw a hatred for Kane Edwards. He recognized that look, that caged beast of emotion begging to be released. At least from that standpoint, Jonathan could tell Rico was telling the truth and that he really must have some score he wanted to settle with Mr. Edwards. Rico then placed his hands on Jonathan's shoulder, and spoke in a calm manner.

"So allow the enemy of your enemy to be your friend Jonathan. Allow me to to help you kill Kane Edwards."

CHAPTER 9

THE DECISION

It was a tight feeling; his brain almost felt as if it were expanding inside his skull. So much in fact that he could sense there was little room for thought. Which was a very ironic feeling because *thinking* was the exact thing that Jonathan was currently trying to do. To say he was in deep thought was an understatement. He did more than just ponder the offer that was given to him. He studied it. Although just as Rico had said the other day, right before he ended their brief rendezvous with the murderous suggestion of killing Kane Edwards; Jonathan was no killer. It was true that Jonathan wanted to get his and Rachel's life back, however not at the expense of taking a man's life. He couldn't kill Kane, he just wanted to bring him down, give him a taste of what justice and defeat was like.

Although perhaps a darker, more sinister side of Jonathan would agree with the idea of dealing with Kane on a permanent level. Thankfully, he hadn't been pushed to that level nor would he allow himself to be. He was better than that. Even with his moral compass still pointing in a safer direction, he still had to admit he could use the help. Based off his previous experience from tangling with Mr. Edwards, Jonathan knew he couldn't go at him alone. Yes, it was true he would be facing Mr. Edwards as a newly reformed man, forged by the fires of battle and hardened by the blows of war. Jonathan also knew this battle wasn't a mere physical one; on the contrary, it would take a lot more. It would take meticulous planning, resources, and brains as well as muscle. He knew that two heads were better than one, and that a team was more powerful than an individual. Besides, if he was going to go after Kane, now was the time to do it. Even though Rico found Jonathan by accident, he still found him, and if Rico could stumble upon him like that, then there was no telling who else might be able to do the same.

They could no longer sit back and idly wait for the opportune time to strike, if there ever was such a thing. The opportunity had been made. Now was the time to seize it and do so with *force*. Jonathan couldn't risk letting the chance to finally set things right slip out of his grasp. It was this reason that ultimately drove him to what he felt was the logical choice; he would partner with Rico and his mini entourage. Though Jonathan knew he would have to consult another person on this decision, since he wasn't the only one who would be affected by it.

He sat in one of the wooden chairs that came with the room while his mind and tried to process everything that was going on. He would have to not only explain his case but if need be, convince her that this was the right play. The room was quiet but only for a second. He watched Rachel's left leg shake as she bounced her foot off the ground in a continuous motion. She concentrated, in a focused zone as she searched the net on the Coloso family. Earlier, she told Jonathan the name rang a bell but she wasn't really sure if it was the right family. The information she looked up along with backyard blogs and scandalous rumors painted a not-so-subtle picture. A picture that spoke if you decided to listen to it and its message was clear; the Colosos were dangerous. Signs pointed to ties with the mob located in Harbor Stone. Jonathan could tell Rachel had a nervous energy about all of this. It was one of the things he learned about her during their recent time together in Olberton.

"They're from the same city," said Rachel, her voice sounding annoyed by her own statement.

Jonathan frowned when he heard Rachel's cryptic message. "Whose from the same city?" he asked.

Rachel looked at him before responding, her eyes giving a glimpse of her hidden concern.

"This Nero Coloso guy and Kane. They're both from Harbor Stone City," she responded.

"Well we knew there was some history based off what Rico said," Jonathan replied, trying to do his best to deflate any hesitations or worries that Rachel may have. He could sense she was a bit uneasy about the whole thing.

"Yeah, but we don't know what that history is, Jonathan," replied Rachel.

"I mean, you heard what he said. He wants to kill him!" snapped Rachel, her beautiful face revealing that it had the potential to showcase anger as she spoke.

Jonathan, trying to get a handle on the situation before it became one, replied, "Nobody's killing anybody. But what we *are* going to do is get our lives back"

"How exactly are we going to do that?" she asked."I mean, trust me, I'm all in for getting back what's mine. But…I guess I'm asking if they're the right ones to help us."

Jonathan's mind continued to run at a solid pace while his ears listened to what Rachel had to say. "I hear you Rach, but you also have to ask yourself another question: What exactly do the people who would help us in a situation like this, look like?"

"I mean really, you're telling me that his father is some supposed crime boss? Well, hell Rachel, sometimes you have to fight fire with fire!" he snapped, his words coming out fast, accompanied by a cold and harsh tone. Jonathan sat back as he listened to the sound of his own voice. It was then when he realized that his anger was focused toward the wrong person. His eyes widened as if a light bulb went off, but in actuality, one did go off. Rachel was the last person on earth who Jonathan wanted to raise his voice to. After everything she had endured with him and some things she endured *because* of him, he couldn't mistreat her. Not even if it was unintentional, he couldn't do it on any level. He immediately apologized, "I'm...I'm...sorry Rachel. I didn't mean to yell." He got up from the chair and walked over toward her. She said nothing to his apology only staring into the cheap screen of his laptop. He placed both his hands on her shoulders and spoke softly,

"Look, all I'm saying is that it may take a kingpin to stop a kingpin. If these two have some violent past, then let this Nero guy, or Rico do the work for us. You know as well as I do that Kane is a dangerous man and this time around I wouldn't mind having a dangerous man or two on our side."

Rachel was silent for a moment. He could hear her soft breath escape her mouth as she let out a deep breath.

"I know," she said. "It's just that if we do this, you have to promise me nobody gets killed. I know Kane's crazy but I'm still not going to be an accessory to anyone's murder. I won't give him or anyone else that level of power over me where I would stoop to that level." She turned around before she said anything else, her soft eyes meeting his. She placed her left hand on top of his as he touched her shoulder. "And you shouldn't either Jonathan, not even for him."

It was clear Rachel wasn't mad at him for the minor verbal assault that took place only moments ago. Perhaps she extended him grace because she knew he needed it, but he wasn't going to ask her about it. He felt that would only belabor the matter. The moment came and it went, he apologized, it was over. There wasn't enough time to beat a dead horse, especially when there were other humans out there who were more deserving of a beating. Jonathan knew Rachel was right. He didn't want anyone's blood on his hands; he just wanted their lives back. As he looked back at Rachel, he knew it was settled, and he knew they were both in. The agreement had been made, and they were going to go through with it. It wasn't a mystery as to what drove the two of them to partner up with a crime family they knew little about. The truth was much more simple and less hard to find. It was the thick cloud of desperation that sat heavily between the two of them. It was so vast at this point that it almost consumed them, regardless of if they realized it or not. The cloud of desperation reached out with its black mass and smoky demeanor and made its way into their minds. It was quite possible that it even had its sights set on their hearts as well.

As to whether the black ether of desperation touched their souls, only time would tell. For now, they were going to do what they both secretly longed for, the private craving that hid behind their closed lips, and had not seen the light of day in a while. Finally the hidden wish would get its due, its public announcement as Jonathan and Rachel sat before their proverbial cake and inhaled as if they were about to blow out the candles while they thought of this special wish. Yes, indeed their wish would soon be granted; soon they would get what they wanted. Soon they would return to Edge City.

CHAPTER 10

RICO AND HIS CREW OF TWO

The day itself seemed to be tired in a sense. The sun's rays were a bit duller and the heat was dry. It felt like some Saharan desert had taken up residence in the small town of Olberton as it sucked up the air's moisture. That wasn't the only thing off about the day. The town itself felt smaller than normal, almost like a latent sense of confinement had crept in the midst of the unassuming town. It was a harder feeling to describe than it was to experience; so this was yet another thing Jonathan kept to himself.

Then again, there was a logical explanation for all of this. It could be due to the fact that a few new big fish found their way into the smaller pond of Olberton and space was already beginning to feel tight. This was all the more reason for a hastily exit. As cliche´ as it was, the town wasn't big enough for the both of them. However, if everything went well like Jonathan was expecting it to, then the need for space wouldn't be a problem, since they would all be leaving soon. Jonathan sat patiently in his seat as he took a moment to stop looking out of one of the large windows of the cafe he was in. He turned his attention to the rest of the room and lifted his head as the aroma of a pleasant mixture of food passed his nostrils. This place was completely unfamiliar to both he and Rachel; it was toward the edge of Olberton. Some of the locals referred to the small stretch of border where the town ended as *the skirts*. This was obviously because it was in the outskirts of town, but still it didn't make it less amusing to Jonathan. It was a small nod to his own past and a pinch of Winterville thinking that would cause people to name the area the skirts. Although it wasn't something for Jonathan to get stuck on, it was merely an observation. He managed to get a look at the name of the cafe as he and Rachel were walking inside. It was called the *"Blue Dress Cafe"*, and Rico was insistent on this location. His knowledge of the surrounding area gave the impression that he had been there before. It obviously wasn't a crime for Rico to be familiar with the town, however more so of a private observation on Jonathan's part, one that made him do some more thinking about the new clan he was about to start associating himself with.

The place was neat and quiet as he looked around. It was more of an old timer's spot; a place Mr. Culgary might like to eat. There were a few scattered couples in the cafe, and all of them looked like they had been there before. Jonathan looked at Rachel as she sat across from him; she was a little more on the reserved side than normal. She didn't really appear to be nervous, just quiet. Her hair was neatly tucked into a ponytail. Jonathan liked when she wore her hair like that. He felt that it gave a clearer view of her lovely face and he admired the fact that even in tough times, Rachel still managed to have a certain level of regalness that circled her like a watchful eagle. She never seemed to let herself get too beat down to the point where she forgot who she was.

Jonathan remembered some of the late-night talks they had back in the city when they first started spending time together. They came from different worlds, which was something Jonathan admired about her. She came from an upper-middle class family. Her father was a high school history teacher and her mother was an executive at a pharmaceutical company. She was close to her father, but she said she didn't classify herself as an over-the-top daddy's girl. She was the middle child of three, and her older brother was her rock growing up, until he died of undiagnosed cancer. She said her parents blamed each other for neither of them catching it, which ultimately lead to their divorce. Her sister Cathey always felt a sense of competition between the two of them, although there never really was any because Rachel was better at everything than Cathey, a harsh truth that caused her sister to resent her over the years,but they eventually buried the hatchet, becoming more civil toward one another as they grew older.

Her mother was the one she never really got along with. By Rachel's own admission, she and her mother were a little too much alike. They were both strong-willed at times and both had a tendency to have a smart mouth. This sometimes led to harsh words and even harsher arguments. Rachel didn't talk that much about her family before, and she talked even less about them now, if at all. Jonathan knew her family had to be worried sick about her, as they undoubtedly heard the news about one of their own being in such a horrible situation. This was yet more motivation for Jonathan to help get their lives and loved ones back.

Jonathan held onto that thought for a moment, until something out of the corner of his eye broke his concentration. He caught a better view of the distraction as he turned his head to watch it come into the parking lot, cloaked in black paint while it glided across the pavement on four wheels. It was Rico's black SUV. Jonathan recognized it immediately from the night he had Marco's gun looking at him with a deadly aggression. The Colosos had finally shown up, and a few minutes past the time Rico said he wanted to meet. Who knows, maybe their tardiness was done intentionally.

Either way, they were here now and it was time for the so-called moment of truth. However, the real question was, how much truth would actually come out of Rico's mouth? This was a mystery that was yet to be solved, but as long as he kept up his end of the deal and helped Jonathan bring down Kane, then everything would be fine. He wasn't really in the mood for any extra side missions that might include tracking Rico down because he did something shady once they got back to the city. He cleared his throat in a calm manner as he watched them park the car. As he looked out the window, he heard a small voice in the back of his head questioning this decision. A certain level of double-mindedness came into play. Perhaps Rachel was right; maybe this wasn't the best idea. After all, Jonathan wasn't naive to the fact that he still didn't know these people. The only thing he knew about them were their names.

So he let out a soft prayer under his breath as he now watched the trio walk through the cafe doors. He prayed this would work for him. He needed it to. He needed these people to do what they said they would. He needed to not feel like he was letting Rachel down. He needed to restore his name as well as hers. He needed to fix the damage to what was done and he needed it fixed...yesterday. Failure was not an option, for his own sanity he had to visualize his desired outcome.

As he silently reassured himself, he watched Rico, Aaliyah and the beastly Marco come walking into the small town cafe. One could tell just by looking at them that they didn't belong there. This wasn't exactly their normal day-to-day environment. The first one he noticed but didn't look at was Aaliyah. He could see her shapely figure cloaked in white out of the corner of his eyes. He knew she was untouchable for obvious reasons. He tried to ignore the unannounced feeling he felt when he saw her, especially since the woman who his heart really belonged to was sitting right across from him in plain sight. That feeling he didn't want to acknowledge had a name, that feeling that sat idly by the night when he first laid eyes on Aaliyah in the parking lot. That same feeling he felt when she showed up the next day at Rachel's hotel room. The same feeling that was secretly pacing around in the depths of his stomach like a restless animal; that feeling was *attraction*.

He was currently engaged in a silent back-and-forth argument with his eyes, an argument he was currently winning. He kept his eyes on Marco for a moment as he stomped his way in the cafe like a tamed bull in a china shop. Marco may not have done any damage just yet, however he was more than capable of doing so. It was almost odd watching him walk in. Jonathan knew these innocent people had no idea that a true monster had just entered their midst. He was a giant in stature and his eyes were dark, almost completely black, like an unyielding abyss that could swallow men whole with nothing more than a deathly stare. He was bald with a beard as pitch black as his heart. He almost looked militant as he walked, wearing a long sleeved black shirt, navy blue jeans and black work boots. Jonathan could tell Marco was a man of few words but much action. When Rico told Jonathan he knew a killer when he saw one, Jonathan could also say the same thing. It was actually something he wasn't really aware of until he just sat there and watched Marco's giant frame walk toward him. Marco was a killer. There was no question about it. Jonathan didn't know too much about Rico and Marco's relationship, but he was prayerful that Rico was able to keep Marco at bay and on a leash.

As the trio finally made it over to the table, a small voice in Jonathan's head said something, "here we go." This was no doubt his inner conscience speaking to him. This was it, and it was time to see what plan they would formulate to get what they all wanted. Even though Jonathan's goals weren't thoroughly aligned with Rico's, they both wanted to defeat Kane.

Before Rico could sit down, Rachel got up and walked around the table to sit next to Jonathan. At first glance, it looked like she was possibly being polite and allowing the three of them to sit down, although Jonathan noticed the faint crease in her skin as she slightly frowned. A subtle sign of her obvious disapproval of the whole thing. However, Jonathan knew her well enough to know she agreed with what they were doing on some level, because if she didn't, she wouldn't be there in the first place. As everyone found their seat, Jonathan clenched his teeth, hoping this would all work. Unlike Marco, Rico was a little more formal, he sat directly across from Jonathan wearing a light grey suit with a white dress shirt that was unbuttoned at the top. Perhaps it was his upbringing or perhaps he just simply liked to dress up. Who knew? Before anyone got a word out, the waiter came over to their table.

"Hey, how's everyone doing today?" asked the waiter.

He was a middle-aged man, Jonathan could tell he didn't really care for his job. He was only pretending to be excited about his job by taking their order. Jonathan could see the burden truth embedded in the man's eyes. He could hear the man's yearning for more out of life as he talked.

Jonathan looked at the guy's name tag, before he introduced himself. It said "Greg". Jonathan could sympathize with Greg about where he was because Jonathan felt he was there at one point too, and now ironically, he found himself in somewhat of the same position. As he thought about this to himself, he also thought about the fact that after today, he would no longer be in the same position, the reason being was that he was going to take action. After all, that's what this meeting was all about. He was about to devise a plan to yet again take control of his life, though this time he would do everything in his power to make it stick. Jonathan's train of thought was cut short as he heard Rico's voice dismiss the waiter from further interruption.

"Hey look Greg, we're fine at the moment," said Rico, his tone slightly demeaning as if to make fun of the man for having a customer service job.

Jonathan wasn't too fond of that, but this wasn't really the time to get offended at things that really didn't pertain to him. For now, he would overlook the insult to the common man and focus on the matter at hand.

"So…do we have a deal, Cross?" Rico asked.

Before Jonathan answered the question, he looked at Rachel, in a way that suggested he was searching for some nonverbal form of agreement, which wasn't really necessary for him to do, since her mere presence suggested that she was in. It was more of a instinctual gesture than him actually looking for her to say something.

"Yes, we're in. But on one major condition," said Jonathan, his tone sharp and exact, making sure his words weren't taken lightly. He leaned in closer toward Rico, slightly bending his body over the table. "No killing.

Neither I nor Rachel are going to be an accessory to murder. I refuse to have a man's blood on my hands no matter how dirty he is. I'll help you stop him, but I'm not killing anybody, period."

His face was stone cold as he spoke his last sentence. He was not a killer, nor did he have to be to get the job done. This wasn't something he could look the other way about. He didn't feel the need to have blood on his hands to be the victor; he wasn't trying to win *that* way.

Rico sat quiet for a moment, glancing over at Marco before responding. He then ran his tongue across his bottom lip as the look on his face suggested he was contemplating Jonathan's comments. "Ok, Cross we'll do it your way. No bloodshed, no body count." Rico's voice matched his calm demeanor. As he spoke, Jonathan watched his eyes to see if Rico meant the words that were coming out of his mouth. It was one thing to say it, however it was another thing to mean it. As Jonathan quickly searched for the truth hidden in Rico's face, he caught a glimpse of something. Within that glimpse was the look of disappointment. It flashed across Rico's face in a hasty manner. Almost like that of a thief in the night, it was gone before someone even knew it was there. Though that wasn't the case for Jonathan. He was able to pick up on things like that when he was looking for them. It proved useful in moments such as these. Jonathan knew the quick display of minor disapproval meant that Rico wasn't truly thrilled about the proposal. However, that was a good thing because this meant Rico was sincere when he agreed not to spill any blood. Jonathan would've had a reason to doubt if Rico didn't show any form of emotion because that probably would have meant that Rico was lying.

"So if you don't want to do it the old-school way Mr. Cross, then tell me exactly what it is you propose to do," said Rico, his voice revealing that he was reluctant to go through with Jonathan's idea. "You *do* know that he's the Mayor now, right?"

"Yeah I know," Jonathan replied. Hearing the mere phrase that

Kane was now Mayor wasn't the most pleasant pill to swallow. Though Jonathan knew things had changed since the last time he was in the city, it didn't make it easier to hear that the man who was responsible for derailing his life in a violent manner was now given more power. The thought of Kane having a bigger and broader reach in Edge City than he did before was a something that almost made Jonathan physically sick.

"So if you know he's the Mayor now, how do you propose we take him down?" asked Rico, his voice sounding irritated at the suggestion of another alternative."Because please believe I have several bullets locked and loaded with his name on each and every one of them." He spoke in a manner that suggested that *his* way was the only sure way to get the job done. Although Rico didn't say it, Jonathan could both hear and see a blanket of arrogance that covered Rico. He could tell Rico believed that he had the best answer to the problem that they were facing.

"So you still haven't offered your alternative method to the equation, Jonathan," Rico said, his facial expression making it clear that he was awaiting an answer.

Jonathan took a second before he answered. He looked at the faces that were before him: Rico, Marco, and even the temptress herself, Aaliyah. His plan was simple, mainly because it wasn't really a plan, nor did he have all the details to it. But he knew that in theory it would work. He just needed help with laying out the groundwork.

"Well, he's gotten stronger so to speak since the last time I've seen him, that means we can't attack him head on." explained Jonathan."We'll take him down from the inside, destroy him from within."

Rico sat there looking off into the distance, not seeming too enthusiastic about the idea he had just given into. Perhaps he was awaiting to hear more details of Jonathan's so-called plan.

"Look, if we can prove he set me and Rachel up, we can take him down." said Jonathan. "He won't be dead, but we'll both still have our revenge. Rachel and I will have our lives and names restored. Plus you and your family can watch him rot in jail."

As Jonathan said this, a sudden pause came up almost mid-sentence. His mind had suddenly remembered an important piece of information. Why did the Colosos have a problem with Kane in the first place? Jonathan still didn't know the answer to that question, and given the situation, he felt he should know the answer. If he was going to be fighting alongside these people, so to speak, he was entitled to know why they were even fighting in the first place. Jonathan couldn't afford to go to war with a man like Kane Edwards and not know his *teammate's* motives. The man they were about to go up against was too dangerous to roll up on half-cocked and uninformed. That was a recipe for disaster and given the man they were dealing with, that could ultimately be a recipe for death. Jonathan wasn't going to chance it. He couldn't.

"You know Rico, you never told me why you and your family have a problem with Edwards," he said, his tone direct with slight suspicion having its way with his vocal cords. "What's the deal there? What did he do to you?" Jonathan stared at Rico, not fully with an attitude but with anticipation of what the answer he was about to receive might be.

Rico slightly adjusted himself in his seat before opening his mouth. He then turned his head slightly in Aaliyah's direction."That psychopath killed our mother!" he snapped. He spoke a decibel level that was loud enough in Jonathan's face but quiet enough as not to alert the whole cafe.

Rachel almost let out a slight gasp as she sat there listening to what Rico had just said. Jonathan's eyes widened slightly as he too was caught off guard at the revelatory knowledge that had just been released upon him. There was also a slight sense of embarrassment and guilt that played an unwelcome part in the equation. Jonathan knew he needed to know what the deal was, but he wasn't expecting that sort of answer. Perhaps this was a not so subtle reminder to make sure he was in the right mode to approach Mr. Edwards. Jonathan would have to make sure he expected the unexpected and was ready for the unknown. This was also a gruesome reminder of the person he was dealing with. This was not a game that they were about to embark on. The dangers and risk were real and could possibly be fatal. These thoughts oddly enough gave Jonathan a sense of comfort. Comfort in the fact that he didn't need to feel so guilty about asking Rico that question, even if it was at the expense of opening old wounds.

"I'm..I'm sorry…I didn't know" said Jonathan, a remorseful tone now taking occupancy in his voice. His words were true. Jonathan had no idea about Rico and Aaliyah's mother, but then again how could he? He also wondered how their mother died. However, the more important question was why was she killed? It was a bit overwhelming for a moment for Jonathan to delve into the thought about how the man he used to work for was a murdering maniac. It was hard to believe that at one point, this maniac offered the promises of helping Jonathan become what he always wanted to be: successful.

Though he couldn't spend too much time wrapping his mind around such things. He was more focused on the matter at hand, that matter being to find out why Rico was motivated to kill Kane. Although now that Jonathan knew the answer to that question, there really was no need for elaboration. This was a quick and abrupt change of pace from his last thought that took place in the gutter fields of his mind only seconds ago. For a moment, he wanted to know what happened to Rico and Aaliyah's mother, then he quietly changed his tune. There was a sense of understanding that began to blanket Jonathan's mind and almost force his thoughts in the way they should go. He thought about how he didn't really like to talk about how his father died. He then rationalized that he could apply that same level of understanding and courtesy to Rico. Due to this, Jonathan refrained from asking what happened to their mother.

Rico was now slightly adjusting himself in his seat, an assumed attempt to regain his level of sophisticated coolness that he had entered the cafe with. "An old wound that hasn't healed," he said. Without much warning, Aaliyah suddenly chimed in with, "and it won't until he's paid for what he did."

Jonathan hadn't forgotten about her forbidden presence at the table. He merely attempted to ignore her, though given the topic of discussion, it was hard not to acknowledge her presence.

"So now you know why we're here Johnny boy," said Rico, his tone surprisingly returning to a calmer level."You could say that we have some serious skin invested in this particular game. So if we're not going to kill him, then we hit him, and we hit him hard."

Jonathan paid attention to Rico's apparent level-headedness that was currently on display. He seemed to snap back to a reasonable level of calm from talking about the man who was responsible for killing his mother. Surely, Jonathan wasn't going to begrudge Rico for showing some raw emotion. He knew what the death of a parent felt like; but he didn't know what it was like to know that the person responsible for your parent's death and was still out there walking the streets. The word "tough" wouldn't probably be the right word to describe that feeling. Jonathan could use his well-known pain about his father's death as a point of reference, so he could only imagine what Rico and Aaliyah felt, and it had to be just as bad if not worse in a way.

"Listen I can promise you this," said Jonathan."We will get him back for everything he's done".

He looked around the table as he spoke, as if he were about to deliver some rousing speech to an army getting ready to head out into battle. Honestly, in a way, that's exactly what was going on. Here they were, quietly plotting on how to take down the king of Edge City. They were mapping out their battle strategy so to speak, while Jonathan was taking a moment to rally the troops. They were definitely about to go into battle and this was a war that was not to be taken lightly in any form. The man they would be up against ruled his territory with a solid foundation and would not be easily moved. If they were going to do this, they were going to have to do it right. Anything less than that would result in dire consequences, possibly even death. The good thing though in all of that was this: everyone at that table knew what the stakes were. They all knew they had to be all in to pull off something of this magnitude. With that being said, Jonathan didn't have to do much talking. He took a silent inventory of the people who were seated at the table. He knew he had two men that weren't afraid to take a man's life, although he wasn't trying to play a double-minded game of switching his position on not killing anyone. He also had to admit there was a sense of security and reassurance that he had those sort of *animals* on the roster. This was an internal thought he knew would stay in place because he wouldn't utter a word to this mode of thinking to Rachel.

It appeared they were all on one accord, as Jonathan sat there for a moment that felt longer in silence than it was in reality.

"So we're really going to do this?" he asked, not in a nervous manner but more of a reassuring way. His eyes looked at Rachel while he asked the question, awaiting an answer.

Rico smirked in his seat, probably laughing at the idea that Jonathan felt the need to ask that question. "Hell yeah, we're sure. Are you?" he asked in a tone that suggested he was slyly testing Jonathan's resolve. "You not getting cold feet on me are you, Cross?"

"No," said Jonathan, almost in annoyance that such a question was asked.

Rico leaned forward in his seat, while putting his elbows on the table, his fine suit looking like it didn't belong in such a place, let alone being draped over a cheap cafe table."Well that's good because we may not be spilling any blood once we get out there, but please believe things can still get dicey," he said.

Then Aaliyah decided to join the conversation, as she had been relatively silent the whole time. "Oh, don't worry Rico, he's a strong man. I've seen him in action," she said. Her flattering words were accompanied by a flirtatious look toward Jonathan.

There was an awkwardness that sat in the air for a bit, however it wasn't recognized by everyone at the table or at least it appeared that way. The ones that seemed to grab a hold to the unpleasant moment were only two people, Rachel and Jonathan. Aaliyah didn't appear to be uncomfortable, but then again why would she? She was the one who made the comment in the first place. It was obvious she did it on purpose, but that didn't stop Rachel from chiming in to let her know that the comment didn't go unnoticed.

"Which is why he has a strong woman," she quipped, her tone and her facial expression appearing to be in no jovial mood as she stared at Aaliyah.

Jonathan was slightly taken aback by all of this. It took him a moment to let what was happening sink in. There was a part of his brain that looked at the fact that he had two gorgeous women seemingly fighting over him, though this wasn't the time to act like a cocky college frat boy because this wasn't something to play with. He loved Rachel and he knew that just because he happened to privately acknowledge that Aaliyah was beautiful, wasn't any sort of excuse to let himself run wild. Beyond all of this, lay the obvious logic like a log in the middle of the road. That logic had a strong and resounding message that vibrated furiously inside Jonathan's skull and it plainly declared: *we don't have time for this!*

This prompted Jonathan to reach over to Rachel underneath the table and place his hand on hers. This was a signal that he knew she would understand; it said many things while not audibly saying a word. This told her that he was with her and her alone and that she didn't need to entertain Aaliyah's childish banter. Though the true test would be if Rachel allowed this nonverbal message to calm the seas of her rapidly brewing storm. Rachel remained silent after her lips pressed firmly against one another. Jonathan could tell she was holding back, her mouth being a cage for the harsh truth that wanted to be unleashed like a wild animal. This was a good thing for the sake of everyone at the table, although mainly for Aaliyah. Rachel held back the rising tides of her emotions so that her tongue wouldn't cause any problems.

Rico seemed slightly oblivious to the whole thing that was taking place at the table before him. It was either that he just simply didn't care, or perhaps he was so used to Aaliyah's antics that he was unmoved by the whole thing. It was a safe bet to assume Rico knew more about Aaliyah than anyone else at the table. Jonathan thought to himself whether Aaliyah's presence on this mission of theirs was going to be a problem. Unfortunately, he already knew the answer to that hidden question and the answer was a hard and uncomfortable *yes.* His private thoughts were interrupted by the sound of Rico's voice.

"So then that settles it," stated Rico, his head on a slight swivel as he spoke, scanning the table for answers, though it seemed like he really was just looking at Rachel and Jonathan to see what their reactions were.

"It's settled," Jonathan replied, his eyes holding an expression that said *I hope this isn't a mistake,* though Rico didn't appear to notice anything out of place in Jonathan's response, so there was no need for him to further question him. While still holding Rachel's hand, Jonathan looked over toward her so that she may speak her mind. However, he was hoping she wouldn't speak *all* of her mind. He was in luck, because Rachel simply squeezed his hand back and nodded her head in agreement. Rico looked at the two for a moment before a huge chester like grin made an appearance on his face.

"Oh the fun we're going to have," he said, his tone of voice soaked with a sense of unnecessary excitement.

Jonathan didn't really like the sound of that, wondering what Rico was alluding to, but he ultimately decided to ignore it. Besides, there was no time for backing out now. If Jonathan wanted to stop running and get his life back, this is what he had to do. Rico slid back in his chair as he then stood up from the table.

"We leave in the morning, that should give you both enough time to pack up your things." he said.

He buttoned his middle jacket button before walking away from the table. Aaliyah and Marco stood up as well. Aaliyah stared at Jonathan longer than necessary, enough to make him feel slightly uncomfortable and long enough to allude to the possibility that Aaliyah was going to be a problem for him on this trip. Jonathan locked eyes with her but only for a moment since he wasn't trying to feed into her obvious games. He held onto Rachel's hand as they both watched the Coloso clan walk out the door.

Jonathan took this moment to take a mental break as he continued to hold firmly onto Rachel's hand. He knew they were about to embark on one hell of a rollercoaster. In a sense, they really were going off to war to fight for their lives as well as their freedom. They were going to reclaim their stolen freedom and rise from the ashes of harsh defeat. Jonathan wanted to win; he had to win. There was no way that he could go all that way and come up short.

Jonathan's eyes followed Rico and his crew of two as they made their way out the door. He continued to watch them as they walked. It was like he was watching them move in slow motion. Perhaps this was due to all the thoughts that found themselves cramming their way into his mind. He noticed Rico came to a slow halt as he turned toward Aaliyah yet again. Jonathan found himself watching Aaliyah silently from afar, so he turned his head to look at Rachel. She too seemed to be taken adrift by her thoughts of her own and she stared out the opposite window towards her left. There was a sense of irony that made its way into the room. Here Jonathan was having private thoughts of his own that he wouldn't be inclined to share. However, he wanted to know what Rachel was thinking about as she looked off into the distance; it was clear her mind was on other things as well. But what things? This was something Jonathan wanted to know. Perhaps he would be able to ask her later as he then turned his attention back to Rico and Aaliyah. The two of them were still talking, although it appeared Jonathan had missed something while he was looking at Rachel. He could tell the conversation between them had gotten heated, at least on Aaliyah's end since she was the one who was yelling.

Jonathan could feel the slight wrinkles forming on his forehead as a frown came upon his face while he watched the outside events unfold before his very eyes. Jonathan studied Rico's face as he yet again looked calm and collected. If he were to take a guess as to what was going on, Rico probably said something to Aaliyah that wasn't currently sitting well with her. Jonathan never had a brother or a sister, so he didn't know how siblings were or how they operated. He was completely unfamiliar with the term *sibling rivalry,* though he wasn't sure whether that was what he was witnessing or if it was something else. It wasn't until Aaliyah shoved Rico when Jonathan noticed another black SUV pulling up to them. Jonathan could tell things weren't quite right and something was going on. Suddenly, Marco picked up Aaliyah by her waist, carrying her with ease. Two men in suits then popped out of the SUV. One moved quickly to open the back door for Marco as he held Aaliyah kicking and screaming in his arms. The other man got out of the driver side door and greeted Rico, who seemed unimpressed with the man given the way he looked at him.

Jonathan looked quickly around the cafe with concern to see if anyone else was paying attention to what was going on outside. To Jonathan's surprise, no one noticed a thing. Everyone was going along with their cheap meals and preoccupied lives to notice that a woman was being stuffed in the backseat of a car. Then again, Jonathan wasn't too surprised given the fact that no one came to his rescue that night in the parking lot. It made him ask the private yet dark question of the so-called character of this small town. Perhaps this small town wasn't so innocent after all. Perhaps, someone did see what was going on and just decided not to lift a finger, though, there was no way to prove this. It was no more than a private thought at the moment, than a public accusation.

It was interesting the difference a few days could make. Just the other day Jonathan was literally fighting for Aaliyah in a parking lot and he didn't even know her. Now here he was a few days later, having had the opportunity to get to know her a little better, and found himself watching her in another predicament. This time, a man was shoving her in the back of a car and Jonathan didn't even move a muscle, although technically, that wasn't a true statement because there was a muscle in Jonathan's body that was moving: his mind. He quickly put this scenario together in his mind and laid out a pretty plausible explanation to what he was witnessing. He thought back to that night in the parking lot when he first met Rico and Aaliyah. At the time, Rico was looking for her and it sounded like Aaliyah was concerned as to whether or not her father sent Rico to find her. Perhaps Rico told their father what was going on, and he wanted his daughter to come home. After all, the way Rachel talked about Nero back at the hotel made it sound like he wasn't a man who was ok with not getting his way.

Jonathan watched as Marco closed the door behind Aaliyah, and took a step back. The other man in the suit hopped back into the driver's seat and closed the door. It looked like Aaliyah wouldn't be making the trip to Edge City after all. Jonathan's private prayers had been answered and Aaliyah wasn't going to be a problem. Besides, Jonathan had the woman he loved sitting right next to him; he didn't need any distraction or temptation to ruin what he had built with Rachel. He watched as the SUV drove off, carrying away what could've been a problem for him. It was better this way. The journey they were all about to take would demand complete commitment as well as focus. There was no room for error nor distractions. It was time for Jonathan to reclaim his life. It was time to come out of the shadows and step boldly back into the light. It was time for him to return to Edge City.

CHAPTER 11

THE APPOINTED TIME

His eyelids were still feeling heavy as the night's slumber slowly but surely released its grip from his body. Jonathan placed his hands on the cool bathroom counter as he looked at his own reflection in the mirror. He stared at himself for a moment in complete silence studying his own face. He was looking deeply within his own eyes, catching glimpses of the warrior roaming around within. He stood there, quietly summoning the warrior because it was now needed. Now was the time for Jonathan to rise and go after what he wanted. Today was the day. He had been dreaming of this day for the last eight months and now it had arrived on the wings of anticipation, guided by the winds of preparation. His time had come, not by a moment of his choosing but it came nonetheless and not a moment too soon. He splashed water on his face and brushed his teeth before he decided to take his morning shower. He had been previously given instructions by Rico to meet them at the same cafe where they met yesterday. It was the same place where Jonathan watched Aaliyah get yanked up by Marco and driven away like some war criminal.

Once he finished his morning rituals, Jonathan got himself dressed. Their bags were already packed and in the car. He watched as Rachel walked out of her room. There was never a moment when Jonathan didn't think she looked beautiful. She was wearing a light grey sweatsuit with a white shirt that matched her white sneakers. Her hat covered the top of her hair as her ponytail draped in the back, stopping at the bottom of her neck. She was quiet as well as lovely. Jonathan stared at her for a moment, making sure she was alright. He knew this day and even the current moment was important to them both. There was a present reality that was just so surreal to him. He knew that what they had been waiting and praying for was around the proverbial corner, although they still had a decent way until they saw their journey come to a satisfied completion. Just the fact that they were taken these very crucial first steps was a powerful thing. It was powerful because it signified the journey was already underway. Truthfully, the journey started back in that parking lot the other night.

They both held hands while they walked down to the car in silence. Jonathan took a moment to soak in the surrounding scenery, as he knew this would be the last time that he saw these things, though he did this in a joyous sense, not in a doom and gloom manner. He was ready to be rid of this town and his false life. Like the shedding of old skin, Jonathan was definitely ready to be out with the old and in with the new.

When they arrived to the car, Jonathan looked at Rachel again, taking time to look into her eyes. For the first time in a while, he saw something in Rachel's eyes that made him feel more at ease about the situation. He saw *hope,* and all that came with it. He saw it bouncing around in her eyes with glee. He could see she was happy, and this did his heart a world of good to see her like that. Although she may not have physically been smiling from ear to ear, he knew how to read her well enough by now to know when she was upset and when she was happy. Jonathan let go of her hand for a moment to put their bags in the bed of the truck they were borrowing from Mr. Culgary. Jonathan knew he was going to be leaving today so he asked Henry and Mr. Culgary to meet him at the cafe near the outskirts of town. From there, Mr. Culgary could get his truck back and Henry could take Jonathan and Rachel in his car to meet Rico.

The disturbance of hesitation paced around on top of Jonathan's thoughts for a moment as he wondered if it was a good idea for Henry to drop them off. The only reason he found himself questioning that course of action was because he didn't want any more unnecessary drama to erupt. Although, it may have been a touch of paranoia instead of caution that caused these thoughts to roam freely within Jonathan's mind. Perhaps it was also a sense of protection. Though Henry was more than capable of protecting himself, Jonathan didn't need someone else getting hurt. However, he didn't want to prolong worrying over the possibility of a negative outcome.

He watched as Rachel hopped in the truck with ease as a blanket of calmness sprawled over her. Things were better than they were yesterday; it was like a whole new world had opened up overnight. A world where Jonathan and Rachel could be free from their false past and start afresh with a new outlook on life. For the first time in a long time, Jonathan was experiencing the same thing he saw dancing around in Rachel's eyes only moments earlier. He too tasted the allure of hope and endless possibilities joyously dancing on the tip of his tongue. A new day had sprung forth and Jonathan aimed to take it for what it was worth. He closed Rachel's door behind her, then hopped in the car as well.

Mr. Culgary's truck had a certain aged aroma to it; it almost smelled like pinewood. Whether they realized it or not, it was a physical reminder of the level of innocence this town and its people held onto. Jonathan started the truck and pulled out of the parking lot. He made his way to one of the main roads before he decided to roll down the window. He studied his surroundings silently as the town's air whisked by his ears. He could smell the unmistakable scent of freedom floating around in the air, ripe with opportunities. It held a certain sense of alluring promise to it that tickled the fancy of his imagination. Oh the things that could happen, once he were to reclaim the life that was previously ripped away from him.

However, that didn't matter as much as it did before, because now Jonathan could see restoration as well as restitution on the horizon. What they were planning on doing could be done, but it would take careful strategy and precise execution on their part. Jonathan knew that with the added touch of Coloso muscle, he would be able to get the job done. He continued to cruise through the streets of the innocent as he noticed something staring back at him through the truck's window. It was that thing that Jonathan encountered before, from his days in Winterville. A creature that once appeared frightening as well as lethal, though it didn't seem to look so bad anymore as Jonathan found himself staring back at its invisible visage. That creature was readily identifiable to Jonathan's trained eye: a creature named *normalcy*. Here he was perusing the streets of a normal town occupied by normal people, there was no dictatorship of power nor criminal underworld lurking in the shadows. Normalcy, it appeared, wasn't so unbearable after all, and in an ironic way he had grown to appreciate its beauty. Its unassuming yet attractive nature caused him to appreciate it, though his underlying hunger for a better and greater life still roamed impatiently within his heart. He now realized there wasn't really anything wrong with what he previously considered a slower paced life. He looked over to Rachel to continue to soak in the atmosphere as well as to accompany his newfound epiphany.

She appeared to be in better spirits than before. The simple sight of joy draped over Rachel's face was almost enough to send Jonathan over the moon. He was pleased to know she was happy. Both of them had spent too long in isolated states of minor depression, but neither one would openly admit that to the other. They both weren't in the best of places for the past few months. Now it seemed they were on the path to starting anew.

Before a full blown party could be thrown, there was still some serious work that needed to be done. For a moment, Jonathan turned his attention off of Rachel as he felt the old worn steering wheel beneath his palms. His hands were a little warm from the natural heat of his own body. He continued to listen to the wind as it sped past his ears while he drove by the streets of Olberton. Jonathan took time to soak in the nuances of the moment. He found himself briefly studying the town's life as he rolled by. He could see a man wearing denim overalls with a dingy white shirt to match. The man looked to be in his late thirties, and he had dark hair and by the look of his face, he hadn't shaved in awhile. There was no judgment in Jonathan's observation, just noticing the man for who he was or at least who he appeared to be. While he continued to drive by, he got a better look at the man's hands; they were dirty and black at his fingertips. This gave Jonathan the impression that he was a working man, probably a mechanic.

Jonathan wondered what the man was thinking as he watched him going on about his day, quietly walking down the street. It was an amazing thing how perspective can alter perception. There once was a time that Jonathan might have silently pitied that man; now it seemed there was an underlying sense of envy floating in the midst. Although Jonathan was aware of the fact that he didn't know anything about the man or his life, he at least knew this man wasn't wanted by the police or wondering how he was going to snatch his life back from the hands of his accusers. For Jonathan, it was an interesting and surreal conclusion. Jonathan now had more of an understanding that there wasn't anything wrong with wanting more out of his life. He just needed to make sure the path he was taking to get the things he wanted was the right one. A path that didn't require him to look nervously over his shoulder in fear of retaliation from a dark deed previously committed. A path he didn't have to lie about or convince himself it was a path worth walking. A path that was legal; one he could truly be proud of.

While Jonathan continued to drive through the peaceful streets, he noticed a certain level of calmness that was present. He took a minute to acknowledge how he was feeling and allowed his brain to chime in with its two cents on the subject. The reason Jonathan was feeling this way was because he thought about how he was now taking the necessary action. He also couldn't help but recall Mr. Culgary's advice about Rachel, and how it was time to show her he would do what he said he would do. Again, he glanced over at her, as he noticed the sun's rays dropping themselves peacefully upon her lovely face. He thought to himself how the old man's wisdom was true. Rachel was now in a relatively good mood compared to her previous murky demeanor that appeared to be taking up residence in the house of her emotions.

Jonathan wasn't exactly able to read her mind, but he could always tell when Rachel was just kind of off. He enjoyed the present truth that things were getting better and moving forward. He gripped the steering wheel with ease and excitement as he allowed those thoughts to float around on a peaceful cloud in the sky of his mind. The midsize buildings continued to pass by in his peripheral vision. The town was obviously in plain sight, but it stopped being at the center of Jonathan's focus the closer he got to his destination. He could tell he was getting closer to the cafe to meet with Mr. Culgary and Henry. Jonathan took a quick look at the speedometer of the truck and thought about Mr. Culgary's generous heart. He not only allowed Jonathan to use his truck, but he also gave Jonathan a job at the old junkyard. That was definitely something Jonathan was thankful for. Mr. Culgary really helped Jonathan and Rachel get back on their feet while they were trying to figure things out. This was all the more reason Jonathan had to make sure no unnecessary drama took place when Henry dropped them off.

The rest of the drive over was peaceful, as the town told the story of its own limits. Jonathan slowly but surely watched while the small-town buildings became fewer in number as he traveled toward the cafe. The roads got a little dirtier as well. Yes, indeed it was evident the surroundings were changing as he got closer to meeting Rico. Much like a domino effect, Jonathan realized the closer he got to Rico, the closer he got to his ultimate goal. He was ready for freedom and all its uninhibited glory it had to offer. The time was now and he was going to milk it for what it was worth. His racing mind came to a steadier pace as he approached the cafe.

Before he could pull into the parking lot Rachel spoke up.

"Do you see them?" she asked, her head on a slight swivel as she looked out the window.

"Give me a sec," Jonathan replied, as he too glanced over the parking lot, searching for those familiar faces.

His eyes searched with efficiency as he scanned the small parking lot looking for their target. The parking lot was surprisingly full, during the middle of the week no less. In the back of the parking lot, to the far left was a dark brown El Camino. It was Henry's car, and reflected its owner well. It had some supercharged muscle under the hood thanks to Henry's private love for speed.

"Got, em," said Jonathan as he pressed his foot on the gas, continuing to move forward in the parking lot. He recognized Henry's mug through the windshield. He looked halfway stern and ready to fight as usual. There wasn't an open spot next to Henry's car, so Jonathan parked in front of the car that was next to Henry's. Mr. Culgary was the first one to get out of the car, and because it was still Mr. Culgary's car, Jonathan was sure the man was ready to have it back. There was a wide and joyous smile plastered across Mr. Culgary's face, as if a long lost love had come home. He was dressed in a short sleeved, light blue collared shirt, and had on khaki pants that played well with his shirt, plus worn down white sneakers to complete the look. Jonathan felt the rubber top of the key as he turned the key in the ignition to cut the truck off. After the truck's rumbling engine went into a cold sleep from being turned off, he thought maybe he should have just left it on. After all, this little rendezvous with Mr. Culgary wouldn't last that long and they'd probably be on their way quickly. He stepped out of the truck first and Rachel followed suit as he heard her door shut, after his.

"Well Mr. Culgary, it's been real," said Jonathan, with a jovial tone gliding its way across his words.

Mr. Culgary smiled, before answering, "Well, that depends on who you ask," he replied.", How you doing, Ms. Elizabeth?"

Rachel almost took a moment to respond to her fake name but not too long that someone would notice. "I'm doing good Mr. C, how about you?" she asked, as she walked up to him and gave him a hug.

"Well hell, I'm doing better now that I got a pretty lady in my arms," he jokingly answered as he put his arms around her.

Jonathan watched as the two of them innocently embraced. Mr. Culgary was a good man, and Jonathan appreciated everything he did for him and Rachel. It wasn't everyday a man would take on some young couple and help them as if they were his own flesh and blood. He needed to meet a man like Mr. Culgary more than he realized. It helped balance out his previous mentor relationship. Mr. Culgary was a much needed, positive reinforcement for him, even though there were times when it wasn't that obvious. He was a strong force of wind, that helped blow Jonathan in the right direction and lent his voice for sage advice. A testament to this truth was the fact that Jonathan and Rachel were actually in a pretty good mood today. They also found themselves enjoying each other's company in a way they hadn't experienced in a while. In fact, Jonathan thought it would be the right thing to do by telling Mr. Culgary that he was right about what he told him.

Jonathan waited for a second and allowed Rachel and "Mr. C" a chance to finish catching up. Rachel took a few steps back and then appeared to direct her beautiful attention toward Henry who was still sitting in his car. Henry was a good man too, like his uncle, but he wasn't always as open and easy going as Mr. Culgary. To see him remain seated in the car while watching everyone else socialize wasn't out of the ordinary. That was sometimes just the nature of *Hurricane Henry,* so there was no need to be offended by his obvious lack of interaction. After all, Jonathan was fairly convinced

Henry had a soft spot for him and Rachel. Not to mention Mr. Culgary happened to let it slip one day that Henry was kind of fond of Jonathan, or "Carl" as he knew him. The subtle evidence of this, was seen in Henry's willingness to continue to spar with Jonathan on a weekly basis. Mr. Culgary made it clear if Henry didn't like someone, he wouldn't have spent that much time in the ring with them, as he did with Jonathan.

Rachel made her way toward Henry's car with a certain smirk on her face, one that suggested she might go over there to start some lighthearted trouble with Henry. Jonathan noticed as Henry lowered his window, and looked prepared for any wisecrack remarks Rachel may throw his way just to see him halfway smile. Although the test to see if Rachel could break Henry and make him laugh, would have to wait. Jonathan's attention had been gently turned from watching Rachel to looking at Mr. Culgary as he steadily approached Jonathan.

"Well, I gotta give it to you Mr. C, you were right," said Jonathan, his voice having a certain matter-of-fact demeanor.

Mr. Culgary smiled, and adjusted his belt before responding "Well, not that it sounds like a complete surprise but what exactly was I right about?" he sarcastically asked.

"Everything really. You were right about everything," answered Jonathan. "You told me it was time for me to start doing what I told her that I would do," he said as he nodded his head toward Rachel's direction. Mr. Culgary smiled again and belted out a hearty chuckle before replying "Yeah, I thought I noticed a lot more pep in her step today and a certain satisfied smile across her face too. Well, looks like you done good son. Gotta admit I'm proud of ya," he said.

These words were a nice compliment that seemed to float gently within the air before they glided down to Jonathan ears. He was pleasantly taken aback by what he had just said. He slightly furrowed his eyebrows as he gazed at Mr. Culgary's, then switched his eyesight off into the distance. It was as if he were actually searching for a memory he could recall of what he might have done to make Mr. Culgary proud. He was having a hard time trying to pinpoint exactly what it was he did to make him say such a thing.

"What did I do?" inquired Jonathan, still unsure of the answer that was to come.

"You did it, young man!" exclaimed Mr. Culgary, in his country twang amplified by the mid-day's heat. "You pulled yourself up son, you didn't stay down. That's the true mark and honor of a fighter; you took some hits and got back up. I've watched you grow in the short time ya been here. When you first got here, you were agitated and run down. You hadn't given up, but I know a weary soul when I see one." Mr. Culgary then lifted his hand and pointed his index finger at Jonathan."And you, young man... were tired."

Jonathan paused as he listened to what Mr. Culgary was saying. There was an eerie truth to the words that were spoken because he knew exactly what he was talking about. What was also shocking to Jonathan was hearing how closely Mr. Culgary was watching him all that time. It made him realize he was actually paying attention to him, and given everything Jonathan had been through, that was a precious thing in his eyes. However, before Jonathan could respond, Mr. Culgary added yet another piece of information to his surprising list of observations.

"Plus to top the cherry, you know how to listen, my boy! You wanna know how I know that?" asked Mr. Culgary, no doubt a rhetorical question that he would soon provide the answer for.

Sure enough, before Jonathan could even move his lips to create a response, Mr. Culgary answered his own question. "Fine, since you're twisting my arm so hard, I'll tell you. Because you're still standing and you're not standing alone." He pointed back to Rachel. "That let's me know you had enough sense to listen to someone other than yourself, because when people only listen to themselves Carl, they can end up in a world of hurt." Jonathan all but marveled at the wisdom that was so freely given, with no hidden strings attached. He could truly value and appreciate the instruction from an older man. Since he didn't always have direct access to that when he was growing up, he would always value it whenever it came his way. There was a wonderful peace that rested in the middle of them in that moment. Neither one of them wanted to disturb its invisible, yet undeniable presence; so they both stayed silent for just a while.

Mr. Culgary walked over to Jonathan with a calm and collected demeanor engulfing his body. He calmly placed his hand on Jonathan's shoulder. He still waited a moment before he said anything else and then he spoke. "I got the gist of what's going on from Henry, plus it doesn't take a rocket scientist to know you're leaving town," he said. "You're going home, aren't ya?"

"Yeah, it's…it's time," replied Jonathan.

Mr. Culgary stood silent, his hand still resting on Jonathan's shoulder. "You gonna face him?" he asked.

Jonathan stood there for a moment with a bewildered look on his face, as he tried to figure out what he was talking about.

"Are you gonna face that Kane Edwards fella when you get back?" asked Mr. Culgary, his words revealing he knew information that was once thought to be a secret.

A cold shock went through Jonathan's body as he felt his heart began to race. He tightened his knees so he still stood strong. Fear tried to creep in, but he was doing his best to keep it at bay. His mind raced with possible scenarios as his ears just processed the jaw-dropping sound of a secret being uncovered.

Before Jonathan could say anything, Mr. Culgary continued to speak."Well, hell, I reckon you would face him son, since he's the only thing standing in your way of your name gettin' cleared and your life restored." Mr. Culgary's eyes were now directly locked onto Jonathan's.

"Oh I knew who you were son, just after a few days of laying eyes on ya. I may be small-town, but no one and I mean *no one* pulls the wool over Mr. C's eyes. Now come on son, take that frog out ya throat and say something."

For the first time in his entire life, Jonathan was actually *speechless*. He heard other people use that very phrase when they found themselves shocked or surprised at something. However, Jonathan really felt his lips were in a locked position, as if they were giving his mind time to come up with a proper response. He still managed to formulate some words, in order to articulate his response.

"You knew…this entire time?" he asked, while lowering his voice, making sure there was no possible way for someone else to pick up their conversation.

"Like I said son, nobody pulls the wool over Mr. C's eyes," declared Mr. Culgary.

Jonathan took Mr. Culgary's jovial advice about the frog in his throat and swallowed in order to get rid of what felt like a bulging knot. He took a deep breath and looked over at Rachel. She was completely oblivious to the conversation that was taking place just a few feet away from her. Mr. Culgary turned his head to briefly glance back at Rachel as well.

"Oh, and I presume that Ms. Elizabeth over there is really *Ms. Monroe*," he said.

Jonathan shook his head in agreement and gently bit his bottom lip. "And you would presume right." he replied, still in disbelief that good ol' Mr. C knew what the deal was the entire time.

Another thought that quickly took up space in Jonathan's mind was that Mr. Culgary was in a way, protecting them. He thought about how Mr. Culgary could have called the police and turned them in anytime. Heck, had this been Edge City, someone in his position probably would have tried to blackmail them. Truly there was a mixture of emotions playing the field at the moment. While Jonathan thought about all of the possible scenarios that could have taken place, a strong sense of gratitude came over him. Then, all of these feelings were followed up by one simple question that had yet to be asked. *Why? Why did Mr. Culgary protect them and keep their secret?* Honestly, this was a question that Jonathan would like to have answered. Sure, he knew that Mr. C was a good guy and that he liked to see people do well. However, when Jonathan first met him, there was really no way for Mr. C to know that Jonathan was worth taking a chance on.

"I don't understand," said Jonathan, while a mild mix of confusion and bewilderment took residence within his facial expression. "Why would you do all of that? Why would you protect us, when you didn't even know us?" His gaze was now calmer yet steady, still with a silent undertone of confusion nesting in his mind.

Mr. Culgary grinned for a second while looking at Jonathan, still not answering the question that was just presented."Well, ya see son I like to think of myself as a pretty good judge of character. And once I knew that y'all weren't who you said you were, I looked into the matter further. I saw the crimes they say you committed and the one little piece that just didn't sit right with me, was that whole attempted murder thing. I've seen some things in my life son, I know an evil man when I see one." Mr. Culgary took another step closer to Jonathan. "And you, young man, are not evil. Fighter? Hell yeah! Killer?...No! Cuz I know a killer too, when I see one, and you ain't that either. So that's how I knew that y'all didn't really do what they say y'all did," Mr. Culgary explained.

Jonathan smirked as he stood there, quietly listening to the old man. "Thank you," were the next words that came out of his mouth. Truthfully, those were the only words he could muster up at the moment. He didn't really know what else to say. There he was, standing in gratitude to a man who seemed like he truly wanted nothing more than to see Jonathan do well. He had to acknowledge a blazing fact that had seemingly shot straight out of the heavens and landed in the midst of their conversation. That fact was as simple as it was powerful; that Jonathan was in the presence of a good man. It had been a while since Jonathan experienced such a thing and he had to admit it was a good feeling, one that could not go unnoticed. He felt the need to say the words aloud.

"You're a good man Mr. C," he said."But I really don't know how I can repay you, sir."

"Hell, youngin' you don't have to repay me. Just go set things right over there in that fancy city, to where you can hold ya head high again," said Mr. Culgary. "I've watched you. I've seen that uneasy look in your eyes. You've been uneasy because you're not settled with things being the way they are. You go back to that city and straighten some things out and I guarantee you, you'll straighten yourself out in the process."

The words of wisdom echoed in Jonathan's ear as their spoken power settled in his mind. He felt himself almost getting emotional over what he was currently hearing. He had been around this man for the last eight months and the whole time, Mr. Culgary was teaching, guiding, and protecting him. He was grateful for the unknown protection he had received and humbled that he thought so highly of him.

"I don't know what else to say other than, thank you," replied Jonathan. "Although I don't really know if there is even more that I could say."

"You've said enough. I know you appreciate it," said Mr. Culgary. "Like I said, you just make sure you set things right for yourself up there in that big city. Oh and make sure you take care of that pretty young lady you've got with you as well. Cause believe you me, the only thing that could make a woman stick with a man through all of that is love. And she must definitely love you son, to tolerate all this foolishness. So you make sure you treat her right and take care of her, ya hear?"

Jonathan shook his head in agreement before allowing his mouth to chime in as well."Yes sir, I will," he said.

He then looked over to his right, slightly past Mr. Culgary's shoulder and noticed Rachel walking back toward his direction. He wondered if he would say anything to her about what Mr. Culgary just told him. Then he thought about it and decided that for the sake of time, it would be better to tell her later.

"You ready to rock?" asked Rachel as she looked at Jonathan before turning her attention to the truck.

Jonathan could tell she was ready to get this so-called *show* on the road. He couldn't blame her. He understood the yearning to be free from the life of running and hiding they had been forced to endure. Now was the time for them to reclaim what was taken from them. Jonathan briefly looked at Mr. Culgary before saying anything back to Rachel. It was almost as if another conversation had been played out between the two of them, except this time it was a silent conversation, only being spoken through their eyes, facial expressions and mutual understanding.

"Yeah," he finally replied."Let me grab the bags and we can roll."

Jonathan wasn't too worried about whether Mr. Culgary would say something to her about what the two of them had just talked about. He figured he would leave it up to him to relay the message back to Rachel. Jonathan grabbed the bags from the back of the truck and packed them into Henry's car. Henry didn't say anything to Jonathan as he walked by the driver side window. He merely made eye contact and waved his hand. It only took a few minutes to get everything Jonathan and Rachel had packed into Henry's car. It seemed Rachel was saying her last goodbyes to Mr. Culgary as Jonathan looked over and noticed the two of them sharing a brief embrace. It was surreal in a way, to fully grasp the truth of what was unfolding right before his eyes. Watching Rachel say goodbye meant they were finally leaving. It meant that they would no longer be reduced to the lies they had to tell to retain their freedom. Jonathan now knew that the current *freedom* they endured came with a price. A price neither he nor Rachel were willing to continue paying.

Rachel made her way back toward Henry's car while and walked directly in Jonathan's direction. He smiled at her, as she got closer. His eyes then shifted their attention to Mr. Culgary once more. Jonathan waved his hand in the air to Mr. Culgary, as he watched a smile appear on his face in the distance. Mr. Culgary waved as he climbed in his truck.

Jonathan then turned his attention back to Rachel as she walked passed him, heading toward the back of Henry's car. Jonathan grabbed the door for her as she sat down inside. He watched her closely as she took her seat, his protective nature seemingly making an unnecessary appearance. Perhaps it was the air of the day that made him a little more on edge. Maybe it was because he knew deep down that today was a good day, but it was also a dangerous one. It was dangerous because it meant they were going back to a dangerous place where dangerous men dwelled. So even in a moment of peace, Jonathan was naturally on guard, ready for an unexpected threat to rear its ugly head.

Jonathan made his way to the passenger side door, opened it, and sat down. The car's air was on high; he could feel the cool rush of air hit him with force as he closed the door behind him. The sound of the leather squeaking as Jonathan took his seat was muffled out by the air conditioner. Jonathan looked directly over at Henry.

"Thanks for the ride," he said.

Henry nodded. "Always a pleasure to help out a fellow fighter," he said. His voice had an uneasy raspiness to it, though there wasn't much that Henry could do to fix that, since it was his natural voice. Besides, Jonathan was used to the sound of less than friendly voices. "So you're headed to the outskirts?"

"Yeah, we're meeting a…friend," replied Jonathan.

It was odd, because the word friend never seemed to sound so misplaced. Especially since he was attaching that moniker to Rico, who was a man Jonathan didn't fully trust as of yet. The only thing that seemed to be clear between the two of them was that they currently shared a common enemy: Kane. Although now wasn't really the time to dwell on whether he fully trusted Rico. All that Jonathan cared about was that he and Rachel made it to the city in one piece.

Henry pulled out of the parking lot, in a hasty manner, not enough to cause a scene but more than enough to catch the attention of the passengers. Jonathan smirked as he felt the ground beneath his seat roll by quickly, under the rolling tires that propelled the car forward. Henry drove as if he were a man on a mission, probably because that's exactly what he was. He at least had an assignment for the next 20 minutes, which was to get them to their next destination. Jonathan looked at Rachel for a quick second as the car continued to move at a pace that was probably quicker than the pace of the small town they were leaving behind. It wasn't long before he noticed the rapid change of scenery as they approached the meeting location. The vegetation had an unrestricted growth to it that only came from human neglect, which basically meant it was allowed to grow in the wild without someone deciding that they wanted to build a shopping mall in that particular location. Henry was silent as the car pushed onward, the only sounds were the air conditioner and the engine making its occasional growl as it flexed its American-built muscle. Jonathan noticed a small country-looking gas station coming up on the left-hand side as Henry raged on. He noticed two black cars and quickly realized this was the place where he was meeting Rico.

"It's over here," said Jonathan, as he peered out the window noticing Rico's truck accompanied by an all black town car.

While Henry pulled into the gas station, Jonathan couldn't help but think of a familiar yet unfriendly face: Adrian. He had spent his fair share of time in a car just like that back in Edge City. Still, the faint thought of a possible double-cross couldn't help but dance its way into his mind. Could it be that perhaps that was the same car he was used to seeing the death-dealer himself riding in? Or was this just an example of Jonathan's sometimes overactive imagination taking an unauthorized stroll down paranoia lane? Jonathan's unspoken guess was on the latter; the more he looked at the car the more he knew it didn't belong to any deadly henchman, or at least not the one that he was familiar with. Jonathan could feel the car slowing down beneath him as Henry pressed his foot on the brake. The gas station looked like an old, worn-down barn, due to the fact that the store actually was made out of wood. The tattered blue paint still left its mark on the wood, a reminder of an older time. The pumps were obviously more up to date, but not too much.

"Stop here," said Jonathan, his voice giving slight hints at his present uncertainty.

Henry put the car in park as Jonathan looked through the windshield to see if he saw Rico. Although, before he could make out a face in the truck, the passenger side door opened. During that moment, Jonathan couldn't help but think of when he first saw Marco's hulking frame make its debut. He thought back to the night in the parking lot when he had a gun aimed directly at his head. Old dark thoughts came up on a new and brighter day; not the best combination. Soon a face he recognized revealed itself as Rico stepped out from the passenger side door. He appeared to recognize Jonathan through the windshield, as he lifted his arms in a manner that seemed to ask, *What are you doing?*

Although no apparent anger seemed to show itself in Rico's facial expression, he appeared to be ready to leave. Jonathan looked at his watch to see if he was late; luckily that wasn't the case. It was only a few minutes past the designated meet time. Short enough where he was still in the window of the societal acceptable window of tardiness. Besides, it wasn't like Rico was a stickler for things like that anyway.

"This is the guy you meeting up with?" Henry asked, as he pointed his finger at Rico.

"Yeah that's the one," answered Jonathan.

The thought of things somehow going sideways prompted Jonathan to quickly unbuckle his seatbelt and step out of the car. He could smell the Pinewood trees that allowed the wind to carry their scent throughout the air. It was a completely different terrain out here, and Jonathan had grown to appreciate its beauty. In an ironic way, he was slightly disappointed he would be leaving the peaceful life he had built over the last several months. His time hadn't been that long in the grand scheme of things. However, it felt like they had been there for almost two years.

As Jonathan stood by Henry's car, he took about two steps forward. "Well, you ready?" Jonathan asked, while listening to the sound of his own voice. Though that question was aimed at Rico, he too quietly contemplated the answer to his own question, wondering if in fact, he was ready as well for what lay ahead.

"Believe me when I tell you, I was born ready for this," Rico answered, his braggadocious tone overlapping his sentence with its heavy verbal weight.

The surprising thing was that Jonathan actually believed him, even though he was drenched in arrogance. All things considered, perhaps it wasn't the worst thing to have someone with supreme confidence to help with the war on Kane.

"Well, that's reassuring," replied Jonathan in a sarcastic tone.

"I aim to please Mr. Cross, mostly myself but on occasion others benefit as well," said

Rico with a sly smile. He remained near the truck, but calmly paced as he talked to Jonathan, almost like a roaming tiger guarding his territory."Well look, I got you your own set of wheels for the drive." Rico pointed to the black town car.

The explanation for the presence of the extra car put Jonathan at ease. At least now he knew why there were two cars instead of just one. He thought about why Rico did this, but he then thought about how he would probably enjoy his own drive back into the city.

"I figured you wouldn't mind having your own space," said Rico. "Ya know, give yourself some time to unwind while you drive."

"Thanks," replied Jonathan, as he continued to look the car over from a distance.

He then came to the conclusion it was time to go, no more stops to make or people to see. It was time for their long awaited exit and the timing was indeed perfect. For the sake of his sanity as well as his relationship with Rachel, they could no longer stay in Olberton. Jonathan turned and looked back as a sign to Rachel that it was ok for her come out of the car. She stepped out as Henry popped the trunk for her so that they could take their bags. Jonathan then turned around to help grab their bags from the trunk.

"The doors are unlocked and the keys are in the driver's seat," said Rico. He spoke louder so Jonathan could hear him as he walked in the opposite direction.

Jonathan turned back and nodded. After he unloaded the trunk, he and Rachel said their goodbyes to Henry and headed toward the car. Sure enough, the door was unlocked and the keys were where Rico said they would be. Jonathan opened the driver side door, he and Rachel sat down simultaneously, meeting in the middle. They looked at each other briefly before Jonathan closed his door. There was a respectful silence for the moment at hand. They both knew what was about to take place. They were on the cusp of the battle of their lives. Jonathan looked out the window and saw Rico's truck pulling out onto the road. Jonathan put the key up to the ignition and paused. He sat there for a second as if giving everything he was about to do a second thought. However, he couldn't stop now. He knew that this had to be done.

"You ready?" Jonathan asked Rachel, as he looked over to her to see what state of mind she appeared to be in.

"Ready as I can be," Rachel replied, as she placed her hand on top of Jonathan's.

Jonathan pulled her hand up to his mouth and kissed it, a sign of his love and gratitude. He put the key in the ignition and started the car. It was time for them to leave. Now was the time for them to do what had to be done. Now was the time for them to face the giant that stood before them. Now was the time for them to return to a place they once called home. It was time to return to Edge City.

CHAPTER 12

THE RETURN

Time has its own way of distorting one's view of something. It's as if time itself is endowed with its own special set of powers. Some say one of the powers that time holds, is the power of perception. When someone stares at something long enough, they'll begin to notice things they didn't see before. The small details that once escaped the glances of the untrained eye, now become visible.

This was something Jonathan noticed for himself as he quietly yet nervously gazed upon a familiar face, except this face was full of features one could easily overlook, or worse, never notice at all. In a way, Jonathan could consider himself to be one of the lucky ones who was able to see the true nature of the face he was currently looking at, catching failing glimpses of its faults as well as its marvelous features. Perhaps there was more to this face than met the eye. Perhaps those who looked upon it were easily fooled for a reason, and that reason was no fault of their own. Maybe they weren't able to see its true identity, because it was hidden. Richly cloaked in enchanting beauty that drew the eyes away and fooled the mind into missing its true nature. Oh yes, this was a familiar face and it appeared to look right back at Jonathan as he drove along. This face, as with any, had an identity, a name to go along with it. Truly it was a name Jonathan would never forget. A name that inspired some and frightened others, a name that would cause its inhabitants and sometimes its victims to give it its proper respect. A name that meant something and could never be taken lightly, the name of a place called: *Edge City.*

Alas, Jonathan had returned to his old stomping grounds. Although some would say it was the city that did more of the stomping than Jonathan did. It had dealt out its fair share of blows toward the young man, although like a true champion, Jonathan rose. He rose to the occasion and allowed his light to shine and his inner strength to show itself.

Jonathan's hand firmly gripped the steering wheel, as a sense of nervousness seeped into the car. It felt like its own separate entity, sitting in the midst of Jonathan and Rachel, feeding off their secret emotions. Anxiety coerced its way through Jonathan's veins as he searched for a calming thought. He found himself in the presence of a rather large being that liked to enforce its will on the people that inhabited its metropolitan body. However, all was far from lost as there was an untold secret that eluded the minds of many. Only a select few had discovered the secret of the city, those who had survived its test and lived long enough to find the truth. Jonathan now found himself privy to this information that seemed to pride itself in being tough to find. The secret in fact was this: the city had a way of rewarding those who could survive its often abusive test. Sometimes the test was physical and sometimes it was mental. No matter what form it took, the test still came, and passing it was entirely up to the individual.

The last time he found himself within its grasp, Jonathan had taken a beating from the city. Now once again, he had returned ready to face the formidable foe. What was yet to be seen was his reward for his willingness to return to the labyrinth. After all, he had just stepped foot into the city and perhaps he would have to face yet another test or two before the reward was manifested. All he knew was that this time, he could not turn back. He was going to have to see it all the way through. He had to finish the mission in its entirety. It wouldn't work if he didn't.

That nervousness he felt only moments ago now seemed to subside as his sense of courage and resolve now wanted to take the stage. Wisdom and caution made their debut as well, as Jonathan thought about the fact that he was still a wanted man. Not only that, but here he was traipsing along in the very city that was the source of him becoming an outlaw. With the wheel still beneath the palms of his hands, Jonathan started to look around and see the familiar scenery he once called home. His next move was a risky one, but then again so was him being back in the city. The sights weren't enough to satisfy Jonathan's senses; he also wanted to add sound and possibly smell to the equation as well. He pressed a button on the driver side door to roll down the window.

"Jonathan! What are you doing?" Rachel gasped, her voice riding high at a concerned pitch.

Jonathan didn't respond. He didn't seem to care about revealing his face out in the open. He rationalized that he knew he was a wanted man, but it wasn't like he was public enemy number one, which meant that at first glance, no one would probably recognize him. Immediately, there was a sense of nostalgia that swept across Jonathan's face. That feeling also entered into his mind as he looked at the people and cars that inhabited the city's landscape. They were the familiar faces of the people that dwelled in the concrete jungle, and as Jonathan remembered, they were all preoccupied with their own lives; going on about their days, some bending to the will of the city without noticing, others trying to boldly defy the mundane. Although the ones who walked in courage weren't always easy to spot, but they were there, walking among the crowds.

Jonathan noticed a random face among the certified masses as he continued to drive down the street, while occasionally glancing at Rico's truck in front of him. He saw another young corporate type, the same way that he once was. The young man had on a black suit with a white shirt accompanied by a stately purple tie. It made Jonathan think back to almost a year ago when he was driving on these same city streets, except back then his heart was filled with optimism and his eyes were ripe with possibilities.

Surely, he thought the sky was the limit as he explored new terrain. He still believed in his greater tomorrow, but he was no longer naive to the ways of this world. These streets had toughened him up in a way he would never forget, nor could he have foreseen.

Jonathan continued to silently study the young man from a distance while glancing at the road. Truthfully, he hoped the best for the poor guy. He prayed that whoever this well dressed, wide-eyed man was wouldn't be defeated. Jonathan knew something this other guy didn't seem to know yet. It was the young and unfiltered pep in his step that gave him away and his walk told a story of youth not yet tainted by the outside world. He had not seen the harshness of this city yet. He knew nothing of the hard blows that he could be dealt if he wasn't careful. Jonathan hoped that whoever the guy was would have the strength to endure and that he would not give up. One thing he knew for certain was that this city was going to deal that guy a few hard knocks, and no purple tie or fancy suit would keep that from happening.

Jonathan then diverted his attention to the city itself as he listened to its call. The old familiar sound of the hustle and bustle of the city, its voice still raw and clear, its roar mighty and ferocious. Jonathan could hear the sound of cars moving and brakes squeaking with horns blaring in the background, being pounded on by aggressive taxi drivers. The pace was still the same; things might've changed for Jonathan, but the city remained the powerful colossus that it was when he first arrived there almost a year ago. Its rhythmic tones almost formed a melody, as if to welcome Jonathan back in some twisted yet sincere way. Then again, it wasn't fair to hold grudges against the city itself; it had no vendetta against one man, although at times it seemed to show favor to some and possible disdain for others. Maybe Jonathan could consider not taking the past personally, but then again, how else could he perceive it? He lifted his head and saw the same ominous metal giants that had clear eyes all over their bodies below, the same giants that appeared to watch people at times, as their height caused them to scrape against the clouds. Perhaps that's why they're known as skyscrapers; indeed the name was fitting. Suddenly Jonathan felt his nostalgic moment being cut short as he heard the sound of Rachel's voice wrapping around his ears.

"Jonathan, are you seriously gonna drive with the window down?" she asked, her voice sounding sharp and slightly disapproving all in the same breath.

He looked over at Rachel and thought it would be best if he just listened and avoided a serious argument. He wasn't really in the mood to have something like that happen on his first day back, although, it probably would be more fitting if something like that were to happen. Perhaps, it could serve as some sort of warped way of saying welcome back. Thankfully, that wasn't about to happen and Jonathan decided to roll the window back up. It wasn't worth the added headache of arguing with her over it; things were already tense enough. While he rolled the window back up, he couldn't help but wonder if he had gone slightly insane. There had to be something going on for him to do what he was currently doing. Who in their right mind would just drive right back into the very city that charged them with these violent crimes? Jonathan realized that insanity wasn't going to get the credit for such a ballsy move. Instead, the inner warrior would get the spoils and courage would be the one to take props for their return. He decided he would no longer run from his problem, and instead he would run toward it with a fury, the likes of which he had never demonstrated before.

The tail lights from Rico's SUV shined bright when he put his foot on the brake. Jonathan in turn did the same, realizing they were at a red light. In the stillness, he thought about a few things. He thought about how a squad car could come pulling up and somehow notice the wanted man behind the wheel. He wondered if this bold move was actually a foolish mistake. Then he thought: how was he suppose to travel around the city? Would he just walk openly in the streets? These were things that didn't seem to come up until now; however, it was a bit too late to turn back now. Surprisingly, he wasn't completely worried because he knew he had two other faces that wouldn't be as recognizable on his side. So if push ever came to shove, which in this city it likely would, Jonathan could use Rico or Marco as his eyes and ears if he needed them. Though right now they seemed to be already playing the role of the eyes, seeing that they were the ones currently leading the way. Jonathan had no clue where they were going. Though he had spent time here before, it wasn't enough for him to get the entire layout of the iron behemoth.

Some of the streets were faintly familiar, but Jonathan began to notice they seemed to be heading in a direction of town he was unfamiliar with. The buildings were still big, just different in appearance. Jonathan followed Rico as they took a right turn onto a street called *Bullet Drive.* Perhaps it was a bad omen or maybe just a fitting name, given the situation. Either way, there was a great chance bullets may yet again fly in these dangerous streets that Jonathan once again found himself submerged. It was the nature of this iron beast known as Edge City to bring out the primal side of some people. Instincts that laid dormant would now have to be called upon, if they were to make it out of this alive.

"Have you ever been on this side?" Jonathan asked Rachel, while looking intently out of the window, studying his new surroundings.

"No, not really but I think we're on the lower south side," she replied."I've heard things tend to be pretty quiet around here."

Jonathan followed Rico down into what looked like a private garage of a rather nice looking building. He watched as Rico stopped in front of it, waiting for the door to go up. As the door opened, Jonathan could now see inside, sure enough it was a private parking deck that was completely empty.

"Yeah. Another parking deck," said Jonathan, a sarcastic tone having its way with his vocal chords.

Rachel looked over at him."Huh?" she asked.

Jonathan silently smirked to himself. "Nothing," he said.

He then released himself from the role of follower, as he pulled out from behind Rico and parked in a spot of his choosing. Rico pulled into a parking spot as well. Jonathan sat for a moment as he cut off the car, letting the reality soak in that he had returned.

Marco was the first one out of the SUV, stepping out calmly, yet ready for war. Jonathan slightly frowned as he suddenly remembered Rico had gotten in the passenger seat back in Olberton and it was Marco who was the one that was driving all along. It was a small thing in the grand scheme of things that the day held, nothing worth commenting over. Jonathan and Rachel hopped out of the car as well. Rico then walked around the corner of the car, exiting from the passenger side.

"Well, you made it Cross. How does it feel?" he asked.

"It'll feel good when we do what we came here to do," Jonathan answered.

"Where are we?" Rachel asked.

"It's called "*The Nine,*" Rico answered, with a strong wave of pride and bravado delivering his sentence. He lifted his right hand, gesturing for them to behold as he stood there proud. "My father built and owns this building. He named it *'Nine'* due to it being his ninth real estate project. No one really knows that he's the one that owns this building and he likes to keep it that way. He secretly owns a few other buildings in the city as well. He likes to have eyes in several places." The pride that Rico felt for his father saturated his sentences whenever he spoke of him.

"That's touching," mumbled Rachel at a decimal level that only Jonathan would hear.

The sarcasm was evidence of her obvious disdain for Rico. Jonathan could tell Rachel didn't fully trust Rico and he couldn't blame her. However, they were in a situation that they both would have to make the best of. Jonathan thought he had escaped those sort of cryptic ironies that only Edge City could offer. Once he stopped to think about it, it was really fitting. His return to the city meant more than just the act of his physical body returning to a certain geographical region. It was more akin to revisiting an old relationship, like some wayward lover trying to strike up an old flame. Jonathan knew how he felt about the city, and it was still a promising place. Only this time around, he had a better lay of the land, so to speak. There were certain things he knew to watch out for now. He couldn't say that he completely felt at home in Edge City, but there was a strong sense of familiarity that in its own way offered an odd sense of comfort.

Jonathan noticed Rico's mouth continuing to move, however he had tuned him out. The movement of his thoughts somehow muffled Rico's voice. Selective hearing perhaps, but either way, it gave Jonathan a moment to feel the presence of the city. If he got quiet enough, he could've sworn he heard the slight whisper of his name. The city itself beckoned him to come back and try his luck again, although Jonathan knew that luck had little to do with navigating this city. In order to make it here, he would have to have a strategy, which was the very thing that he wanted to talk about next. However, it seemed that Jonathan's private thoughts were interrupted by Rico's response.

"Well, how about we take this party upstairs, kids. I'll show you your rooms," said

Rico, his words sounding promising as they ran through the air.

Immediately, Jonathan found himself snapping back into the moment. "Sounds like a plan," he replied.

He glanced over at Rachel as she simultaneously reached for his hand. She was strong, there was no question about that. However, it was good for Jonathan to see that simple gesture he had made pass the wall of her emotional barriers and that she trusted him. He held her hand as they allowed Rico to lead the way. Marco followed behind the group as the watchful eye.

They walked through the empty parking deck, with the resounding echo of Rico's dress shoes clanking against the cool pavement as he led the way. There was a gray door with a polished stainless steel handle that Rico stopped at once he got to it. He pulled out a key and opened the door. Jonathan walked behind Rico as he had Rachel's hand still in his, and she walked behind him.

Once they entered the door, they were all greeted with the sound of an AC unit blasting its power. Jonathan could feel the immediate shift in temperature, as the nice cool air ran alongside his face and continued its run on the rest of his body. They entered a well-manicured hallway with white marble flooring. One could tell this was a building that was going to be used to host high-end clientele. Jonathan couldn't say that he was really surprised at this; on the contrary, it was starting to make perfect sense. After all, they entered the building through a private parking deck. Not to mention, if this Nero guy was anything like his son, he probably took a liking to the finer things in life. With this in mind, things began to make more sense and the pieces formed a more cohesive picture. The hallway itself wasn't a very big one. There was a nice black and white painting of a city skyline. By the looks of it, it could have been a painting of the city itself, but Jonathan wasn't one hundred percent sure. Opposite the painting were two elevators. Rico walked to the elevator closest to him, which happened to be the one on the right.

He pressed the button to call the elevator. "It's been a while since I've been here," he shared.

They stepped onto the elevator once it arrived, its metal doors welcoming them with open arms, so to speak. There was an odd feeling of vast emptiness present; although they had just entered the building, Jonathan could tell they were the only ones inside. The elevator ride was quiet in a slightly awkward way. There was really nothing for Jonathan to say. He was still wrapping his mind around the fact that he had returned to the city. While he continued to study his own thoughts, the elevator stopped. Again, the doors opened, except this time, there was no hallway, only a small waiting area, with the same marble floor. Jonathan was too wrapped up in his own thoughts at the time to notice that Rico had pushed the PH button on the elevator when they arrived at the penthouse floor .

Rico walked forward, pulling ahead of the group, naturally because he was the one holding the keys. Rachel looked over at Jonathan when she noticed the words "Penthouse" on the top of the door.

"Moving on up in the world," she sarcastically whispered to Jonathan.

He looked at her and gave her a smirk that represented his amusement. By now the two of them were no longer holding hands. Jonathan noticed Rico's hand on the doorknob as he was opening the door. In that moment, Jonathan couldn't help but think of his old condo in the city. The pride he felt when he received the keys to his first place was a moment that he wasn't willing to trade. It was an odd thing really, this tumultuous relationship he shared with the city. It was something that couldn't be explained to any outside party, they would have to experience it for themselves. These thoughts played as a backdrop while Rico opened the door. It was time for Jonathan to let go of wandering thoughts and focus on the present moment.

Besides, it was turning into the type of moment that could not be ignored. The door to the penthouse was now open, and the grand entrance had been revealed to the newcomers of the group. This time, Rachel went first as she took a step forward; Jonathan moved next but slightly out of sync. They had just re-entered a realm of luxury, one that Jonathan had almost forgotten about. As soon as Jonathan walked in, he noticed that the place was immaculately staged to perfection with fine furniture. The immediate display of opulence was the famous floor to ceiling windows that he once enjoyed from his time previously spent in the city. The city skyline seemed to dance with every step that Jonathan took, gazing upon the majestic splendor--that was Edge City.

"Well, welcome to your new home," stated Rico, as he threw up his hands in a grandiose gesture. "Try not to get anything on the carpet," he sarcastically added, although with the tone of his voice you couldn't always tell if he was joking.

The place itself was a meeting of two styles, a bit of contemporary elements combined with a more traditional flare, including those with a more seasoned design palate. Undoubtedly, this was a physical manifestation of the father/son duo who probably shared ideas on this particular project. Jonathan continued to look the place over, as did Rachel. He noticed her as she slightly veered off to the left running her hands along the top of the bone-white leather couch. The couch itself rested nicely on top of the high-end grey carpet that lay beneath it. Jonathan's attention briefly wandered to the flat screen tv, his eyes looked up to the two-story ceiling right above them. He caught a glimpse of the upper level balcony, which was probably where most, if not all of the bedrooms were. It was a surreal feeling once Jonathan took a moment to acknowledge it. He didn't quite imagine this warm of a welcome when he envisioned himself coming back to the city. Nor did he imagine he would have any outside help who agreed with his vengeance endeavor. His eyes returned back to the windows, that captured the beauty of the city nestled in a still shot frame.

"Well, feel free to look around," said Rico, his voice actually sounding warm and inviting in a sincere way.

Jonathan had a bit of a delayed response. He was still preoccupied with his current view. He studied the top of some of the buildings that were off in the distance, remembering when all of this was new to him. He then turned and looked at Rico and nodded his head in agreement.

"I'm going upstairs. Not really used to being in the car that long," said Rico, revealing his lack of host skills. He didn't bother to show Jonathan nor Rachel where their rooms where before he decided to head up the contemporary glass staircase, although he did manage to *tell* them.

"Oh, and before I forget, Marco gets the room down here. Your rooms are upstairs," he commented, as he pointed his finger toward the top of the stairs. "They're the rooms that aren't occupied," he sarcastically jested, while lightly laughing at his own joke.

Rachel smiled without saying anything to Rico, but Jonathan heard her sarcasm loud and clear from where he was standing. He knew Rachel in a different way than the rest of the them did. He saw her face while she offered up that empty grin; he knew she was agitated. Rico and Marco appeared to vanish at the same time, leaving them to fend for themselves in the confines of the penthouse. Jonathan walked over to Rachel and gave her a hug, she nestled her head in his chest as he put his arms around her.

"Thank you," she said

Jonathan squeezed her tighter, "Don't thank me just yet," he said."We still have to slay the dragon. And you know as well as I do that this dragon won't go down without a fight."

Jonathan turned his head and again looked outside of the giant glass windows. They revealed the concrete jungle that lay before him. Somewhere out there, deep in the jungle, the dragon Jonathan spoke of was waiting. A violent creature that took no prisoners and would devour those it came in contact with, a creature that they aimed to confront once they devised a proper game plan. Jonathan was ready; now was the time. Starting tomorrow they would begin their quest to wage war against the beast. Hunting season was now in session.

CHAPTER 13

DETECTIVE MERCER

While Jonathan was plotting his next move, the city itself was still very much alive and active. It didn't wait on anyone, and it moved to the beat of its own drum, that is of course whenever it felt the urge to move. Lives were still being lived and the days would continue to rise and fall. However, there was something else that lived in the city with the rest of its inhabitants. Within the city streets there lay a force, a force that existed to combat the evil that would manifest itself through the presence of crime. This force was none other than the police force of Edge City; *The Edge City Police Department* to be exact.

Truthfully, today was no different than any other day in the life of a cop. However, this wasn't just any cop; in fact this man wasn't a cop at all. He was actually a little bit higher up on the payroll of the law enforcement hierarchy; he was a detective. Detective Sebastian Mercer had made his mark on the city the best way he knew how: by making arrests. He was honest and hard working, and he never liked to see the bad guy come out on top. He couldn't stand to see injustice survive in his presence, so as one could imagine, he had his fair share of tough times in Edge City. He was currently out closing a case. The day itself was calm. It was about 75 degrees outside with a strong chance of arrest. He found himself located deep in a part of town known as The Gallows. It wasn't the nicest, nor was it the safest part of the city. It was a place where darkness liked to show itself strong when given the opportunity.

Detective Mercer was currently handcuffing a known drug dealer known as The Mint. They were in a dirty back alley behind what looked to be a makeshift meth lab located in the bottom of an apartment building. Apparently the Mint, who's real name was Ralph, had a reputation for providing his clients with the freshest *ingredients* he could get his hands on. Word got around, and eventually when his caseload lightened, Detective Mercer paid him a visit.

"You should know that some of the guys down at the station got a real laugh at your street name," Detective Mercer said, with a strong dose of sincerity riding alongside his words. The point was to let Ralph know that he was serious about people really laughing behind his back about his lackluster alias.

"Hey, my dude, can it with all the jokes and lighten up on these cuffs man!" demanded Ralph. He was currently lying face down on the concrete with his $400 designer shirt getting its fair share of newfound scuff marks from being exposed to the filth that laid on the ground.

Detective Mercer was a fairly built man, his body still holding onto the muscle he put on from college football days. At times like these, it served him pretty well as he tackled Ralph earlier and put an abrupt end to their chase. He bent down and leaned in as if he was going to whisper in The Mint's ear.

"Listen to me when I tell you, you're in *no* position to negotiate with me," he responded, his voice sounding rock solid and authoritative. He was a man who didn't like to be trifled with, especially by those whom he deemed to be the underbelly of society. "So do yourself a favor and be quiet before I decide to break something."

They locked eyes, each one representing the silent conversation between crime and justice, that for now would remain one-sided and in the favor of justice. Besides, there was nothing left for Ralph to say, or at least nothing that wouldn't cause him to get his jaw broken. Mercer had a reputation of his own and he was considered on the street to be a man of action more than words. He was one of the pitbulls of the department; he'd get a hold of something and wouldn't let it go. This may have aided in the thought process of Mr. Mint as he decided to keep all remaining comments inside his mouth. Detective Mercer stood and looked around for a moment, the air had gone still. Mercer kept quiet as well, with silence having its way.

Mercer stood about 6 foot, 2 inches tall. His hair was short and unshaven stubble covered his cheeks and around his mouth, but not in a way that made him look like a slob, rather a way that suggested there was a certain look he was going for. He wasn't a small man and didn't get spooked easily. Detective Mercer turned his head, now looking back toward the door of the apartment building that he had pushed Ralph through about 5 minutes earlier. There were faint thuds that were now coming from the other side of the door. It was a sound that made Detective Mercer lower his hand, so it would hover above his gun that was safely resting in its holster. Suddenly, the door flew open with a sense of purpose, as if it wanted to be released from the very hinges that kept it tied to its frame. Although the real purpose behind the door flying open like that was dressed in a dirty red shirt and ripped blue jeans. The man had an even dirtier pair of sneakers that seemed to complete the look of a guy who was probably up to no good. There was a look of panic plastered on the face of the man who came bolting out of the door, obviously for good reason; there was a police officer that was about a few steps behind him screaming as loud as he could

"Freeze! E.C.P.D!" shouted the officer.

The man kept running, but there appeared to be a delayed reaction of surprise. The man didn't realize he was heading into the path of Detective Mercer, or at least by the time he did, it was too late. Mercer already had his gun drawn. The man's eyes stared at the gun before they moved to see the man who was holding it. Mercer held the gun steady as he aimed at the man's head, normally this was the part where Mercer was suppose to tell the assailant to get down on the ground. However, that's not what happened. Mercer said nothing as he allowed his gun to do all the talking for him. There was a look of stillness in Detective Mercer's eyes. A certain stillness that spoke, and it said that he had no problem with killing a man.

Perhaps the criminal could see this and understood the look in Mercer's eyes for what it was; a warning. One that shouldn't and ultimately wouldn't be taken lightly. The man stopped as if he had hit an invisible wall. He locked eyes with Detective Mercer, while breathing heavily. Mercer stayed locked on his current target with his gun aimed steady, just in case he needed to let a round fly from the chamber.

The man stood there for another few seconds, then he was abruptly tackled from behind by the other officer who was chasing him. Detective Mercer lowered his weapon and looked down to his left. He noticed that good ole' Mr. Mint was in the same place that he left him, lying face down on the concrete in handcuffs. Detective Mercer walked over toward the cop, his name tag said *Johnson.* Mercer stood there quietly before he said anything, he looked as if he was studying the cop who was clearly new to the force.

"That was a nice takedown," said Mercer. "Next time try not to let him get so far in front of you."

The cop was young, and he had a look of eagerness as he looked at Detective Mercer. It wasn't something that they taught at the academy, but nevertheless the eagerness was present in the young officer.

"Yes sir," the officer replied as he did his best to multitask by cuffing the assailant and responding to Detective Mercer.

Detective Mercer watched as the officer finished making his arrest. It was a sight that Mercer was familiar with. He had the look of a man that enjoyed seeing justice properly served. Indeed, today was a good day in the eyes of the law. A few less criminals on the streets, thanks to the valiant effort made by Detective Mercer and the rookie cop. Although the rookie had much to learn, an honest arrest was still made.

"Alright let's get these two fine citizens downtown for processing," instructed Detective Mercer.

"Yes sir," answered Officer Johnson.

It was the usual routine from there, round up the bad guys, put them in the car, and head back to the station. A mundane process that lead to a greater outcome, helping to clean the streets. The route to the station was a scenic one, although this was probably not the case for those that found themselves in the back of a squad car, like The Mint. There were people going on about their daily routines as Detective Mercer's undercover car rolled its way through the city streets.

The police station itself was a pretty stately looking building, at least for its age. The words Silver Edge City Police Station were carved out in stone on the front of the building. The letters all but jumped from the building as they stood boldly in a three-dimensional fashion. The rest of the building was made of brick, with modernized glass doors toward the entrance. It was all but obvious that the building had been around for a while and received a face lift. The renovations, although a nice touch, didn't take away from its true meaning, nor did they take away from the righteous spirit of the police department and what it stood for. It was really more of an atheistic adjustment for the productive citizens and officers of Edge City to enjoy.

Inside the precinct was where the real magic took place. There was a certain hustle and bustle within the walls of the station. If those walls could talk, they probably would've been silenced by the public due to the unsightly knowledge they would reveal. Edge City had seen more than its fair share of corruption, and it had the history to prove it. Some of the history was housed in that very building, living a divided existence. Some evidence of the history's life was tucked away in case files. Some were on display in photos that were framed and hung on the walls.

A few quick strides and Detective Mercer was well on his way to his desk. Just a few steps behind Mercer's heels was the rookie cop picking up the slack while escorting their guests in cuffs. Within the precinct, Mercer received mixed reviews. There were pockets of praise from some of the cops in admiration of his good example. While others who had grown numb to the crime in the city, viewed Mercer as too much of a boy scout. This two-sided coin was on full display in the department this afternoon.

"Got yourself another one huh?" said one officer as he tipped his uniform hat toward Mercer, his gesture showing a sign of respect.

Mercer said nothing, only a half grin that represented his answer. There were several onlookers, even the ones who weren't Mercer's biggest supporters that were present as well. Sometimes their stone cold silence spoke volumes to a man that was very skilled at observing things. It was often a look in their eyes and a minute frown perched on their lips that earned them the moniker of *hater*.

Mercer parted ways with the rookie, and he continued to head toward his desk while the junior officer escorted the two criminals to processing. He arrived at his desk, which was almost indistinguishable from the others when looking at them from afar, except that his was a lot neater than most.

Mercer could see Captain Herschel Briggs's office from his desk. A few times, Mrs. Briggs had come down to the station with a freshly made batch of her sweet potato muffins. During some of her visits, she let her nickname for her hubby slip out, as she said "Love you, Hersheys!" No doubt the play on his name was also a nod to his chocolate complexion. A few of the guys tried to make fun of the captain about his pet name; it didn't end well for them. Mercer wasn't the type to make fun of anyone's name, whether it was a nickname or not. This probably stemmed from the fact that his first name was Sebastian, so he was the last person who was qualified to make fun of someone else's.

Captain Briggs had a large glass window in the front of his office, though it was probably so he could look out, than it was for people to look in. The captain was currently on the phone and by the looks of it, he was in a good mood. That was always a good thing for those who were fortunate enough to be within constant yelling radius of the captain. Mercer managed to stay on the good side of Captain Briggs, so he was rarely on the receiving end of one of the captain's tirades.

Mercer took a seat at his desk and sat quietly for a moment. Though the stacks of paperwork and cases were filed neatly, they still called for his attention and couldn't be ignored. In the pile of cases on his desk, there was one that was slightly sticking out and had red tape on the side of the folder. A stranger could tell that this folder was probably of some importance. Mercer looked at the folder and pulled it out, his hands moving swiftly and meticulously, as if he was a gifted surgeon. He laid it flat while moving it toward the center of his desk. He looked at the folder before opening it, studying its every detail. There were several tabs sticking out from the top of the thick layer of papers that were in the file. The tabs were color coded, only recognizable to the one who made the system. Mercer placed his hand where there was a blue tab that was sticking up from the top. He opened the file from that tab, his eyes met a picture that was clipped to more stacks of papers with notes he had made about this particular case. The picture held a face that was important to the case. In fact, it was a picture of the primary suspect. That suspect was Jonathan Cross. Detective Mercer lifted the picture and studied Jonathan's face as he had done many times before.

"Tell me you're not still chasing dead-end leads on that case!" said a voice from behind

Mercer's shoulder.

Mercer turned his head, with a look on his face that suggested he knew who the voice belonged to before he turned around. "If it's on my desk, then it's unsolved and I don't like unsolved cases, you know that Chuck," answered Mercer.

While Mercer was talking, he got a full view of the man he was speaking to. His name was Chuck Roberts, and he was another officer at E.C.P.D.; a pretty good cop too. A lot of people, including Mercer, thought Chuck had what it took to make detective. Although Chuck never displayed the desire to make it to detective, he still had what it took to be one.

"Shouldn't you be out somewhere checking the meter?" asked Mercer in a sarcastic tone.

"Now, why would I do that when I could be in here messing with you?" Chuck replied, with a smart aleck question of his own. "That case is like the white whale of Edge City right now. No one has seen the kid or anyone else involved for that matter." Chuck nodded to Jonathan's picture as Mercer held it in his hand."I mean really, how the hell does some snot nose punk from the middle of nowhere steal from a man like Mayor Edwards?" he asked, his voice carrying through the air with a sense of confusion hiding in his undertones.

Ironically, there happened to be some news coverage of a live speech that Mayor Edwards was giving. Mercer could see the TV mounted on the wall on the other side of the room. Even though he was unable to hear what Mayor Edwards was saying, he could still get a good look at the man. There he was, draped in a bespoke suit standing in an array of power, while addressing the people of the city. Mercer studied Mayor Edwards intently for a moment, the same way he had studied Jonathan's picture only moments before.

"I don't know Chuck. But that's what I plan to find out," he answered. "That's what I plan to find out."

CHAPTER 14

THE DRAGON OF CITY HALL

Sometimes the best laid plans don't always work, but when they do, they require synergy, commitment, and focus. Those involved have to make sure that they're moving on one accord; simultaneously synchronizing their individual movements with one another. In short, everyone has to play their part, and if they want it to go off without a hitch, they have to play their parts well. This was the consensus and the current topic of conversation between Jonathan and his newfound crime family.

"He's giving a speech today," said Rico, hunched over on the edge of what looked like a custom-made sofa in the living room. "It'll probably be a few hundred people in attendance, maybe even close to a thousand." It was just past 11:00 am and Jonathan was still thinking in circles about what they were planning to do. After almost a year, he was going to lay eyes on the man who stole his life. Jonathan's calm outward demeanor didn't give the slightest hint of anxiety or fear. These emotions were kept aggressively at bay within the hidden depths of his mind. They didn't have permission to surface at this time. They would only bring him down and he couldn't allow that to happen. Jonathan was bound and determined to show Kane Edwards and this city that he was a new man. A man that wouldn't go down without a fight, a man that would stand up for his own justice.

"Ok, so to be clear, this is just a reconnaissance sort of thing, right?" asked Jonathan.

"Oh yeah, Johnny boy, that's all that's on the menu for today," answered Rico."You don't run at the lion head on. He'd see you coming from a mile away. No no no, we'll use some of the Coloso magic to shut him down." boasted Rico, his vocal cords displaying his own pride.

"Well I hope so, because believe me when I tell you that this man is no one to play with," said Jonathan with strong agitation in his tone. His voice acting as a testament to the history he shared with this man, who was now going to be their intended target.

"This lion could see you coming from ten miles away. Hell, he may even know that we're already here." continued Jonathan

Rico and Marco both looked at Jonathan for a moment, their eyes appeared to examine his demeanor without commenting. Perhaps they were truly listening, or maybe they weren't. Jonathan wasn't too sure just yet, but he was also slightly surprised with himself for that comment. Though it was true that he wondered if Kane already knew of his presence, it was highly unlikely.

"Relax Johnny boy, your old master doesn't know we're here," Rico firmly retorted with his own agitation now entering the conversation.

Jonathan was on the opposite couch when he leaned forward and clenched his fist for a moment. "My *master?* What the hell did you say?!" snapped Jonathan.

Before Jonathan could move an inch and do something that he would possibly regret, he felt the touch of a rather soft hand on his left shoulder. He knew who it was before he turned around. Rachel had that sort of affect on him. Unbeknownst to the rest of the group, Rachel had the ability to calm the raging seas on Jonathan's emotions without the use of a single word, although now they all were currently bearing witness to her silent powers.

"He doesn't know we're here Jonathan, and save that anger for when it counts," she said.

Jonathan rubbed his hands together and sat there in silence for a moment. He then looked back at her, long enough to see the look in her eyes.

It was a look that told him they were going to get through this, just as they had before.

"Look, all I'm saying is that we have to be ready and prepared when we face him," he said, this time his voice returning to an acceptable decibel level."I'm not afraid of him anymore, but I still know that he's extremely dangerous and we have to approach him accordingly."

Rico looked as if he gave a slight thought to what Jonathan was saying. His face frowned before he spoke. "And all I'm saying is that we're dangerous too," he replied.

Rachel suddenly interjected, "Yeah, but he's also smart, Rico. Don't underestimate him like that."

"Ok, ok, goodness. The two of you need to relax," explained Rico.

All the while, Marco said nothing during the whole exchange. He merely sat there and watched. This wasn't really the sort of thing that required his kind of expertise, but no one really noticed, there was a silent understanding that he was the muscle, the strong-arm that was capable of flexing when they needed it to.

Rico continued to explain his whole take on the situation. "Look, we'll handle this with care. This isn't my first day on the job," he said, his bravado and arrogance coming back to join the verbal party. "I'm not new to this line of work; I come from this."

"I get that, but you're new to him, and in his world that can be the difference between life or death," replied Jonathan. "I just want to make sure that we don't get caught when we show up to his speech. He has eyes everywhere. I'm sure it's even three times as much now since he's the mayor. He'll be ready for the unexpected, so we have to be ready as well," he explained, with Rachel still standing behind the couch.

"Ok, you win, I promise we'll be real careful," said Rico reassuringly. "He won't know we're there and believe me when I tell you he won't see any one of us coming."

Rachel had now walked over to the frontside of the couch and took a seat next to Jonathan. They were a team in this; they had to be or else something like this wouldn't work. However, Jonathan wasn't concerned about whether he and Rachel were on the same page. He knew they were good. His focus was making sure he and Rico saw eye to eye. He knew what the supposed plan was; they were going to basically conduct a semi-stake out of Kane and see what they could find out. He was scheduled to give a speech later this afternoon in City Hall. Rico thought this was the perfect time to get close enough for a look. Jonathan wasn't initially thrilled about the idea, but the more he thought about it, the more he decided to give in. The last thing that he wanted or needed was to have drama inside their newly formed *group*.

"Ok Rico, we'll do it your way on this one." said Jonathan, with a small mound of hesitance hiding behind his voice.

He was going to go through with it, but there was a hidden nervousness that swirled around in his stomach. The thought of making a move like this was risky in Jonathan's eyes, but he already said he would do it, so he planned to see this thing through. His only hope, although silent in nature, still existed, and that hope was that he wanted everything to go smoothly. After all, he was a wanted man and he didn't want to get arrested on his first real day back in the city.

Once the conversation ended, they all went their separate ways to their spot of the penthouse. Rachel would sit this particular mission out; Jonathan didn't really want her there, and Rachel didn't want to go either. However, she didn't have to say she didn't want to go; he noticed it earlier by the look in her eyes and the masked tone of her voice. Either way, if something were to go horribly awry, at least the two of them wouldn't go down. Before Jonathan knew it, he was dressed and ready to go. In fact, he was already moving. It was like the brief time of preparation for what lie ahead of him had come and gone. The next thing he knew was that he was walking to Rico's SUV. There was a calmness that Jonathan recognized as he approached the blacked out car. It was that familiar calm before the storm, Jonathan had become eerily familiar with this level of calm. He didn't view it as a good thing, merely a pause before a possible violent action. One thing was for certain, a storm was coming. It just unclear as to whether the storm would hit today or tomorrow. Either way, Jonathan had mentally prepared himself for these present moments he was now experiencing.

He got in the car, and closed the door behind him. It was the first time he had actually been inside this car, and it was the same one Rico pulled up in, that night in the parking lot. Jonathan sat behind Rico, who was in the passenger seat. The sound of Marco closing the door with a certain level of force sent a rush of air brushing against Jonathan. Within that gust of unexpected wind, he caught the scent of Marco's cologne. For a man who was extremely deadly, he apparently had good taste in cologne. The scent was pleasing to Jonathan's nose, in some way it seemed to put him at ease. Perhaps it allowed his mind to think of something else for a moment, other than the thing they were about to do.

"Alright fellas, let's get this show on the road." said Rico, his voice sounding oddly enthusiastic for such a risky assignment. Perhaps Rico's comfort around danger was more of a strength than Jonathan realized. A strength that could play to their advantage, because they would need all the help they could get.

Marco pulled off, silent as always. He had the look of a man that was ready for war at a moment's notice. Again, this was something they would need in the surely coming war that awaited them all.

It was midday, so the sun was out, displaying its power as the skyscrapers reflected its immense rays. Jonathan leaned his head slightly against the glass looking at the city that had left him wounded once before. He still marveled at the city's beauty, a sight that he hadn't seen in almost a year. He was back, although his return was in secret he knew that he would soon be vindicated in public. Although to do so, he would not only have to play his cards right. He would almost have to play them perfectly if he and Rachel were going to make it out of this alive and restored.

He could see that the city was vibrant as usual, not missing a beat. There was a certain rhythm that took place in Edge City and Jonathan would be lying if he said he didn't miss it. However, the trip down memory lane would have to be cut short today, because there were more pressing matters at hand. Jonathan never went to City Hall when he lived in the city, so he watched to see if he recognized any of the surrounding area. It was an unfamiliar scene really; there was nothing that stood out to him enough to tug on his memory bank. Edge City was colossal in size, so it was only natural that Jonathan hadn't seen all of it yet. Besides, the last time he was in town, he didn't really have time to take in all of the local scenery.

The rest of the car ride could be summed up in one of Jonathan's single thoughts. To be honest, this thought wasn't just a random thought, but one that kept itself in a state of repetition. *"Are you ready?"* was the question the silent thought asked its host. Jonathan had not only waited for the moment that was now arriving swiftly, he trained for it as well. Still, with all of that under his belt, he couldn't help but feel a small layer of anxiety underneath the fight and desire that he held onto. He acknowledged the thought and subconsciously answered his own question and the answer was *yes*. Yes, he was ready, not only because he felt it, but because he had to be. There was no other option that could get the job done, and he had to be ready for this. For the sake of his life as well as Rachel's, Jonathan had to be ready to face the dragon. He was ready, the fight awaited him and he awaited the fight.

It was a good thing too, because Jonathan looked up and noticed a sudden change in the scenery. They had arrived at City Hall. There were cars everywhere, and people filled the steps of the city hall building. The building itself was a work of old industrial beauty. In fact, it reminded Jonathan of the art museum that he went to last year, the same museum where he met Mr. Edwards for the first time. A night that he wished he had the power to erase altogether, a night that subsequently lead to other nights that were sometimes filled with pain. A night that lead to countless sleepless nights.

So perhaps it was poetic irony that he was now entering a building during the *day,* that reminded of him of a building he went to at night, that changed his life. Maybe this could be a reversal of the things that went wrong; prayerfully he could make those things right.

"It's game time, kids," said Rico.

Jonathan could hear the excitement in his voice. It was an interesting observation, he didn't want Rico to be too excited. He didn't need him to do anything stupid. Not now.

"Ok, but it's like you said, we're just having a look, seeing if we can gather any information, right?" asked Jonathan, a question that he wanted to hear Rico answer for his own reassurance.

"Yeah, no worries Johnny boy, we're just having a close look," replied Rico. "You can learn a lot from your enemy by watching him. That's something that my father taught me. We'll see his security detail, how many he carries with him versus the ones we're not supposed to see. We'll watch him, how he moves, how he reacts to people and how people react to him. We're here to hunt him, Johnny." Rico's tone took a more serious approach in the air as he turned around to face Jonathan.

"Stop looking at him as the predator, because he's the prey now. He just doesn't know it yet." The words that left Rico's mouth spoke volumes to Jonathan.

He did his best to hide the emotion from appearing on his face. He didn't want Rico to know he was impressed with what he just said. He never heard a man refer to Kane Edwards as prey. Either Rico was a complete madman, or it was something else that was so extraordinary that Jonathan doubted it could be possible. That something being that maybe, just maybe, Rico was just as serious with defeating Kane as Jonathan was. This rogue thought and absurd idea, didn't seem to be so crazy after hearing the bold words Rico had just spoken. This gave Jonathan a certain level of reassurance about the whole thing, however he still didn't verbally respond to Rico, only offering a simple head nod. He left room for Rico to prove himself and his weighty words.

Marco stayed silent through it all as he drove to an available parking spot next to one of the meters across the street. He parked the car, then they all got out in unison, stepping boldly to their assignment on one accord. It was an unexpected feeling, but Jonathan felt a certain level of added security. Although he had been fully aware that Rico and Marco were aiding him in taking Kane down, it was only in this moment, when they were about to enter the lair of the dragon that he truly felt their support. Jonathan realized that this time around, he wouldn't be fighting alone, and that was a beautiful thing.

While Jonathan walked across the street with his newfound team assembled, he heard the faint sound of warfare in the air. He could almost hear the battle cries of those who had charged the dragon before, only to come up short. Though there was no need for fear, because that emotion didn't belong here. After all, today was only for observation and reconnaissance. There would be no bloodshed, at least not today, although there was the very real possibility that the day would come that blood would be spilled; maybe sooner than they all thought. However, on that day, Jonathan vowed to himself, that if it came to it, the only blood that would hit the ground would be that of the dragon.

The trio began to make their way through the amassing crowd as they moved toward the front entrance. Jonathan looked around for a moment before he lowered his head; he was still a wanted man. He could all but laugh at the absurd boldness that he was currently displaying. Here he was, in broad daylight, going to spy on a man who framed him, while still keeping his head on a swivel so that he wouldn't be arrested. Jonathan looked toward Rico's direction; he would only catch a glimpse of him as Rico made his own way through the crowd. There was no need to look for Marco at this point, so the three of them went their separate ways. They were now making their way deeper into the dragon's lair and from the looks of it, the dragon had been busy.

The look of some of the people in the crowd had a familiar glimmer in their eyes that Jonathan recognized. It was the same glimmer that he once carried, especially when he first met Kane. A spark that spoke of wonder, amazement, and admiration for someone who he thought could change his life for the better. It was that same look that now appeared on some of the innocent faces in the crowd. Thinking that their newly appointed Mayor Edwards would change their city for the better. They had been seduced by the lies that he undoubtedly fed them with a silver spoon.

Jonathan made his way inside the building where Kane was giving his speech. Security was in sight but there were no checkpoints people had to pass through. This meant Jonathan didn't have to worry about anyone checking his ID. He looked around for a moment, still being cautious to keep his head down, hoping that no one would notice him. Jonathan was counting on the hustle and bustle of the day to aid him in staying invisible. To his pleasant surprise, it actually worked. No one was paying any attention to him; they were all too occupied with themselves to notice him. That was until Jonathan felt a hand touch him on the shoulder.

He stood still for a second, his mind going to places it shouldn't. He hoped he wouldn't have to resort to drastic measures if he had been identified. Then the next sound that he heard was a woman's voice.

"Excuse me sir," she said.

Jonathan turned around to see whose hand the voice belonged to. When he turned around, there was a small petite lady with brown hair wrapped in a ponytail. She had to be no taller than five feet with a stack of papers that appeared to be her equal in body weight.

"Yes?" he answered as he looked directly into the woman's eyes. He stood there staring at her while searching her eyes to see if there was even the slightest hint of her recognizing him. He appeared to be in luck today because she had no idea who he was. He couldn't help but notice the name tag she was wearing. Her name was written in black sharpie: Monica.

"Would you like a flyer?" she asked, her voice sounding pleasant, as if she were actually excited to be there.

Jonathan paused for a moment before responding; he was thankful that it was an innocent encounter. "Yeah sure," he answered. He figured it was the *normal* thing to do. Besides, he could learn some information from the flyer, so he took it and walked off. He was still being cautious by keeping his head low as he walked away. He used the flyer to act as his cover for keeping his head down.

As he glanced over the flyer, he saw that it gave directions to the auditorium, where the *mayor* was currently giving his speech. While those words ran across Jonathan's eyes, he processed the sentence to understand what it really meant. In his mind, the translation meant that he was about to lay eyes upon the man who had attempted to destroy his life. A flashback of him standing face to face with Kane in his office entered his mind. Certain memories liked to reappear in his mind from time to time. He yet again thought about the first time he met Kane, that night in the museum. Jonathan wondered where he would be now if it wasn't for that moment. What would have happened if Jonathan didn't approach him that night outside of the museum? Yes, the deadly "what if?" game came into play. Although as fast as it came in, Jonathan made sure that it went out just as quick. It wasn't time for what if's? It *was* what it was; although he was aiming to change what it was now into something different. Something that allowed him and Rachel to be free, something that would restore his name, something that would allow justice and vengeance to be served.

Jonathan made his way to the auditorium. He could hear the faint rumblings of a crowd as he moved closer to his destination. There was also the sound a muffled voice that was speaking over the crowd, no doubt from the help of a microphone. This voice belonged to the person who was speaking to the crowd, and Jonathan knew exactly who that was. Ironically as he approached the auditorium, he found himself alone walking down a hallway. There was a sign straight ahead at the end of the hall that sat right above a set of wooden double doors. The sign read "Auditorium." Alas he stumbled upon the final door into the deep lair of the dragon. With every step, Jonathan clenched his fist tighter as the muffled voice became clearer. Yet again, he heard the invisible battle cry of the fallen, those who once tried to stand against the dragon, only to find themselves engulfed in the scorching flames of the dragon's life-taking breath. However, Jonathan would not be like the rest, for he had already tangled with the ancient beast before and lived to tell his own tale. Today, he found himself back in the lair of the beast, ready to wage war, only this time he was not alone in his efforts. Although he didn't see his other warriors, he knew they were somewhere behind those set of double doors. It seemed that Jonathan would be the last to arrive to this lethal party, but that was ok because he knew he was ready.

He stood in front of the double doors, he clutched the right door handle in his right hand, and pulled it open. Once he opened the door, he saw flashes of light in the already well-lit auditorium. The flashes were from some of the cameramen, who were probably working for some of the local news stations. The seats were filled as people were sitting down overlooking the lower level of the room, where the stage and podium were, and where *he* was. Jonathan had unknowingly entered the upper level of the auditorium, which was actually a good thing. It gave him a better view of the entire room, and ultimately a better vantage point of the beast itself. Jonathan walked in the aisle between the seats so he could peer over the ledge and look down upon the monster he had came to see.

There he was, or more appropriately, there *it* was: the beast that was encased in human flesh. The thing that disguised itself as a man, a man who was ruthless in power and fatal in execution. A man that had elevated his own warfare by now planning to take over the entire city. A man who once held Jonathan's life and his hopes in the palm of his hand. The same man who closed that hand and crushed Jonathan's life and left it in ruins. The man who had become Jonathan's focus for the last 8 months, the man who Jonathan came to see. The man who called himself *Kane Edwards.*

There he was, standing in all of his lethal and corrupt splendor. He was a monument to his own power, as he stood there unashamed and seemingly proud of his position. He had elevated his own status by becoming the mayor, a feat that Jonathan unknowingly had a hand in almost a year ago. He briefly thought back to how he helped frame the Mayor Caesar by breaking into his house and placing a envelope on his bed. That envelope contained evidence that would have ruined the his reputation and credibility within the city.

While Jonathan looked upon the man he planned to exact his revenge upon, he felt his heartbeat. Surprisingly it was steady; it moved at a warrior's pace. Jonathan knew battles lied ahead, so he had prepared himself mentally and physically for them. This current display of calmness had been eight months in the making; Jonathan was ready. He looked upon Kane with a fixed level of focus, the kind that refused to be broken or distracted for even a moment. Kane was sharply dressed as usual. A navy blue suit that was surely bespoke, from the way it hugged his frame perfectly. Jonathan could see Kane was neatly groomed and put together, looking flawless for his audience. So flawless as if he were untouched to be exact. He was completely unscathed by the damage he had done to Jonathan and Rachel for framing them for crimes they didn't commit. Although Jonathan was far off, he could see the void in Kane's eyes from where he was standing. He could tell that there was no sign of remorse or concern for any previously committed sins, though this wasn't a shock to Jonathan. At the end of the day he expected to see this, to see Kane going on about his life with no concerns of the past. There Jonathan stood staring, while holding back memories that he wasn't fond of. He looked onward as he yet again found himself looking at the man as he stood high above a crowd telling them what he wanted them to hear.

"People of this great city, you have bestowed upon me your ultimate level of trust," said

Kane, his voice sounding as strong and as regal as ever, a true man of power. "I promise you, I will take this city to new levels, ones that you never thought possible if you continue to trust me."

While Kane's words of promise filled the air, Jonathan looked around the room, catching glimpses of the faces that were in the crowd. He saw hope in their eyes, he saw the trusting expressions as they listened to their mayor, the one whom they had elected to oversee Silver Edge City. He saw belief, but he also saw something else. He saw indifference scattered among them, as well as doubt in some of the people. Jonathan recognized what those things looked like from his own experience. He had become versed in certain emotions. Though he never thought he would feel this way, he was actually happy to see some skepticism among the people. This let Jonathan know he wasn't alone and everyone wasn't on the Kane Train. A certain amount of encouragement stemmed from this observation and it was a good feeling, especially since Jonathan was way behind enemy lines at this point.

After noticing this, Jonathan noticed someone else, someone he didn't think to look for. Someone who he could never forget, but ironically this person had briefly escaped his memory. There the man stood to the far left of the podium, touching the outer lines of the shadows, the death deliverer himself: Adrian. The Edward's family secret; Kane's younger, silent, and to most people nonexistent, brother. No one knew that the two were related, at least not to Jonathan's knowledge. No, this was a secret originally kept between blood, but had now spilled into the ears of another.

Jonathan took his eyes off of Adrian for a moment, looking for the rest of his new crew. He didn't see Marco or Rico anywhere, and to their credit that was probably for the best. That meant they were doing a good job of blending in and staying unseen, just as Rico said they would. Jonathan looked back at Adrian while catching bits and pieces of the speech that Kane was currently delivering. This could have proved too overwhelming for other people, with the current rush of memories that were all but overtaking Jonathan's hidden thoughts. Fading glimpses of Jonathan and Adrian driving around at night flashed before his eyes. The secret meetings, the nightly errands, all of those distasteful things that made up his past experience in this city came oozing to the surface at the sight of these men. He remembered things that he desperately wanted to forget but couldn't, although in light of all this, Jonathan proved himself to be strong by being unwavering in his current mission. He knew he was there for a purpose and not just any purpose, but a purpose that would not be denied. The place was full, but Jonathan honed in on his specific task; after all, he was there to gather information. He scanned the stage that Kane was on, looking past the podium and studying the edges. He counted four men standing in the shadows behind good ol' Mr. Mayor, including Adrian. Jonathan then directed his attention to the seats in the front row on the lower level. He scanned them carefully looking for more men in suits that were guarding the mayor; he counted another two. It was the way they dressed as well as the obvious ear pieces that gave them away.

Although Jonathan made sure to take into account that these were just the men that he could see, he knew that it wasn't uncommon practice for political officials to have hidden security. These were the ones that you weren't supposed to see, the ones in plain clothes blending in with the crowd. To an average person who had no dealings with a man like Kane Edwards, they may think this level or security was a bit much, even for a mayor. However, Jonathan knew better; he was thoroughly initiated in this man's methods. Suddenly, his concentration was derailed by the uproar of the crowd's powerful applause. He looked immediately at Kane, locking in on his facial expressions, wondering what words had just left his mouth to warrant such a response. There was a cheshire-like grin buried deep within Kane's face, but Jonathan was able to see past the facade. He knew there was ill-will and violent intentions behind that smile. If only these people knew who they were dealing with. While the people were still standing Jonathan glanced at Adrian for a moment, he noticed something. Adrian was staring directly at Kane. In fact, he seemed to be burning a hole in his back. There was a certain emotion that swirled in Adrian's eyes, and then danced on his face. Even though he was at a distance, Jonathan could see it moving. It looked familiar to him and this emotion had a name, it was called *disgust.*

Adrian seemed to be angry as he stood there, cloaked in silence and dipped in shame while he gazed at his brother who seemed to get all the glory and lived in the limelight of success. Although there was contempt and jealousy now playing on the field, Jonathan thought it would be more appropriate to dub this beautiful thing he was witnessing as a *window.* Yes indeed, his window of opportunity may have just presented itself in an unsuspecting manner, but Jonathan was still happy to take it. A cheshire-like grin soon found its new residence on Jonathan's face as the wheels of his mind began to churn. He now saw a new weapon that had formed during his absence, a weapon that he could use in his fight against Kane. A weapon that was close to home; Jonathan saw it now, clear as day. He would fight the beast from within, killing it from the inside, in a way that the beast wouldn't see coming. Jonathan would do so by turning the dragon's own flesh and blood against it. He would use Adrian to get to Kane.

CHAPTER 15

WISDOM OF THE WARRIOR

"I'm telling you, I know this can work." explained Jonathan, his voice sounding sure of his own idea.

He stood there presenting his case to the rest of the group. They were all assembled in the lavish living room of the Penthouse that was immaculately perched within the skyline of the monolithic city. For a moment, it was quiet in the room, long enough for everyone to hear the rain while it danced its droplets alongside the building, hurling down from the dark and dreary sky above. Jonathan knew what he was saying sounded a bit off, but he just needed them to understand the logic that found itself currently trapped in what appeared to be foolishness. The eyes of his current crowd didn't seem to be convinced, with Rachel in particular appearing very apprehensive.

"Jonathan, you want to do what?" Rachel asked, her tone of voice sounding agitated as well as unconvinced.

"You sure you wanna do that, chief?" chimed in Rico. He sat on the couch with a mixture of Crown Royal and Coke waving around in his glass that found itself stiffly nestled within his hand. His legs were crossed as a doubtful smirk danced on his lips. "I mean look, I know you were close to these guys, but even by my standards that sounds like a risky move."

"I know what it sounds like but trust me," Jonathan explained, his frustration slightly rising as he noticed that he wasn't really getting through to them.

The only one who didn't have anything to say was Marco, but then again he never really said much. Rachel sat in a love seat that was next to the couch where Rico was seated. She was wearing a pair of white sweats with her hair in a ponytail. Since her hair was pulled back, Jonathan was able to get a full view of the doubt that was cast over her face. He understood what he was saying sounded insane, but he knew that it wasn't. He remembered when he first discovered this secret. He knew then that there was a possibility Adrian would turn on Kane, given the right opportunity. That belief was still there, and the plan could still be put into play, he just needed a way to get to Adrian. He would ultimately have to get a private face-to-face with the man, something that wasn't exactly going to be an easy feat. Now that Adrian was keeping company with the mayor, Jonathan would have to figure something out, but first he was going to have to convince the rest of the group.

"I know it's possible. You gotta trust me on this," affirmed Jonathan.

Again there was a pause in the room, before Rico responded."Look Johnny boy, I know you guys got history, I get that whole angle. But do you really wanna go behind enemy lines and see if you can strike up a conversation?" Sarcasm laid its heavy burden on his sentence.

Jonathan noticed Rachel shook her head in response to Rico's comment. He could tell that she probably agreed with what Rico was saying. Heck, even Jonathan had to admit that when Rico put it that way, it didn't sound like the wisest idea.

"Look, in case you haven't noticed, this is war. There's no negotiating when it comes to war," said Rico.

"Actually sometimes there is," replied Jonathan

It was then, when Rachel decided to throw her hat in the ring. "Yeah but Jonathan, are you sure this is one of those times?" she asked. "Look, let's not forget who these people are. They're not really the bargaining type. How do you know that he won't shoot you on sight?!" Rachel's voice sounded sharp and agitated.

Jonathan rubbed his hand alongside his head, and he could feel the hair under his palm. He stood there frustrated in the moment. They weren't understanding where he was coming from. That much was being made real clear to him, but as he continued to speak, he was getting nowhere rapidly. He decided to let wisdom have its way and end the conversation; he was skating up hill at this point and there was no need for him to fall to realize that.

"Ok, just relax. You're right, I'll leave it alone," said Jonathan

He watched as Rachel ran her hand along her forehead, and yet again he saw a look on her that he didn't like. It was that face that said she was *tired,* but the fatigue she was displaying didn't seem merely physical. He knew it was more emotional than anything else.

"We're getting close Rachel," said Jonathan, hoping to reassure her that the end was indeed in sight, they just had to stay the course.

Rachel looked at him for a moment, before saying anything. "Yeah," she replied, her voice now sounding more defeated than anything.

Jonathan knew what she really meant when she said that. It was more so a "yeah I've heard this before" type of response.

Rico took another sip of his drink before he said anything else. "We're here to help Johnny boy, so let us do what we do," he said. "Marco and I know how to handle a man like this. We've seen his type up close and personal, and your girl is right. These aren't the type of people that you talk to, these are the type you shoot first, then have a conversation with them." said Rico with a sadistic look that found itself growing on his face. Jonathan also shot Rico a look, one that spoke for itself; it was a look that reminded him that he didn't want any killing to take place.

"Oh relax, Cross, we won't put a bullet in him, even though that would end all of this pretty quickly," mentioned Rico, with a devilish grin gliding across his face yet again.

"But what we'll do is catch him off guard and get him to come clean."

"What, Rico?" asked Jonathan, with a his own level of annoyance starting to show on his face. "Wait, I just said that I wanted to talk to Adrian and you said no. But now you're telling me that you want to talk to Kane?"

Rico put his glass down on the coffee table in front of him before he leaned up to the edge of the couch."Trust me, our conversation versus your conversation will be completely different," answered Rico. He turned and pointed at Marco who was peering out of the floor to ceiling glass windows of the penthouse, standing like a watchful guardian.

"People tend to confess their sins when Marco is present. We'll handle Kane," reassured Rico.

It was then that Rachel decided to chime in with an idea of her own.

"Jonathan, maybe you should let them handle it this time. A different approach may be what we need," she explained.

Jonathan took a deep breath and held silent for a moment as he studied the face of the woman he loved. He wasn't going to argue any further, and he would let this go, at least in their eyes.

"Ok," he replied, staring at Rachel with a look that suggested he had conceded to the sway of the room.

However, in the inner churning of his heart and mind, he was nowhere near giving up on his plan. He knew that he would talk to Adrian with or without their help. He was going to go through with it. The inner warrior told him to stay the course and hold true to his own convictions. Now wasn't the time to give up on something just because it wasn't the most popular idea among the masses. He knew that it was a good idea; he also knew he could get through to Adrian and vowed to do just that.

CHAPTER 16

THE FACES OF DANGEROUS MEN

As of late, Jonathan found his proverbial plate pretty full; this was something he anticipated, but it was still taxing nonetheless. Due to this, the ever so calm and collected Rico suggested the guys have a night on the town. Jonathan wasn't completely convinced that Rico was solely looking out for him. He knew Rico had his own agenda to add to the evening. The dead giveaway was that Rico initially tried to entice Jonathan with a raunchy evening that included countless bottles of alcohol, a gentlemen's club, all followed by a bite to eat. Jonathan managed to convince Rico that the first two items on the to-do list wouldn't be in the best interest of keeping a low profile. Instead, he suggested they skip straight to the part where they got something to eat. There was an obviously lower statistical possibility that they would get in any sort of trouble while eating a late-night dinner.

Jonathan wasn't really familiar with that part of town, so he didn't really have any suggestions for restaurants. This didn't stop Rico from coming up with an entirely new idea. He told Jonathan that he knew the owner of one of the restaurants that was around the corner from the penthouse. Even though it was after hours for most restaurants, Rico assured Jonathan that they would be able to get in.

For once Jonathan didn't argue with Rico, because it seemed innocent enough to work. After all, he didn't mind VIP treatment; he hadn't experienced that since the last time he was in the city, that is before things got rough of course. He also wasn't too worried about Rachel, who opted to stay home for the evening. He knew she was safe within the confines of the hidden sanctuary of the penthouse. Besides, no one even knew that Rachel Monroe and Jonathan Cross were back in town. Their presence had not been revealed and would remain in the shadows until the appropriate time. Though one would question if Jonathan wanted to stay invisible, why walk the streets at night? He relied heavily on the fact that people were too occupied with their own lives to remember a story about a young man who was accused of some harsh crimes. However, he wasn't completely reckless; he didn't plan on being a total fool and walking around in broad daylight everyday, thinking he was untouchable.

It had been a long time since Jonathan had seen the night's sky of the city. While the three of them walked on the sidewalk, Jonathan took the time to allow his senses to soak in what was happening around him. He felt the cool breeze of the night's wind brush alongside his face and glide on his lips. He could almost taste the atmosphere itself: it was a mixture of wildness, opportunity, optimism, and danger. Some would call it an acquired taste but there was a time when that taste was comforting to Jonathan. A time when his innocent eyes hadn't yet seen the horrors that existed in this city. Now it was nothing more of a reminder to keep his eyes open and to stay alert.

There were always sights to behold in Edge City, if one would just take the time to look. The stars lit up the sky, showing their light with pride as they scattered themselves for all to see. Everything from the buildings, to the darkness of the concrete, where Jonathan's feet trampled, everything there had beauty to it. It was there for all to see, but few appreciated it the way Jonathan did. Perhaps it was the country boy in him that was still in awe of a place like Edge City. He didn't want to show it, but deep down Jonathan still found himself impressed by the magic of this place. The wind hovered above his head as he made his way down the sidewalk, howling like some wild animal as it moved swiftly in the air. Jonathan didn't think about asking Rico where they were going because it was close, so he calmly followed his lead. Jonathan occasionally glanced at some of the cars that were driving down the street. It was always nice observing the movement of city life.

Another thing Jonathan bore witness to was the interaction between Rico and Marco; there wasn't much of any to be honest. However, Jonathan refused to believe what he saw on the surface; he knew that there had to be more to them than what he saw. On the outside it appeared to be a simple boss and employee relationship, but Jonathan could tell Marco was loyal.

Marco's loyalty was a certain type that couldn't be bought; this was something that was earned through blood, sweat, and probably more blood. Jonathan recognized that sort of loyalty well, since he had seen it before when he encountered Kane. He remembered Kane's favorite henchman, Percy, who was Jonathan's only point of reference for a man like Marco. This made Jonathan think a little deeper as he realized that the source of the loyalty probably had less to do with Rico and more to do with his father. That was something that made more sense. He wondered what Marco had done over the years, although Jonathan honestly had a pretty good idea. He knew those deeds were far from pretty. He knew Marco was a killer; that much was true. Besides, Jonathan realized it was best not to know too much about Marco. He had learned not to let his curiosity get the better of him, especially not at a time like this. Jonathan could tell they had arrived where they were going as the three of them crossed the street. There was a restaurant on the corner with large windows in the front, that had the drapes closed. Jonathan thought it was interesting that the place used drapes instead of blinds, but he wasn't one to judge. There was a neon sign above the window that said *Casper's*. Although the neon sign was turned off, it still caught Jonathan's attention.

"Ok fellas. Get ready for some serious chow," said Rico. "It's been awhile since I've been here, they better still serve that caramel pie I love."

At this point, Jonathan was standing behind Rico. He couldn't see his face, but he could hear his voice. He could tell that Rico was being sincere. He appeared to let his guard down and looked forward to a normal evening. This alone was enough to ease Jonathan of any previous concerns he may have had.

When they arrived at the front door, Jonathan noticed the lights were off; he could barely see inside. Even though it was dark, he did manage to see a figure moving closer toward the door. The more the figure moved, the more was revealed about the mystery person moving in the darkness. When the person finally arrived at the door, Jonathan got a better look. It was a short old man; he was bald, wore thick glasses and had on a white apron that wasn't so white. The man unlocked the door and smiled wide at the sight of Rico.

"Ah ha, my boy!" said the man, his eyes fixed solely on Rico.

Jonathan could see the pure joy that seeped through the man's eyes; it was clear Rico meant something to this man.

"Mr. Palairo, it's been a long time," said Rico.

The man smiled and stretched out his arms as he said, "Indeed it has my boy, indeed it has. I'm always honored to have you."

"I appreciate you allowing my friends and I to eat here so late. Thank you," said Rico.

Mr. Palairo shook his hand at Rico as he shook his head in unison, "No, no," he said. "I owe your father everything, everything I tell you," said Mr. Palairo. "Me keeping the restaurant open is a small thing; it's the least I could do."

Rico entered the restaurant first, Jonathan then noticed that Marco stood to the side, allowing him to walk in front of him. At first this was slightly surprising to Jonathan because he knew Marco was looking after Rico, but he didn't think Marco would extend that type of gesture to him. It didn't take Jonathan long to take him up on it as he followed suit, walking behind Rico. The lights came on in the restaurant as he entered. Immediately the place was illuminated with lights from the ceiling shining brightly on everything beneath them. He could now properly see his surroundings and he had to admit, he liked what he saw. The restaurant had a very old world feel to it. The walls were made of brick that you could tell had stood the test of time. The hardwood floor was that of dark oak that sprawled its beauty out for all who entered *Casper's* doors to see. There was a mixture of wooden tables and booths that filled the restaurant. They had a nice bar nestled toward the left side. This was a nice place, fit for Edge City. If Jonathan had to guess, especially given the brief conversation between Rico and Mr. Palairo, this operation was probably bank rolled by the Don himself, aka Nero.

Jonathan thought about how powerful Rico's father probably was. He hadn't had the opportunity to meet the man; however, Jonathan wasn't really in a rush to meet another man as dangerous as Kane Edwards. For now, he would gladly deal with the son of the urban monarch. These were dangerous times that Jonathan found himself currently encased in, so he knew that having a connection to a man like Nero could prove to be beyond useful. Although the connection being Rico was enough for now, Jonathan wasn't sure if he needed the head of the mob to get involved in his business. These thoughts found themselves fading as he caught a whiff of that caramel pie Rico must have been talking about. This evening may have been unexpected and impromptu, but it was still appreciated. The simple act of going out to dinner felt like something Jonathan didn't think he would encounter here in the city. It felt like another dose of normalcy; perhaps this is what another young man might experience when out on the town with his friends. Although, Jonathan definitely wasn't confusing Rico or Marco as his friends; he knew better. No, what they had was nowhere near friendship, but strictly a business relationship. At the moment, they all had a common enemy; this was the reason for their alliance and Jonathan didn't lose sight of that.

There was no need to get things mixed up. He understood what the situation was and he planned to govern himself accordingly. While Jonathan continued to look around, he realized he was actually pretty hungry and was ready for a bite to eat. Jonathan watched as Rico took a few more steps to the center of the restaurant. He had a slow yet steady stride. It was as if he wanted everyone else to notice him, even though by Jonathan's count there were only four people in the restaurant. This wasn't counting the possible chef that could've been in the kitchen in the back. Perhaps Rico was more in his element than Jonathan realized; even though he knew Rico had been to the city before, he still didn't know how much time he spent there. It was quiet inside, as well as it should have been since it was after hours. Again the VIP feeling slid its way into Jonathan's mind, something he hadn't experienced in a while. Although it was a small thing, that feeling was still there, resting below the surface.

"Let's grab a table, shall we?" said Rico, as he walked toward the tables that were in the middle of the room.

Jonathan let his guard down once he realized this was actually going to be a quiet evening with minimal drama. The three of them sat down at the table, and it wasn't long before Mr. Palairo came over.

"What can I get you gentlemen to drink?"

Rico answered first, as it was obvious to Jonathan he was in his element. The more time he spent around Rico, the more he seemed to learn about him. He could tell that Rico's element was any place where people knew his name and his reputation. This place fit the requirements for his egotistical needs.

"You know me. I'll have a Coke with some Crown Royal of course," said Rico, his mouth seemed to water as he gave his order.

Jonathan went next, "I'll have a lemonade if you have some," he said. He looked at Marco once he finished, wondering if he was going to participate in the dinner as well.

"I'll take a glass of water, no ice," said Marco, his voice was rough but steady at the same time. Just by listening to him talk, you could tell this wasn't a man to mess with. Jonathan noticed that even though they were having a night on the town, Marco didn't order any alcohol — a true testament to his discipline. He knew that Marco was the "about his business at all times" type, so he probably wanted to keep a clear head and remain sober. Honestly it made sense, on the off chance that something were to go wrong, he wanted Marco to be alert. He wasn't mad at Marco's show of restraint; if anything he knew it was the mark of a professional.

"You see Cross, this wasn't so bad," said Rico, as an eerie smile formed on the left side of his lips.

"Well, the night is still young," said Jonathan, a dose of pessimism getting the best of his vocabulary at the moment.

"Man, he really did a job on you didn't he?" asked Rico.

Jonathan knew the *he* Rico was referring to; he paused for a moment before answering. "Actually, yeah he did Rico, which is why we can't screw around, because he's dangerous."

"Yeah, I know he's dangerous, which is why we were telling you earlier that your plan about Adrian was crazy," Rico replied.

Jonathan ran his thumb alongside his knuckles, keeping his irritation inside. There was no need to let his temper get the best of him, even though he was growing weary of bickering with Rico. His anger was partly due to the fact that he knew more about Kane than Rico did, and sometimes he felt Rico didn't realize that. It wasn't so much that Jonathan wanted to prove he was right all the time; he just didn't want Rico to get any of them hurt by underestimating Kane.

"Well, we'll just have to agree to disagree," said Jonathan.

"Fair enough," replied Rico. The tension at the table was starting to rise, until it was disrupted by drinks.

"Ok gentlemen, here are your beverages," said Mr. Palairo; he had a wide smile on his face as he put down the drinks.

He looked like a genuinely happy person. Perhaps his generosity didn't stem from the pockets of Mr. Coloso alone. Perhaps this man was simply grateful for the things he had. Either way, it was a nice show of light in a dark city.

"Ok, are we ready to order?" asked Mr. Palairo.

It wasn't until that moment that Jonathan realized he hadn't even noticed that the menu was sitting right in front of him. He knew he wasn't really ready because he hadn't looked at the menu. He figured he would look quickly as Rico and Marco gave their orders. By the looks of the menu, the restaurant served a little bit of everything, from burgers, to seafood, to steak dinners. For the sake of time Jonathan figured he couldn't go wrong with a classic bacon cheeseburger, so he ordered that when Mr. Palairo got to him. When they had all ordered, there was a silence that tried to creep its way over the table. That was until Rico kept the silence at bay by announcing he had to go to the bathroom. Jonathan wanted to shake his head in disbelief at Rico's boisterous ways but he kept his annoyance on the inside for no one to see.

He watched Rico make his way past the table and fade into the back of the restaurant, going around the corner. He kept his stride strong and confident as he made his way to the bathroom. It appeared Mr. Palairo had left the table as well after taking the orders, and went back into the kitchen. Rico suddenly found himself walking down a very dark hallway. Normally, a person could get lost in spots that were *that* dark but it was a short hallway so it was impossible. He ran his hand along his mouth as he pushed the bathroom door open. Again, he was met with more darkness.

"Come on Mr. P, you slipping on the light bill, what's up?" he asked aloud, speaking only to himself.

Rico took a few steps in, far enough to hear the door close behind him.

The darkness had now consumed the room. It spread its shadowy power throughout the space it currently occupied. He was powerless against the unknown abyss that had suddenly presented itself in the form a restaurant bathroom. He reached in his pocket to fix his current problem by using the flashlight on his smartphone. This way he would be able to shed some light on the situation so to speak. While he reached in his pocket, there was a faint noise that presented itself. It sounded a lot like a man breathing, though Rico wasn't able to figure that out until a strong and hard punch confirmed his suspicion that there was someone else in the bathroom with him. Rico was unable to react as the hard blow left him unconscious.

Back at the table, Jonathan attempted to make some small talk with Marco, although it wasn't really working out for him. Jonathan looked at Marco, trying to discover if he could get past his icy persona and see if there was a beating heart behind those death dealing eyes. Jonathan scanned Marco's face as if he were looking for something and indeed he was, he wanted to see how much monster Marco was made up of and how much humanity he had left. Jonathan knew Marco was the real deal, and that he was a killer. The bodyguard whose body count was probably sky high at this point in his career.

"If you don't mind me asking, how long have you been with the Colos-os?" asked Jonathan; his mind wondering if he were going to get an honest response to his question.

"A long time," answered Marco, his eyes looking to the left before he turned his whole head in that direction.

This current display of ice-cold focus caused Jonathan to turn his head as well, to possibly catch a glimpse of whatever it was that had more of Marco's attention.

"Something's not right," said Marco, his voice sounding confident of his instincts.

Jonathan didn't know what he was referring to that made him say something like that. However, he had learned something from his time in seclusion; he learned to trust his instincts and his instincts were telling him to listen to Marco. Marco rose from the table with a certain level of authority that he seemed to be encased in. Jonathan could tell he meant business and something was definitely wrong. He was now on high alert himself, as he turned around to see if there was something he could possibly pick up on. He noticed Mr. Paliaro had not been back with the food yet. By the time Jonathan turned back around, Marco had gotten up from the table and headed toward the bathroom Rico went into.

Marco wasn't just a big man, he also had the lethal skill to accompany his hulk like frame; he wasn't a man to mess with. He turned the corner where he had last seen Rico and noticed the hallway was dark, though he also noticed there was a light switch close to where he was standing, a switch that Rico missed. Marco tried to turn it on but no lights came on; his face frowned in the darkness as he pressed on down the hall.

There was a glock nestled neatly in the holster that was on Marco's waist, although he hadn't yet reached for it. He arrived at the bathroom door and turned his body, putting his shoulder into the door. He then pushed the door open with his bodyweight, and as he pushed the door open he was able to reach his hand inside. His hand now engulfed in the darkness of the bathroom as he felt against the wall for the light switch. This time the light worked and suddenly the bathroom was illuminated, and that's when he saw Rico's body lying on the floor. Marco pulled his gun from his holster with lighting speed guiding his hand. He pushed the door open violently as he made his way fully into the bathroom. He quickly scanned the room with his gun, checking to see if whoever did this was foolish enough to stick around. The room was empty besides him and Rico. Marco quickly went over to Rico and put his finger on the side of Rico's throat to feel for a pulse.

He was still alive, just unconscious. Marco turned and stared at the door; it had closed behind him as he walked in. He scanned the bathroom again making sure he didn't miss anything before he left. He quickly moved to the door and pulled it open with his gun aimed steady. He wrapped his large hand around the door and opened it slowly while looking around; no one was there. However, he noticed something he didn't see the first time, there was another door, directly across from the bathroom. Again, he pointed his gun in front of him and moved with a swiftness that would surprise most for a man his size.

He slowly opened the door. From across the hall there was a bright light that made its way into the equation. The light was bursting from the crack of the door as Marco opened it. The more he opened the door the more that was revealed to him; it was a door that led to the kitchen. He could see the brightly illuminated scenery that lay before him as he walked forward, moving slowly like some lowly tiger searching for its next victim. The smell of the caramel pie that Rico was so fond of filled the air, along with the aroma of some food that was in the early preparation stage. There was a faint sound of a man crying as Marco continued to move with a militant-like posture through the kitchen. Marco paused once he found the source of the sobbing sounds that he had heard earlier. It was none other than Mr. Palairo. He was sitting upright against the industrial sized refrigerator, while holding his wife Mrs. Palairo with his hand over her mouth. The two of them both had tears running down their faces. Mr. Palairo looked like he was attempting to muffle the sounds of his crying wife, as he failed to keep his own cries at a low decibel level.

"Please forgive me. I'm so sorry!" he cried, his voice cloaked in fear.

"He said he would kill my wife and make me watch if I said anything!" cried Mr. Palairo. Marco stood there with his gun drawn, his eyes giving a cold stare to Mr. Palairo, although this time there was a contradictory action taking place within the depths of his eyes. There was suddenly a fierce fire that had been ignited in the back of his normally icy eyes. Perhaps this was a sign of Marco's rising rage that would soon be put on display for those who were unfortunate enough to be in his immediate vicinity. To the fortunate grace of Mr. Palairo, Marco hadn't pulled the trigger yet; he simply responded with a question.

"Who?" he asked.

Then without warning, Marco's question received a violent answer as he was grabbed from behind. The mystery attacker quickly moved his arm to grab the gun out of Marco's hand, but clinched his wrist instead with an iron grip. Marco immediately put his head down and lowered his chin to the top part of his chest, a maneuver that successfully prevented the attacker from properly choking Marco. The attacker tried but was unable to get a good grip around his neck. Marco continued to demonstrate that he was versed in hand-to-hand combat as he quickly dropped his gun. Once the gun fell near his foot, he swiftly kicked it away, sending it sliding across the kitchen floor. He then immediately delivered a strong head butt by lifting the back of his head, directly into the face of his attacker, followed by an almost simultaneous strong elbow to the attacker's midsection; this swift combo was enough power to loosen the grip of the attacker. Marco yet again capitalized on this moment and released himself from the attacker. He turned around to deliver yet another stinging blow, but his punch was caught mid air, putting a sudden halt to the blunt force behind one of his punches. Marco was a strong man, a monster in disguise, a killer by nature, so it would take a man of equal size and ferocity to match him. It was in that moment when Marco got a good look at the man who was bold enough and, by the looks of it, strong enough to challenge him.

The face that Marco was looking at was unfamiliar to him, but familiar to another: Jonathan. This mystery man was mighty indeed, and he too was dangerous, like Marco, with his hands undoubtedly dirty from his own bloodied past. It was none other than the muscle of Kane Edwards himself, Percy. A clash of two titans was about to begin, and in the middle of a kitchen of all places. Percy was still holding Marco's fist squarely in the middle of his own gargantuan hand. The two of them looked each other sharply in the eyes, their gazes intense as they were cold. Although the moment was short, their icy eyes still made contact, chilled from the harshness of all the horrors they both have witnessed over the years. In that moment, it was animal against animal, killer against killer. Soon they would prove who was the most dangerous predator between the two of them. Percy fired off a hard right punch to Marco's face, an unmistakable retaliation against the slew of hits he previously endured from Marco's short lived assault. Percy didn't let up as he followed his punch with the same arm by bending it and striking Marco with his elbow directly in the face. All of this took place quickly, as he still had a strong grip on Marco's fist. He was skilled in being the muscle in every situation; he had broken many men over the years and it showed as he continued his counter attack against his opponent. Percy released Marco's fist as he went in closer to his body in an attempt to do damage to his midsection. However, Marco was no easy match, as he too lunged toward Percy in that moment. Their mountainous bodies collided right there in the kitchen, making a solid thud, loud enough for someone else to hear it.

That someone was none other than Jonathan, who sat in his seat wondering what had happened to the rest of his dinner gang. Jonathan turned around quickly, staring in the kitchen's direction. At this point, he had built up enough instinct to know when something was wrong. In that moment, there were too many things that weren't adding up correctly for him. He knew that by now, Rico should've been out of the bathroom and that Mr. Palairo should have checked on them regarding their food at least twice by now. Jonathan had also been counting the minutes since Marco had left the table, thus adding another person who was gone longer than necessary. Then, to top it all off, he was now hearing sounds of a thunderous crash coming from the kitchen. All of these things pointed to the subtle truth that was floating around the atmosphere like the calm before the storm. Jonathan rose from the table quickly but also quietly; he knew it would be unwise to make too much noise. After all, if there was danger nearby like he suspected, he didn't want to attract any attention to himself.

Had this been a year ago, his heart would probably be pounding out of his chest while his mind raced at a million thoughts per second. However, time and experience tends to change people, and a transformation had definitely taken place within Jonathan Cross. He moved toward the kitchen door with a steady and stealthy stride. His eyes were fixed on the door to the kitchen as he heard more commotion coming from the other side. He could feel the warrior within him rising up, his inner power answering the call of the current situation. He was ready. This was the type of moment he had prepared for during his time in Olberton; the unexpected moment. The moment when he wasn't counting on danger to show up but it did anyway. Jonathan knew the possibility of things like this happening were high because he knew that nature of the beast, this beast called Edge City. Well, Jonathan told himself he wasn't going to come up short this time; he was going to come correct.

He made his way closer to the kitchen door, and all the while he kept hearing thuds and violent grunts muffled in the background. At this point, there was no doubt in Jonathan's mind that two people were fighting in the kitchen. The only real question that he had was "Who?" Who was fighting in the kitchen? An answer that would be revealed in the next few seconds. Jonathan was now standing directly in front of the door with his hand gliding slowly in the air. However, before he could push the door open, it swung open the other way with solid force, knocking him back. He stumbled for a moment, before quickly regaining his footing. He had taken harder hits than that in the ring, though his focus quickly shifted as he noticed the cause of the door hitting him was now standing in the middle of the doorway.

There was an eerie silence that crept its way into the room, along with a faint yet foul scent that spread its aroma through the room. It was a scent that the innocent were unaware of and would go by undetected by those who had not experienced its presence before, or fell victim to its power. Jonathan knew the scent because he had been around it before, it was the smell that would often lay in wait during violent situations unless it was called upon. A distinct odor that Jonathan knew existed only because the cloak of innocence had been lifted from his eyes as well as the rest of his human senses: the smell of death. This aroma seemed to follow a certain man because this man always seemed to live in a deathly realm. A man that Jonathan wasn't expecting to encounter this quickly upon his return to the city. A man that sent unpleasant memories rushing toward the memory banks of Jonathan's private thoughts. A man whose eyes could seemingly capture a man's soul if he so desired. A dangerous man that had ironically been on Jonathan's mind, and now said man was currently aiming a gun directly at Jonathan's forehead. A man who was used to doing the dirty work of Kane Edwards, a man named Adrian.

Jonathan stood still as he stared back at Adrian, while the sound of gladiator warfare blazed loudly from Percy and Marco as they fought in the kitchen. Adrian stood still as well, both feet firmly planted on the floor. He had the look of a man who had been sent on an assignment and was ready to see that assignment through to its completion. However, Jonathan noticed something, besides the fact that he didn't currently have a bullet lodged in his head. He noticed there was something different about Adrian while he was standing there in murderous silence. He noticed that there was something resting on Adrian's face, something that was odd to see on Adrian; that something was *hesitation*. It was unlike him to pause like this, and by now Jonathan pieced as much of this current puzzle he was dealing with together. Jonathan knew that somehow Kane found out that he was back in Edge City, a fact that Kane probably became aware of from the daring stakeout move that Rico swore up and down was a good idea. This meant that in typical Kane Edwards fashion he sent his agents of wrath to do some dirty work and eliminate a potential problem.

Honestly, Jonathan wasn't too surprised. After all, Kane was the master of these sort of things, which was something that made him extremely dangerous. He knew the risk of going after him because he knew what this man was capable of, something he was trying warn Rico about.

However, as Jonathan stood there with a gun being pointed in his direction, he felt the original rage come flooding back into his veins. The rage that caused him to train as hard as he did while he was in seclusion. The same rage that gave him the courage to return to the city. Jonathan took a breath, which ushered in a calming sensation as he stood there. It covered his body as some sort of invisible shield, surrounding him. Still there were no words spoken between the two of them, giving time for the inner warrior to arm himself as he stood tall; indeed, the warrior was here and he had something to say.

"Well, I see he still has you doing his dirty work," said Jonathan, his defiant tone coming from the depths of his stomach.

Adrian moved his fingers around the handle of the gun he was holding, appearing to get a better grip. "What would you know about it?" he asked.

The sound of his scratchy voice piercing the still air sent memories hitting Jonathan's mind. Jonathan boldly took a step forward as he continued to speak. "What would I know?" he asked sarcastically. "Oh come on Adrian, Don't play me like that. You know good and well what I know about it. Not only that, but you know *what* I know about it, too." Jonathan's bold and defiant combination existed in his every step.

Adrian seemed calm as he held his gun in place aiming it directly at his head. However, Jonathan had a strong feeling that he wasn't going to kill him.

"Look Adrian, I'm actually glad you're here because I wanted to talk to you," he said, his mind thinking of the fact that perhaps he could sway him as he had originally hoped. If he could just talk to Adrian, he felt he had a good chance of convincing him to help their cause and help take down his brother.

"Take another step and I'll put two in your face. It'll be a closed casket funeral kid," said Adrian, in a sharp and stern voice. The raspiness of his voice made the threat sound more menacing, which in turn helped it sound more believable.

It appeared that the violent command fell upon deaf ears as Jonathan continued to move closer to him, as if he knew he couldn't be harmed, even though that couldn't be further from the truth. Jonathan was more than capable of being hurt, however in this moment he didn't act like it. The absence of his fear made room for his strength, and he was prepared to handle whatever may have come his way. At this point, Jonathan had walked all the way to Adrian and stood directly in front of the gun with his chest touching the tip of the it.

"Just put the gun down and we can talk about it," he instructed, his voice sounding sure of itself as the words came flowing out with an abundance of ease. While he waited for a response from Adrian, he calculated how long it would take for him to snatch his gun. He knew he had been training and his reflexes were faster than they were before. There was an anxiousness that entangled itself up in the joints of his body, ready to explode and reveal his newfound physical abilities. After all, he knew Adrian was a dangerous man, and he didn't want him to have the upper hand if something were to pop off.

Adrian continued to stand in silence with no sign of lowering his gun, but one thing was clear: he was definitely hesitating. Jonathan knew that by now, Adrian had more than ample time to pull the trigger. Jonathan was ready to make a move as he stood there, seemingly calm and collected on the outside. Deciding not to hesitate a moment longer, Jonathan let the warrior within have his day and unleashed his physical prowess as he swatted Adrian's gun from his hand with seemingly great speed. For a split second, Jonathan was surprised that his maneuver actually worked; however, there was no time to waste, and he had to act quickly. He knew that he had just made a move on a dangerous man, and he was going to have to follow through with his decision. There was no room for error at this moment, and he had to be all in with going toe to toe with Adrian.

At this point, Jonathan had enough confidence in himself pull off such a gutsy move. His eyes watched the gun fall but only out of his immediate sight; he never saw the gun hit the floor. Instead, he stayed focused on his intended target. He followed up with a strong and swift uppercut toward Adrian's jaw. While Jonathan felt his hand connect with the bottom of his chin, he thought to himself that he didn't really want to fight Adrian. After all, this was the man that he hoped would side with them in their efforts to stop Kane. The only reason he currently had his fist in this man's face was due to the fact that Adrian had a gun pointed directly at him only a few moments ago. He decided to get his point across by following up with a strong combo, he immediately threw two solid jabs, one at Adrian's chest and the other at his nose. Adrian grunted as he stumbled back from feeling the blunt force of Jonathan's new found power.

Jonathan moved closer with a quick step, not wanting Adrian to recover as he followed up with a right cross and then a left one. In that moment, he felt his confidence swell to new levels. Here he was, literally punching a man that he feared months ago, and there was pride nestled comfortably in every blow from his fists. Pride that Adrian was currently becoming acquainted with whether he liked it or not. He was still standing while taking the onslaught of punches that Jonathan was throwing, that is until he caught one midair. Jonathan hesitated for a moment as he watched his fist stop inside of Adrian's time-worn hand. His eyes then moved to the small stream of red liquid coming from Adrian's nose. He was expecting a counter punch but what he got instead was a hard and sharp kick to the crotch. Jonathan felt his knees buckle and his stomach sink from the pain traveling through his body. He let out a gasp, as if he was trying to breathe. Adrian then lunged at Jonathan with an almost tangible fury that accompanied him. He headbutted Jonathan twice in swift succession before putting his leg behind Jonathan's leg and slamming him directly on his back. Jonathan wasn't surprised Adrian had fight in him. In fact, he was surprised it took this long for him to attack, though Jonathan's mind quickly began focusing toward the pain he was currently feeling. Adrian now stood over him stomping on his stomach in rapid succession, He was all but paralyzed by the pain.

Then suddenly, the pain let up for a moment as a loud thunderous crash sounded off its power within the room. It was the gladiator match that was previously taking place in the kitchen, now arriving in the middle of the restaurant. Percy and Marco came crashing through the kitchen door, their monstrous frames attached to one another in an all-out war between two trained killers. It seemed the two of them were a solid match for each other as neither one of them appeared to have killed the other, yet. This momentary distraction was more than enough for Jonathan to seize his seemingly divine opportunity and swiftly kick Adrian behind his left leg, causing him to stumble. In the few seconds that Adrian used to regain his footing, Jonathan had sprung to his feet like a prize fighter in the twelfth round. He saw the gun he had smacked out of Adrian's hand over near the bottom leg of one of the tables. He quickly darted across the room, almost flying as he reached for it. Jonathan didn't know if Adrian was right behind him or not; either way he knew he had to move quickly. He wrapped his right hand around the gun, he could feel the thick cloud of tension and anger fill the air. At that moment, the atmosphere was deadly to say the least; Jonathan noticed Adrian had tried to catch him before he got the gun. He stood there while something crawled around the edges of

Adrian's eyes, something else that he hadn't seen on Adrian's face before. It appeared to be anxiety, lying in wait on his face, though it was only discernible to the trained eye. Jonathan stared back at Adrian before glancing over in the corner and seeing the havoc that Percy and Marco were inflicting on one another. It was like watching two lions in the wild fight mercilessly over territory, neither stopping until the other took its last breath. For the sake of sparred bloodshed, Jonathan put the gun in the air and fired two rounds into the ceiling. The light from the barrel of the gun flashed quickly as the bullets left the chamber. He felt the gun kick back in his hand as he wielded the life-taking weapon. Suddenly, there was a stillness in the room that had not been there before; Percy and Marco released their lethal holds on one another. Adrian stood still; this time he was the one who would have to await instructions as Jonathan stood with the weaponized authority nestled firmly in his grip.

"Ok gentleman, I'd say that concludes our little soirée for the evening," Jonathan exclaimed with an odd mixture of sarcasm and sternness in his tone.

"Now as you all know, I just fired this gun and I'm sure someone heard it, which means the police will be here within the next 10 to 15 minutes. So how about we all live to fight another day?"

The room was still silent as he looked around, staring at the faces of these dangerous men. He knew that he was surrounded by killers and oddly he seemed unfazed by their deadly presence. Perhaps it was due to the fact that he had become acquainted with this level of violence. He also wasn't surprised to see the ugly face of violence again in the often cruel streets of Edge City. However, this time around he knew how to respond to it. He watched as Rico suddenly appeared from around the corner of the bathroom hallway, rubbing his face. He then noticed Percy heading for the door while still facing Marco with a certain ferociousness in his eyes. Adrian stood there for a second, before replying, "He sends his regards."

Adrian turned around, walked toward the door, and then like a cloud of smoke, they quickly vanished. Percy and Adrian moved like the professionals they were and only left there proof of carnage behind.

Jonathan put the gun down on the table and looked at Marco and Rico. He said nothing. He only looked at the front door that Adrian and Percy had just walked out of. He stared at the door like someone who stares off into space when daydreaming; but Jonathan wasn't daydreaming. He was looking off into the not so distant future. He saw another battle coming because he knew it wasn't over. Indeed, he and his newfound crew had awakened the ancient beast and invaded its territory. Only time would tell what would happen to this group of brave knights looking to slay the beast. However, one thing was certain: the dragon had been awakened and tonight made one thing clear; it was out for blood.

CHAPTER 17

PANDORA'S BOX AND THE GOLDEN SILENCE

There was a thick blanket of emotion that seemed to lay on top of the air, making it feel heavier as Jonathan breathed. Perhaps he wasn't the only one to feel that way as he looked around the penthouse. The gang was all assembled and they were all brewing with their own separate feelings, which contributed to the emotional blanket that was present. They had all tried to speak their peace about what had just happened. Only a few hours had gone by since the restaurant brawl. Jonathan was aware of what it meant, although he wasn't convinced that Rico and Marco understood the severity of the situation. He would do his best to explain to them exactly what was going on.

"This is what I was trying to tell you Rico," affirmed Jonathan.

"It's started now; he knows we're here. There's no telling what he'll do!" His voice was quick and sharp due to the agitation that accompanied it.

Rico was holding a warm white washcloth that had dampened blood stains on it, the liquid evidence that Percy had given him a strong first impression. For once, he didn't appear to have a whole lot to say; perhaps his ego was bleeding more than his nose. He sat there with a look of slight embarrassment and irritation floating on his face. At least that was the way it appeared to Jonathan, because he had seen that very same look before on his own face at times when he looked in the mirror. His days from tangling with Kane in the past had matured him in more ways than one. He recognized certain things now at a quicker pace due to his own personal experience and growth.

"Look, I'll give it to you ok. You were right," said Rico. His voice was subtle, but not from fear; it sounded more like embarrassment as it hit the air.

Rachel stood off in the distance near the kitchen, peering out of one of the floor to ceiling windows that overlooked the city. It was dark out and no one had drawn the blinds. Perhaps it wasn't on anyone's mind to do such a trivial thing. Jonathan noticed she was standing over there but he didn't want to say anything to her. He knew what he wanted to say to Rico, but not to Rachel. She was different. He knew that she had been through this before, and for her sake as well as his, he wouldn't let it end the same way it did before.

"Well, it is what it is now," said Jonathan, his tone coming down from its irritated high. "He knows we're here and he'll come for us from any and every angle he can think of. I've found that when it comes to him, you have to do what you can to be one step ahead. We have to be ready for anything and expect the unexpected. Also we need to be more on the offensive than defensive side of this thing."

Jonathan stood there strong, calm, and collected. At this moment, he had become the teacher, schooling those who needed to be educated in the ways of Kane Edwards. Not only that, but he was also prepared for war. He was merely blinded by this blitz attack, as they all were. He knew that was the sort of thing that could happen, he just didn't know when. Jonathan took his attention off Rico for a moment and looked at Marco, and he noticed that he seemed unfazed by all the comotion. Jonathan kept his take on Marco's demeanor to himself; he knew Marco was a true warrior and would adapt to the situation.

"Let me ask you this, Rico, how secure is this place?" asked Jonathan.

"I mean I know we're in the penthouse and all but how secure is the building itself?" "There are cameras all over the building and we can see everything from the security control room downstairs; plus there's only one way in the building and one way out," Rico replied.

Jonathan mentally reviewed his answer before saying anything and simply responded, "Good to know. The reason I asked is because we have to be ready now. With this man, you never know what to expect. In fact, he may already know where we live. I mean hell, how did he know we were at the restaurant in the first place?" By the time he was finished, Jonathan was shouting, his emotions slowly rising again.

Then a soft voice entered the testosterone filled equation.

"Jonathan," said Rachel.

The mere sound of her voice had proven to be more than enough to calm the raging seas of his emotions in the past. This time seemed to be no different as Jonathan took a deep breath upon hearing the voice of his beloved glide to his ears from across the room. He could tell what she was doing by saying his name and why she did it in the first place. It was a subtle and gentle reminder that there was no need to add reckless emotion to this already complicated situation. Now was the time for calm minds and deliberate actions, not hot tempered reactions.

Rachel looked at him with slight worry swirling in her eyes, yet she said nothing. Jonathan didn't know what she was thinking; perhaps she just didn't want to add more stress to the situation by speaking her mind. He could sense Rachel was more uneasy than she was pretending to be. He knew that she didn't like playing the whole damsel in distress role, and he also knew she preferred to rely on her own strength. However, he watched her learn to trust in him more, which is something that he always wanted her to do. He took a deep breath before saying anything else.

"Well, if tonight has taught us anything, it's that we have to be ready for *anything*," said Jonathan, his tone now accompanied with calmness.

The mood in the room was still somber, but Jonathan saw this as an opportunity to lead. He wasn't about to sit back, not at a time like this. He had grown into himself, and he had become a better man than before. He knew he had to be strong because this moment and other moments to come would require strength. He was prepared to display that strength and he needed everyone else's to be on the same level.

He noticed Marco was quiet as usual, but there was a hidden anger that lay in wait in the depths of his eyes. At this point, no form of rage could hide itself from Jonathan's eyes as he had experienced that emotion too well for it to ever go unnoticed in his presence. He knew that Marco would go the distance if he had to and after tonight. Jonathan wasn't so apprehensive about that anymore. He didn't want any blood to be spilt, but he also understood that there could possibly come a time where bloodshed may not be avoidable. If a trigger ever had to be pulled, he knew that Marco's would be the finger to do it, not to count out Rico, but he knew Marco was a natural when it came to violence.

"It's been a rough night," stated Jonathan as he looked out of the windows that displayed the landscape of the nefarious city that he had returned to.

"You're telling me," chimed in Rico, with a look of disappointment plastered over his face that had seemingly slipped its way into his voice as well. "Let's just start fresh in the morning. We can attack the day and anything else that needs attacking tomorrow," Jonathan continued.

"Because make no mistake, the attacks have begun, but from here on out, I want *us* to be the ones doing the attacking." In that moment, the warrior within Jonathan spoke and he too let his presence be known.

This was a new day, a new time, with a new man standing at the helm of the situation. He was not the man he was before, and in that moment, those who were unaware of that became acquainted with the new him. For this reason, Jonathan knew he had the element of surprise on his side.

He knew Kane had no idea of the growth that had taken place within the young man that he tried to frame. From that standpoint, Jonathan looked at this revelation that currently remained unknown to Kane Edwards as his secret weapon, a weapon he planned to use.

Rico and Marco headed upstairs toward their rooms, while Jonathan and Rachel stayed behind. He still had a few things he wanted to say to her, after all they hadn't really had a chance to talk much since he got back to the penthouse. She was still standing over by the window, her face was worth a thousand words at the moment. Jonathan continued to silently study her mood as he approached her. He wanted to check on the woman he loved and make sure she was ok. He placed his hand softly on her shoulder. Rachel stared out the window for a few more seconds before she looked at Jonathan. The city's skylight was illuminated by the millions of nocturnal lights that shined bright at this time of night.

"Look, things are going to be different this time," he told her as he pulled her closer into his arms.

Rachel lifted her soft arms and embraced Jonathan, reciprocating his kind love. "I know, things are already different," she responded, her voice sounding light yet tired.

He could tell that she was tired in more ways than one, so he simply squeezed her a little bit more and kissed her softly on her forehead. The night stretched out its powers of slumber and they both headed upstairs. They were exhausted from a long and hard day in the city.

The next morning was tranquil at first. As Jonathan opened his eyes, he laid there in the peace of the moment and didn't really move. There was a naive thought that came into his mind while he lay there sprawled across the bed, under the expensive covers that came with the fully furnished guest suite he was currently occupying. Those naive thoughts whispered faint ignorance on the top layers of his mind. It told him that maybe if he stayed there, then nothing would happen. Maybe if he stayed in a peaceful state, then everything negative would go away. Jonathan frowned at the idiotic sentiment of such thoughts as he wondered its origin.

He continued to look around the modernized guest suite, it was nice, as it held a certain touch of lavishness to it. He could see the bathroom from his bed, making him think of drenching his body in a warm shower, his morning ritual. He lifted himself up toward the edge of the bed and slowly stood to his feet. He took a deep breath, as a form of mental preparation to take on whatever surprises the day may bring. He then walked into the bathroom and took a shower. By the time he completed brushing his teeth and putting on his clothes, he caught the rising sound of voices coming from downstairs, although it sounded more like one voice in particular that was speaking at a higher decibel level than what someone would normally use if they were calm. Jonathan rolled his neck clockwise as he did a final stretch before heading out the door. It appeared the day had already begun downstairs and he was going to see what all the fuss was about. He wasn't sure what time it was but he knew it was too early for any foolishness. Then again he remembered where he was and he knew the city itself didn't care about what time of day it was; the city was always ready to serve someone a raw deal if it saw fit. Jonathan could only hope that whatever was going on downstairs, wasn't too serious. He hadn't even eaten breakfast yet. He made his way down the upstairs hallway that was made up of some sort of expensive hardwood. The closer he got to the stairs, the more the voice he initially heard, became clearer. He could tell that Rico was the one talking and he didn't sound too happy. He was able to pick apart certain words as he stood at the top of the stairs getting ready to head down.

He heard Rico say, "That's not my fault." Which was shortly followed by, "Well listen Princess, you made your own bed, now lie in it."

It was that second line that got Jonathan's attention as he wondered who exactly was Rico talking to and what metaphorical bed did this person need to lay in? Jonathan now found his legs moving at a diligent rate of speed down the stairs; it seemed that the rest of his body didn't want to wait on his mind to speak. His eyes were guilty of their own agenda as well as they started peering down the steps searching for the answers to these newfound questions that had recently presented themselves. He was now near the bottom of the stairs and could clearly hear the sound of one voice and one voice only: Rico's. It must have been Rico's loudness that he heard upstairs that somehow made him think there were two people downstairs. He turned around from the stairs and was now facing the living room, looking directly at Rico's back, he realized he was on the phone. However, there was no way of knowing who he was talking to. Jonathan normally wasn't the type to keep tabs on people's private conversations. However, given all that was going on, he wanted to make sure he didn't get any unexpected surprises. There was a certain level of mental frustration, due to the fact that he secretly wanted answers and was expecting to get them upon his arrival downstairs, but it appeared he would have to wait a little bit longer.

"I don't need you here right now," said Rico. "I think you're better off right where you are."

Jonathan stood there in silence, hoping to possibly get some form of information by listening to Rico. It was obvious that Rico didn't know he was a few feet behind him, listening to his conversation and making sure everything was on the up and up.

"Well, I think you'll be fine where you are," said Rico. "Oh...and if you try a stunt like that again, Pop might break both of your legs, even if you are his daughter." Rico chuckled at his own words.

It was then when Jonathan realized who the mystery person was that Rico was talking to; it was his seductress of a sister, Aaliyah. He rolled his eyes at the thought of her. He knew that she wasn't a good person for him to be around. Now that he knew that Rico was talking to Aaliyah, he admitted to himself that he didn't need to sneak around. He began to walk toward Rico and purposefully coughed to make his presence known. Rico turned around and nodded at Jonathan, offering a non verbal hello. Jonathan responded by doing the same thing. In that moment Rico wrapped up his conversation, "Well I'd love to stay and chat but I gotta go. Try not to do anything stupid in my absence," he quipped right before hanging up the phone. "Well, Good morning Johnny boy." He turned around to fully face Jonathan."You've got mail." He bent down and picked up a small brown box with duct tape on it that was sitting on the couch. On top of the box was a piece of paper taped to it. The paper had a message on it that read: *When you're ready to talk.*

Rico held the box in his hand and said, "Well Johnny boy, it looks like you were right, and you've been right all along. Looks like your boy does like to play games." He tossed the box in the air over the couch.

Jonathan caught the box and looked at it, rubbing his fingers gently on the piece of paper. He looked back at Rico and paused before he uttered one word. The word that told him everything he needed to know before he opened the box: "Kane," he said.

"He's not wasting any time," said Rico.

Jonathan stared at the box for a moment before opening it. He then simultaneously began opening the box and responding to Rico. "And neither can we," he replied.

He ripped the box open with his hands and noticed there was an old flip phone inside. He held the box in his left hand while flipping the phone open with his right. It appeared the phone had already been pre-programmed with one contact already listed. The contact read, "Future." Jonathan smirked and shook his head as he read the contact name. He stood there and wondered the meaning behind the name, but then the answer came to him. He knew that was another sick and twisted joke by a madman. Jonathan knew that the contact was a direct line to Kane himself. The whole "future" thing was no doubt his way of letting Jonathan know that he can still have a future with him. Jonathan had become versed in the ways of Kane Edwards and had learned some of his methodical tactics. He had to admit he was slightly confused at the hidden message. He wondered why Kane would still extend an open hand, especially after last night. Though he wouldn't be fooled that easily, he knew that this so-called olive branch would come equipped with some evil intention.

"You gonna call him?" Rico asked.

Jonathan paused before answering the question, while a quick thought flashed before his eyes. He wondered if he should talk to the rest of the group before making such a move. Then as he thought about it longer, his mind was able to answer his own question. For starters, there was no rest of the group once Jonathan really stopped to think about it. There was only Rachel and Marco, which in all honesty, Jonathan knew he didn't really need to talk to Marco because he wasn't the talking type. Not only that, but Marco wasn't the one really making the decisions. He was there for backup, the muscle so to speak. That left Rachel. She was someone who Jonathan would listen to. She was his anchor. Even though that was true, it was apparent by the pace in which Kane was moving that he wasn't wasting any time and neither should Jonathan.

Jonathan looked at Rico for a moment before dialing the contact number. He took a deep mental breath while he tossed the box back over the couch. He knew that by dialing this number, he was opening pandora's box. There was no telling what would be unleashed by calling Kane, however Jonathan knew deep down that it had to be done. He also may not have had all of the answers of what would happen, but he had some idea of what to expect. Jonathan knew with this man, he had to expect the unexpected and be as ready as he possibly could for anything. He pressed the call button and put the phone up to his ear.

Naturally, as he heard the phone ringing, his mind began to run wild. He knew he had to be strong because of the overflow of emotions and memories that came rushing his way in that moment. He thought back to the countless struggles this man put him through,not to mention the life threatening danger. It seemed that with every pacing ring of the phone, Jonathan's heart began to pump a little bit faster. He knew that at any second Kane could pick up that phone and reintroduce him to a world of hurt. He tightened his fist as he stood there waiting for the inevitable to take place.

The phone rang again, and then suddenly it stopped. Jonathan awaited to hear the familiar voice of a psychopath hiss in his ear, however he was sorely disappointed. The only voice that Jonathan heard was that of the voice prompt, as he was instructed to leave a message after the beep. Jonathan hung up without thinking, his reflexes acting in sync with his emotions. He wondered if this was another game and if he should've even called the number in the first place. Perhaps this was a road that he really didn't need to go down. Maybe he should just attack the enemy instead of trying to have a conversation with him. After all, this was a dangerous man Jonathan was dealing with. He stood there in silence for a moment while he stared at the phone, wondering what his next move should be. The silence was golden while it lasted because this was a valuable moment he found himself in. He needed to be still and quiet while he thought of his next step.

Rico spoke up asking a question that didn't need to be asked. "He didn't pick up the phone?"

Jonathan kept his emotions from forming on the outside of his face before he responded to him. "No," he snapped, unable to refrain his annoyance of being disrupted from his brief solace. While he stood there in deep thought, something came to his attention. It was so obvious now that it had come to his mind, a mere observation that slipped in unnoticeably.

However, he caught hold of it now and brought it to Rico's attention out loud.

"He knows where we are," he said, the sound of revelation presenting itself boldly in his voice.

Rico looked at him with his own surprised look. Jonathan could tell Rico hadn't paid attention to this simple yet obvious fact of how Kane knew where to send the box in the first place. "Probably the same way he knew we were at that restaurant," he affirmed. "Your boy's good, I'll give you that. And I should have known better, I'll give you that too. But I'm good too, Cross, and we're good together. We can handle him."

However, Jonathan wasn't quite convinced of the words that were coming out of Rico's mouth. He knew what it would take to bring down Kane. He studied the busted lip Rico currently displayed. He looked at that lip as a small piece of evidence that he may not have given the situation the proper respect it was due. They now had to be ready for anything; the dangerous game that was once played had now begun anew. Jonathan still held the phone in his hand and stared at it for a little longer; still no ring. Rico stood off to the side, appearing as if he too were beginning to become drenched in deep thought. There was no telling what was going on inside that head of his, and Jonathan really didn't have the energy to figure it out. His own thoughts were enough for him to handle. He heard the sound of Rico's footsteps moving as he looked up to see what he was doing.

"You know what, it's early and I'm still kinda tired. I'm going back to bed," said Rico, as he walked past him with his head slightly tilted toward the floor.

Jonathan could tell Rico was agitated and he couldn't blame him. He knew that this is what time spent in Edge City could get you, anger and frustration. It was a lethal combination dealt by a lethal city; the city itself spared no feelings. The room had somehow gotten still in the last few seconds without warning and Rico seemed to have disappeared faster than expected.

Suddenly, Jonathan ironically found himself alone in a penthouse full of people as he stared out of one of the windows in the living room. It was a view that he couldn't help but stare at; the city had a mesmerizing power that refused to be ignored. It was almost like a venus fly trap. It would draw an unsuspecting soul in close and then without warning, snatch them into submission. Jonathan knew this, but still found himself gazing upon the iron built backdrop.

He figured he would go out onto the balcony to get a bit of fresh air. While he walked toward the sliding glass door leading to the balcony, it dawned on him that he hadn't been on the balcony since he first got to the penthouse. Jonathan stepped out on the sprawling balcony that stretched alongside what seemed like half of the penthouse. There was high-end furniture on the balcony, a glass table with chairs as well as a nice sofa for lounging. Jonathan took a seat on the sofa as he listened to the sounds of the city. The way the wind rustled past his ears felt as if the city was whispering the secrets of these often treacherous streets. He closed his eyes as he listened to its ominous voice.

It was then that he heard another sound: the sound of a phone ringing. He quickly opened his eyes. When he looked down, he saw the word "Future" pop up on the caller ID. His heart began to beat at a rapid pace. He would've been lying if he he said he wasn't nervous. He knew who was calling him, what that person represented and what they could possibly do to him. He didn't take too long to react; he had no choice. He answered the phone. Jonathan put the phone up to his ear, and said nothing. However he didn't have to, because the person on the other end had no problem speaking.

"Alas, the prodigal son has returned," said the voice. Indeed it was the voice that had sent chills down countless spines. A voice that contained the power to arrest people in fear with a single word. A voice that needed no introduction, a voice that belonged to Kane Edwards.

"Jonathan, my boy, are you there?" asked Kane, his voice penetrating through the speakers of the phone, making it sound as if he were actually right there with him.

Jonathan took a deep breath and clenched his right fist as he leaned forward on the sofa. This was the moment of truth and he couldn't let anything but firm strength come forth from his lips. He had to be strong. He had to let Kane know he wasn't the same person he once was. Things had changed. Jonathan had changed.

Armed with this knowledge, Jonathan finally spoke: "I'm here, what do you want?" he asked, his tone of voice sounding blunt and short.

"Oh come on now, young man, don't be that way," said Kane. "We haven't spoken in a long time. Surely you're as happy to hear from me as I am from you." Kane's demented way of thinking showing itself strong in his words.

Jonathan felt the tamed rage of the warrior within starting to boil over but he had to keep his emotions in check. In this moment, he couldn't allow himself to unravel. He just couldn't afford it. "I'm about as happy to hear from you as some poor soul that just found out they had cancer," he sharply replied.

"Well, well, aren't you the bold one these days?!" replied Kane.

Jonathan rose from his seat so he could walk around as he talked. He felt the need to be able to move. For whatever reason, it calmed him. "And you should know that I'm here to stop you," he declared.

For a moment, there was silence on the phone before Kane responded. "You can't be serious. You're a wanted man, in case you forgot," he said. Jonathan could almost hear the smirk forming on Kane's face as he spoke those words.

"Oh believe me, I'm serious," answered Jonathan. "I mean, don't get me wrong, the city is nice and all but I didn't come back here for the sake of sightseeing."

"Yes, I must applaud you, you've taken quite the bold move by coming back here. I must admit, that I'm thoroughly impressed. Oh and let's not forget last night's performance, from what I hear you did exceptionally well!" gushed Kane.

Jonathan felt the inside of his stomach beginning to churn as he felt disgust moving around in his intestines. He could hear the old narcissistic and demented ways of Kane come alive again in Jonathan's life, just by hearing him speak.

"This is all a game to you isn't it?!" snapped Jonathan.

"That's the spirit!" declared Kane.

"Show me you still have some fight in you! But to answer your question Jonathan, yes. It is a game that I plan on winning. Me becoming mayor was just my latest move in this game. Now listen to me, I can give you what you want Jonathan. You can still have your freedom, son. You can still have the life you always wanted." The underlying feeling of deception lived on his every words.

"I have the power to give you what you want. I can make you free again. Not to mention I can return the life of your favorite lady, Ms. Monroe, to normal."

Not that Jonathan was taking the false bait, but even he had to admit that hearing those words sounded very tempting. Jonathan's mind churned for a moment, wondering how on earth Kane could do something like that. After all, he was a wanted man, accused of murder. How on earth could Kane get rid of something like that? Nevertheless, Jonathan stayed silent for a second, as if he were giving unspoken permission to allow Kane to continue his explanation.

"Tell you what, meet me tomorrow afternoon in Fedman Park at 2:30 and we'll discuss your future." said Kane, his voice sounding sure of itself. Jonathan noticed that even this man's *voice* moved across the air like a snake, slithering and sidewinding its way into the ears of whoever was listening at that moment.

Again, Jonathan was silent as he walked around. He had been put on the spot, and there was no one there to bounce the idea off of nor did he have time to talk it over. He knew two things; that it was inevitable he would once again come face to face with Kane, and that he had to make a decision, and soon. He also knew he still had Adrian in mind as his secret weapon.

"Well Mr. Cross, what say you?" Kane asked

Jonathan took a deep breath before answering, "I'll be there."

"Great, then it's settled. I'll see you tomorrow," replied Kane.

Before Jonathan could say anything else, the next thing he heard was a dial tone. The quick cut off of the conversation reminded him of days he would rather forget. It seemed that he would soon be strolling down memory lane yet again, by tomorrow afternoon.

He stood there with the breeze of the air dancing over his skin. He could feel the sun's warm rays behind the wind coming in strong. He also felt something else; he felt that someone was watching him. He turned around and to his surprise, Rachel was standing in the doorway behind him. With all of the commotion with the phone call, he must not have heard her open the sliding door. She stood there as if standing in silent judgement of Jonathan, but she said nothing. For a moment, they only looked each other in the eyes.

Then Rachel spoke, "That was him, wasn't it?" she asked.

"Yeah," Jonathan replied. It was a simple response to a simple question. He didn't have the energy to go into detail.

Rachel took a step toward Jonathan and closed the door behind her. He met her halfway as she walked into his arms. She was silent as he held her, placing her head deeply within his chest. It was as if she wanted to bury herself within the comfort of his arms while hiding from the dark situation they faced. Jonathan knew he was yet again going to face the beast. He also knew the beast couldn't be trusted, so he wouldn't show up with naivety by his side. On the contrary, he would show up with preparation. Kane had no idea of the man Jonathan had become, and it was time for an introduction.

CHAPTER 18

FACE TO FACE

It was odd, really; the absurdness of it all defied logical thinking. Clearly there was not one rational thought present from either party when orchestrating such an event. It was unapologetically bold and foolish all in the same breath. Here they were, two men who had found themselves in the public eye, acting as if no one knew who they were. Kane Edwards had now graduated to a higher social status as the mayor of Edge City. Jonathan Cross, on the other hand, was a wanted fugitive on the run, his true innocence still unknown to the world. Nevertheless, they were front and center in broad daylight for any prying eyes to see; yet they oddly found themselves alone.

It was 2:30 in the afternoon, the time Kane had so elegantly requested. Jonathan felt more alive than usual today. It was like his senses were in overdrive as if he possessed supernatural abilities. He heard the birds chirping in the park, and he could almost hear the flap of their wings as they flew overhead. He felt the blood moving through his own veins as his heart pumped with excitement and force. There was a whiff of possibilities in the air, and Jonathan could all but taste its sweet nectar as it floated high in the atmosphere. Most importantly, he could see his intended target, the obsession of his rage walking closer toward him in the middle of the day. Even Jonathan had to admit, the man looked regal and debonair as he laid eyes on him.

When he stopped to think about it, that was probably a part of the appeal, maybe that's why some people didn't see him coming. Due to his charming and authoritative ways on the outside, people knew nothing of the real Kane. Jonathan pitied whoever had the fate of being shown the unforgiving iron fist that Kane ruled with. He was walking toward him in a three-piece, navy blue pinstripe suit. It had been a while since Jonathan had seen the dragon in full view, up close and personal like this, and it was an experience to say the least.

However, he would prove himself to be quite the reformed man, having developed new skills of his own. He had the courage to match the lion heart that he carried within his chest. Now was the time to use it, but he had to make sure that his mind was along for the ride as well. He noticed Adrian walking a few steps behind Kane as well as a black SUV on the curb near the sidewalk. Jonathan's eyes surveyed the scene as Kane walked confidently toward him. He almost couldn't believe that there was really no one out there to see the mayor and a wanted man meeting face to face. He couldn't be too shocked at the whole thing. After all, Kane prided himself on being the king of Edge City. So it was only right that he knew when people would be out and about and what time the park would be empty.

Jonathan stood still, with his feet firmly planted in the neatly green manicured lawn. The park was well cared for, which wasn't too much of a surprise; it was located in a nice area of the city. He looked as Kane's short walk came to a smooth stop. Kane stood there for a moment, looking Jonathan up and down, no doubt noticing the new muscular shape on his frame.

"I see your free time has been good to you," said Kane, while arrogance and sarcasm danced on the top of his words.

"My time was a lot of things, but *free* definitely wasn't one of them," replied Jonathan. "Jonathan, Jonathan, Jonathan, I must admit this is quite a mess you've gotten yourself into," said Kane.

Jonathan smirked and shook his head at Kane's comment. He knew what it was meant to do and he really didn't want to let it get to him but it did. He learned that Kane had a way of reading someone and targeting their buttons and then pushing them violently once identified.

"You mean this is quite the mess that *you* got me into," he replied, as he stiffly stated the obvious facts.

Kane stood there draped in a full garment of his own arrogance, while shining in the self-produced rays of his ill-gotten glory. He responded, but not in the way Jonathan was expecting or hoping he would.

"Do you still want everything?" he asked, with a cold stare locked on his face. His eyes seemed as if they were looking into Jonathan's very soul. This question immediately sent memories rushing back into Jonathan's mind like an uncontrollable flood having its way with the land. His thoughts ran wild and with force, all the while carrying the load of a vivid memory, that memory being the very first night that he met Kane. Jonathan remembered when Kane had asked him the question of what he wanted and Jonathan's response was "*everything*."

"I have the things I want. I just *need* my freedom," stated Jonathan; he had matured in his thinking along the way and his answer was proof of that.

"Hmmm," Kane responded."Well, that brings me to why I asked you here today, Jonathan. I want you to come back and work for me. When I told you I was impressed on how you handled yourself last night, I meant it." Kane's complimentary charm covered his sentences very thickly. "You still have that fire boy! I can still mold you!" Kane exclaimed, moving his hands as if he were a spirited orator giving a riveting speech.

"Oh, you already have," said Jonathan. "Trust me, I've been molded just fine."

"Is that so?" Kane asked.

"It is. After all, that's what you wanted right?" Jonathan sarcastically asked."For me to be like you."

"Oh, now you know you still have a long way to go to be like me," Kane interjected.

The conversation itself was heavy and it was made even worse by the thick cloud of tension. So thick in fact that it was becoming more of a block than a cloud. It was interesting, or maybe just paradoxical, how such a beautiful day could be so dark at the same time. However, such was the nature of Edge City; things were sometimes both up and down, left and right at the same time. Men like Kane saw to it that characteristics like that of the city stayed alive.

"Now as I have stated, I've given you an offer Jonathan. If I were you I would take it. I'll give you a day to decide and then I'll expect an answer. Because I've temporarily decided to overlook the fact that you've brought the living blood of my enemy into my domain," Kane snarled.

Jonathan thought about Kane's words for a moment before realizing exactly what he was talking about. Yet before he could say anything, Kane confirmed his unspoken thoughts.

"You aligning yourself with the Colosos was an unwise move to say the least," instructed Kane.

"Well, from where I'm standing that looks like a smart move to me," replied Jonathan.

"That's because you're still standing…for now. Don't go too far down a road you can't turn back from," Kane advised, with a calm yet unpleasant voice.

"I bet you wish someone would have told *you* that when you were my age," quipped Jonathan.

"I don't wish for anything son. I *make* things happen," Kane declared.

At that moment, Jonathan noticed that Adrian had walked up behind Kane and was standing off to the right of him. Through all the intense conversation, he failed to notice the silent threat that was now in his presence. Jonathan looked at Adrian while Adrian looked at him; an unspoken interaction was taking place. The look that Adrian revealed seemed to be a mixture of both approval and shame. Jonathan didn't know what to make of it but it was there all the same.

Kane turned his head and noticed Adrian; this was probably some cue to let Kane know it was time for them to leave. After all, the man was now Mayor of the city; surely he couldn't be gone too long without being accounted for. Kane looked at Jonathan for a second, staring him down with those predatory eyes. He said nothing, he only looked before turning around and heading to his car. Jonathan watched as Kane and Adrian walked away. He stared as they went back to their corrupt day and even more corrupt lives. He knew he wasn't going to take Kane's offer. He also knew what rejecting that offer would mean. However, Jonathan wasn't afraid of his retaliation because this time he was prepared for war.

CHAPTER 19

THE WARNING

These sort of conversations could oftentimes be unpleasant, but that didn't mean they weren't necessary. For the sake of cohesion with the group, Jonathan knew he had to tell Rico about what happened. The outcome of his honesty was a conversation that resembled more of an argument. Jonathan found himself having to defend his own actions to someone he felt hasn't made the best decisions since they arrived to the city. Rico was annoyed to say the least, but Jonathan felt Rico should've been smart enough to see this coming. He should have known that the phone call to Kane would turn into more, and it did.

"I'm just saying Cross, you gotta keep us in the loop here!" snapped Rico. "You can't just go around meeting with the enemy without informing your people. Your rogue actions affect the rest of us and vice versa, smart guy."

They had already been at it with each other for the past ten minutes and Jonathan was getting bored with the topic.

"Look I knew this was going to happen at some point, so I wanted to do it on my terms without me being forced," explained Jonathan. "Now you gotta get with the program Rico and remember why we're here in the first place. If I told you once, man I've told you a thousand times that we cannot underestimate this man! We have to take the fight to him, sitting back and waiting on him to bring it to us is a bad move; trust me."

"Yeah well, so is not talking to the rest of the group before you go making a move," quipped Rico.

A hot stare came over Jonathan's eyes as he glared at Rico. His anger was begging to be released from the dark depths of his human nature, so it could unleash punishment upon the one who caused offense. However, at the moment, Jonathan's wisdom outweighed his emotions and he decided to take the moral high ground. Although the view from the high ground wasn't always nice, and sometimes that made Jonathan want to come down and straighten some things out. Lucky for him there was someone present who was able to bring some calmness to the room.

"You both have valid points that you need to think about," said Rachel, with her angelic voice invading the current hostile atmosphere.

"And you both bring something to the table that the other one doesn't. Look, I worked for this man for a few years and I know a thing or two about him. This is the type of thing he does, without even trying, he'll try to bring division. I've seen him do this with other rival companies. He would try to tear them apart from the inside, and often times it worked, which made it that much easier for him to take them down." The room was quiet after her truth and voice of reason had been revealed. Neither Rico nor Jonathan said anything to rival her words in that moment. Rico rubbed his head and headed toward the kitchen, undoubtedly to grab himself a bottle of wine. Rachel watched him as he walked by, same with Jonathan; then they simultaneously turned to face each other. They looked at each other for a moment without saying anything. Then Jonathan mouthed the words "I love you," to Rachel. She smiled and mouthed "I know, you too." It was then that Jonathan realized he hadn't really spent too much time with Rachel lately. Although, he was well aware of the fact that this wasn't exactly a vacation they were on, he still wanted her to know that she mattered. After all, she was half of the reason that he was going up against Kane Edwards for a second time. The other half was that he wanted to be a free man again, not one running from the law because he was framed. He also wanted Rachel to have her life restored to her; she didn't deserve to be punished for his mistakes. While he looked deep within the love of her soft eyes, he thought of a plan that was beyond bold. Then again, it was nothing new for Jonathan to come up with a bold idea.

"Look we need to go somewhere tonight," said Jonathan.

While he was well aware of the fact that he was a wanted man, he also knew he was a man in love. That for now, was more than enough to make him want to risk it for her.

Rachel looked at him and said, "Jonathan we can't."

"Why not?" he asked.

"You know why," she answered.

"Yeah I do but who cares?" Jonathan responded

"Well the police might if they catch us," responded Rachel, with an overflow of sarcasm coming from her lips.

"Yeah *if,* but they won't," Jonathan said.

"You seem so sure of yourself lover boy," she seductively whispered.

"I'm sure of you," answered Jonathan.

"Well then it's settled, a dangerous and carefree night on the town it is," said Rachel, again sarcasm being present.

Jonathan pulled her in for a hug, with a smirk on his face while he held onto her. It was settled between the two of them, they would have a night of fun, a night of peace, perhaps a night of normalcy.

Upstairs was a bit of a different story, where another conversation was taking place. Inside the master bedroom of the sprawling penthouse roamed Rico Coloso. He paced back-and-forth while he talked on the phone, his every step seemed awkward and nervous. Perhaps it was who he was talking to that brought about the discomfort. It was none other than the Don himself, his father Nero Coloso. It appeared Nero was checking in on his son, asking for a status report on his last dealings in Edge City.

"You wanted to prove yourself," said Nero, his voice was calm yet intimidating even to his own blood. "So tell me, what exactly have you done over there; behind enemy lines?"

"I'm closing in on him sir, I'll bring honor to the Coloso name," Rico answered.

"Oh, I've already done that son; hundreds of dead corpses over. I've earned enough honor and respect to last me two lifetimes. The Coloso name stands just fine but we're here talking about your name," explained Nero; his earned wisdom cutting through any unnecessary commentary.

"He's proven himself to be a worthy adversary, as you have said" replied Rico. "But I will prevail over him father."

"You did the right thing, sending your sister to me and telling me of her whereabouts, for this I give you the opportunity to handle this on your own," explained Nero.

"If you bring down Kane Edwards, you'll have your higher place in the family. However, if I have to get involved, I'll bathe the city with Kane's blood and I'll let this Cross boy take the fall," said Nero, his words sounding solid and iron clad with no deviation from their original intent. "Not to mention, I'll take this as the final sign that you're not ready for this line of work."

"I understand father and I won't fail," said Rico.

"Good," said Nero, these were his final words before he hung up the phone, leaving Rico in dark silence.

A horrible option had been placed on the table and if Rico didn't end this whole thing soon; then his father would. One thing was absolute; if Nero Coloso came to town, it would be a dark day for *all* of Edge City.

CHAPTER 20

NIGHT OF NORMALCY

Due to previous experience, Jonathan learned that an average night in the city, could prove to be deadly. However, tonight was something different, it was a bit of an oxymoron to be honest. It was an expected yet unexpected night for him. On one hand he knew he and Rachel had made plans to take a risky shot at normalcy; so that much he was expecting. However, the unexpected part was the feeling the night itself brought about in Jonathan. While he and Rachel walked the Friday night streets of the iron paradise, Jonathan felt joy. Not just any joy either, but a joy that he could see and feel; in fact it was all around him. The joy splashed over his entire body as he held Rachel's hand walking in the night's cool breeze. He could see that same joy ingrained within the very pores of Rachel's face, even in the small creases that formed at the edge of her mouth as she smiled. She held onto Jonathan's arm with both of her own as she looked up at him. Jonathan's theory of hiding in plain sight seemed to work… almost too well to be honest. There was a sense of false reality deep within the whole thing; the fact that they were wanted fugitives, yet enjoying a nice stroll on their way to dinner. Although, tonight Jonathan chose to focus on other things, instead of the glaring negative aspects of what he was dealing with in his life. Tonight was about him and Rachel getting a chance to breathe…a chance to love and to live.

They had parked in a parking deck around the corner and were currently walking to their intended destination; a pizzeria. They both wanted something simple, something light-hearted. They both agreed, they needed a night like this. Jonathan could see the bright blue neon letters spelling out *The 83rd Slice,* an obvious nod to its other location, *The 75th Slice.* Jonathan remembered he ate at the 75th street location the last time he was in the city, they had great pizza. He could smell the work of the kitchen's culinary mastery oozing out of the restaurant and dancing its way out into the street. It was a meal worth looking forward to with company that he loved. They walked into the restaurant and waited to be seated; the hostess that greeted them was a nice middle-aged woman by the name of Tiffany. Jonathan had his arm around Rachel as he looked around the restaurant while they walked to their seats. They sat in a booth near the back, a location that was a little less out in the open. After all, he felt that he was being daring enough just by being there; no need to push his luck. Jonathan sat across from Rachel so he could get a good look at her as they enjoyed their time together.

"I love you," he said.

"Love you too," replied Rachel, her voice sounding like angelic music to his ears.

The atmosphere of the restaurant was light and lively, exactly what the two of them were looking for. Thankfully, no one was the wiser to their daring night out and no one knew their situation, so there was no room for judgment. They were wanted by the law but still in love enough to share a meal together. It was the thing movies were made of. Jonathan looked around and scanned some of the random faces that were surrounding him that night. He wanted to make sure there were no surprises in his mist. Tonight was going to be peaceful and dare he say down-right normal. He wanted to give Rachel a taste of regular life again, one without running from some deranged mastermind who's trying to destroy their lives.

Tonight, the troubles of the outside world weren't allowed to come into their personal space. Jonathan took a deep breath and relaxed his shoulders as he began to share casual conversation with the woman he loved. They talked about their plans on what they'd do when all of the current unpleasantness was behind them. The amount of optimism that still resided between the two of them was inspiring to say the least. It wasn't long before they ordered their food and had a large pepperoni and Italian sausage pizza sitting in front of them. The laughter present that night was enough to make both of their souls smile. Jonathan knew for a fact he was smiling hard on the inside. He continued to look at Rachel as she folded a thick slice of pizza and took a huge bite.

"I love you for being you," stated Jonathan, while his eyes studied the target of their affection.

It was something about Rachel in Jonathan's eyes, he always saw her beauty in all that she did. It wasn't just her physical beauty that Jonathan noticed, it was her beauty to be who she was without asking anyone for permission. Rachel was strong but also vulnerable, she was sassy but still had a relaxed attitude, quite frankly she was many things at once. She was a beautiful complexity, she was constantly growing in Jonathan's eyes, reaching to new heights, while at the same time revealing new depths to herself. Jonathan felt it was an amazing experience to be with her. It was nice to just sit across from her at a table, with a warm pizza sitting between them. This was what it was all about for Jonathan, being able to live a happy life with the woman he loved. He was ready for more of this type of peace, this type of joy and this type of life.

The love they shared seemed to create its own atmospheric bubble that was currently surrounded their table. They found themselves nestled safely within the bubble they had created, with no distractions from the outside world. That was until an unexpected occurrence took place outside the bubble. Actually, it happened at the front door of the restaurant to be exact. A small shift in the air, brought upon by a certain presence that had just entered the room. Unfortunately, neither Jonathan nor Rachel knew who this mystery person was who personified this new presence, nor did either of them notice this person at all once they arrived. Although, it always does the hunted some good to know when a new hunter has come into the equation. This new hunter had just finished with his shift and was ready to unwind with a cold one and a few hot slices. The hunter had a name and a badge to go with it: Detective Sebastian Mercer; the man who had been assigned the all but forgotten case of Jonathan Cross and Rachel Monroe.

Detective Mercer made his way to one of the smaller tables as he followed behind the hostess. He took his jacket off from his dark brown suit and put it on the back of the chair. He wore the look of both weariness and hunger, as he took his seat. It looked like the day had been long and hard to him by the way he sat in his seat while looking at the menu. Though for his sake and the sake of Jonathan and Rachel, it would be good if he didn't noticed the two fugitives sitting in the back of the restaurant. There was an awkwardness that floated around on top of the air in the room, something was off yet no one noticed. Prayerfully, things wouldn't end on a sour note that night, however there was no true way of knowing what would happen just yet.

The night went on as Jonathan and Rachel finished their meal. At this point, most of the pizza was gone except the last four slices. They would prove to be a delectable reminder of tonight's evening as leftovers for tomorrow. Jonathan raised his hand to grab the waitress' attention. He asked for the check and a to-go box. The waitress smiled and two minutes later his request had been fulfilled. Jonathan looked around the restaurant for a moment and surveyed the room; nothing stood out to him as his eyes searched his surroundings. Rachel walked in front of Jonathan as he carried the to-go box, walking behind her. Jonathan could see the front door as he made his way through the restaurant that was still fairly crowded. Unbeknownst to Jonathan, Detective Mercer was sitting off to Jonathan's left at a table of his own. Mercer was finishing his third and final slice of meat lovers pizza, while drowning it down with his last swig of beer. Then it happened; Mercer casually looked up and caught a glimpse of a young woman and a man walking out of the restaurant. A normal sight upon first glance, but a lingering gaze gives someone's eyes more time to properly study what they're looking at.

Detective Mercer got a good look at the young man who was now opening the door and walking out of the restaurant. It was a face that was in two places at once, the first place being in the current moment right before Mercer's eyes. The second place being the case file on his desk that contained the photographs of Jonathan Cross and Rachel Monroe.

The door closed behind Jonathan as he walked out onto the street, he felt the night's cool breeze brush against his nose. It was as if time had slowed down a notch or two as Jonathan made his way down the street with his arm around Rachel. He was very much present in the moment with her, his senses were in high gear as he could feel every emotion that presented itself. He could also hear every sound in the distance, even the squeaking brakes of the taxi cabs and the sound of a door opening behind him. Although it was the next sound that got his attention the most, the sound of his name being called. It was loud enough to break the slow motion feeling of time and slap it back into proper speed.

"Jonathan Cross!!" shouted a mysterious voice.

Jonathan stopped in his tracks, as he dropped his arm from around Rachel. Jonathan didn't recognize the voice but he knew the sound of authority coming from it. It was a sound that said it knew who Jonathan was and that it wanted Jonathan to answer to its power. Indeed Jonathan recognized the authority that resided in the mysterious voice, deep down Jonathan knew that it was unmistakable authority. It was the authority of a police officer; one that had obviously noticed Jonathan and knew who he was. Jonathan placed his left hand on Rachel's back and slightly pushed her forward, a sign to tell her to run. A tear welled up in Rachel's eye as it became apparent by the look on her face, that she too recognized the verbal authority.

Jonathan turned to face the voice who held the authority; and it was then that he saw Detective Mercer for the first time. From Jonathan's point of view, half of Mercer's face was covered in blue from the brightness of the neon blue letters that spelled the restaurant's name outside. There they stood, two opposing forces on the sidewalk just a few feet apart from each other, facing off as if they were in an old western. However, this was no western nor movie, there was no bail of hay that came blowing across the street, and Jonathan didn't have a gun. However, he knew that Mercer did, because Jonathan could see the gun in his holster.

"Don't move!" shouted Detective Mercer.

Jonathan stood there in the eye of this new storm that just blew in front of him. He stood firm as he looked at Detective Mercer, "You don't know what you think you know," said Jonathan.

"I know that I just told you not to move!" Detective Mercer shouted, as his hand moved closer toward his holster.

Jonathan's mind was racing as he ran through his list of options but to be honest there weren't many to choose from. He knew he couldn't stand there and let this cop pull his gun on him or that would be the end. Jonathan had to move quickly within the rapidly closing window that he had. Without hesitation, his legs felt as if they bolted from under him, almost dragging the top half of his body…as he made a run for it. All while shouting, "Run, Rachel, run!!" In that moment they both ran as fast as they could, Rachel dropped the pizza and headed straight for the parking garage where they parked Rico's car. Jonathan on the other hand, purposefully ran into the middle of the street, while Detective Mercer gave immediate chase.

"Freeze!" Mercer Shouted, as he ran intensely after Jonathan, putting himself in harm's way as he too ran into traffic.

Jonathan couldn't afford to look back as he watched for cars in his immediate vision, silently praying in his mind that he wouldn't get run over. He could hear the tires of the cars racing on top of the black pavement. Once Jonathan's left foot touched the curb he knew he had arrived safely to the other side of the street. He looked back for a moment to see if this mystery cop was still behind him and sure enough he was. To Jonathan's favor, Detective Mercer was caught in traffic as he was dodging cars.

Jonathan felt his legs pumping hard beneath him, he had never run so fast in his life! He was now on the sidewalk with pure adrenaline coursing through his veins. He felt the nights air rush against his body in resistance as he ran down the street, even knocking a few people over in the process. Jonathan knew he couldn't stay directly on the sidewalk in plain sight, so he darted down a dark alley. Detective Mercer was in hot pursuit as he ran full speed, allowing his glory days of playing football to shine through his physical prowess. He managed to catch a glimpse of the alley Jonathan had turned down; by the time he got there Jonathan was gone. Detective Mercer then stopped and drew his gun, while still breathing heavily. There was a fence toward the end of the ally, a fence that Jonathan climbed over only moments before Mercer had arrived. With no sign of Jonathan in sight Mercer let out a shout of agitation, "Agh!" he screamed.

Meanwhile, about a half block over, Jonathan laid low on the corner of another ally while on the phone with Rachel. She had made it safely to Rico's truck in the garage but Jonathan could hear the emotion in her voice on the phone. He could hear her crying; as he talked to her he glanced around the corner to see if he saw the renegade cop anywhere in sight. Jonathan told Rachel where he was and within two minutes he saw the black SUV, pulling up to the corner. He hopped in the passenger side door, burdened with the weight of his own guilt. His arrogance of parading around in plain sight could have cost both of them their freedom or even their lives. What started out as a nice night proved to be something else entirely, it was a harsh reminder of the world Jonathan was living in. It reminded him he wasn't in Edge City for roses or date nights; he was there on a mission. He had temporarily forgotten he was armed with a purpose and a desire to exact his revenge. He lost sight of the goal for a moment and if nothing else, tonight proved one thing…it was time for Jonathan to make his move.

CHAPTER 21

DOUBT AND A PHONE CALL

It was the next morning, bright and too early to be quite honest. Nevertheless Mercer was on the edge of his seat as he gave Captain Briggs his account of what went down last night.

"I'm telling you chief, it was him!" declared Detective Mercer, the excitement in his tone wrapped in the sureness of his words.

"There I was eating a slice and I noticed this scumbag walking out of 87th like he didn't have a care in the world. And on top of that she was with him, the girl…Rachel Monroe! They're here in the city!"

It was apparent that Detective Mercer was well on edge at this point, he seemed to be wound up tighter than usual. Perhaps it had to do with the fact that Captain Briggs didn't seem to be too concerned or convinced about what Mercer saw. There the Captain sat, in his old leather chair that had seen better days. It was something he received from the department about ten years ago. His demeanor told the tale of a man who wasn't really in the mood to deal with anything he didn't want to hear at an hour like this. The air itself was thick and there was a doubt that seemed to be growing in the room like an entity of its own. The doubt was present, at the other end of Captain Briggs' office, it took up space in the corner as it grew. Its invisible presence only seen on its host, and it appeared that Captain Briggs was its current host. Captain Briggs leaned forward in his chair, with his hands folded together while covering his mouth. He then lifted his hands.

"So you're telling me, that Jonathan Cross, the young man whose wanted for attempted murder and stealing from the man who is now the mayor of this city...is suddenly back in town?!" snapped Captain Briggs, the tone of his sarcastic comment was obvious as it was blunt.

Detective Mercer rubbed his forehead in response to the Captain's obvious disapproval. "Look Cap... I know how it sounds, but believe me I chased the guy," said Detective Mercer.

"You chased him? And then what?" asked Captain Briggs.

"Well I lost him, he ran in the middle of the street, it was a mess," answered Detective Mercer

"How do you know for sure it was him?" asked Captain Briggs.

"I mean really you said it yourself that you had a few. Maybe you thought you saw something you really didn't see. Hell, maybe you wanted to see it, giving you another crack at a high-profile case." said Captain Briggs.

Detective Mercer fidgeted in his seat and sat back, while biting his lip. "Come on, that case happened years ago, this isn't that," he said.

"I've closed dozens upon dozens of cases since then and you know it."

"Look, what I know is that there is no way I'm gonna let you reopen this thing without hard core evidence that I can see with my own eyes!" shouted Captain Briggs."Now I want you to let this go and get out of my office! Because there is no way Jonathan Cross and Rachel Monroe are back in Edge City, and besides I don't need any shit from the Mayor on this!" Captain Briggs continued, his voice sounded like it was irritated for being used like this so early in the morning.

"He had the case closed because he didn't want any of that negative press messing with his public perception as Mayor. And there is no way I'm about to go against his wishes because you think you chased somebody after you had a few beers and some pizza!" shouted Captain Briggs, while slamming his fist on his desk

Captain Briggs then pointed his finger at the door and gave one last shout, "Now get outta my office and get to work on some *real* cases!"

Detective Mercer tilted his head with his eyes steadily focused on the floor, and didn't bother to look back at Captain Briggs. He merely got up from his seat and headed out the door. There were other officers at their desk as Detective Mercer walked out of Captain Briggs' office. A few of them watched Mercer as he walked out of the office. They had a look on their faces that suggested they knew Mercer had just been chewed out, however no one said anything.

Detective Mercer went back to his desk while he mumbled some not-so-nice words about the dear old Captain. Once back at his desk, he stared at Jonathan's case file, complete with the background bios and known associates of both Jonathan and Rachel. Detective Mercer rolled his chair slightly to the side of his desk and looked into the glass windows of Captain Briggs office. The shades on the Captain's windows were still up, so Mercer could see inside. The Captain was on the phone with somebody, appearing as if he had gone on with his morning without a second thought to Mercer. Mercer pushed the chair back toward his desk, and picked up the file as he intensely stared at Jonathan's picture. His eyes then scanned over Jonathan's personal information and he saw that the contact number was to a Marianne Cross. He looked at the number and then the phone at his desk; for a moment he stared at the phone before he picked it up. He then dialed the number that was on file for Mrs. Cross and leaned back in his chair. He heard the phone ringing and waited patiently to see if anyone would answer. It appeared the Detective was in luck because Mrs. Cross picked up.

"Hello?" answered Mrs. Cross.

"Mrs. Cross, this is Detective Sebastian Mercer from the Edge City Police Department."

"Oh for goodness sake, I don't know where he is and if I did I wouldn't tell you!" snapped Mrs. Cross. "Now you listen to me, my Johnny boy wouldn't do any of the vile things that y'all said he did!" Mrs. Cross talked quickly as if she didn't want Detective Mercer to get a word in. "Now I understand how that may sound coming from his mother but believe me...I know my son. I raised him...and I know he's innocent."

"I don't doubt that you know your son ma'am," said Detective Mercer. "In fact, that's what I'm counting on. I don't need you to tell me where he is, because I *already* know where he is."

The phone got quiet on the other end, giving testament to the fact that Mrs. Cross was all ears.

"I know he's here in Edge City," said Detective Mercer. "What I want to know from you is, what happened? What went down between him and the Mayor and why is he back?"

There was an eerie silence that crept over the phone, a few seconds went by and neither party said a word, until Mrs. Cross spoke up.

"Look here, I don't know why you guys are still calling me about these lies you placed on my son! Now, I'll tell you this, you wanna know what happened then you should ask your two-bit hustling Mayor! Ask him why he closed the case around the time he was going to be sworn in as Mayor!" demanded Mrs. Cross. "Ask him why would he give up so early on a case that was was going to arrest the young man who *supposedly* tried to kill the Mayor's trusted bodyguard!Tell him to explain how Jonathan elevated in the company so quickly and why he had Jonathan spend so little time at the office but instead was always at his side!"

"Tell him to explain how a young man from a small town convinced one of your Mayor's loyal employees at the time to help embezzle a million dollars!" Mrs. Cross' voice was as harsh as a thousand storms as she demanded multiple explanations.

"Ma'am I..." said Detective Mercer, but was cut off by the mighty wind that came in the form of a mother who was ready to fiercely protect her son.

"Now you call me back when you can give me some answers and maybe I'll answer one of your questions, that by the way, I have been asked a million times over before by some of your colleagues. So please leave me and my son alone!" snapped Mrs. Cross as she abruptly hung up the phone.

Detective Mercer hung up the phone slowly, as that marked the second time that he had been yelled at this morning, all in his first hour of work. He rubbed his head and continued to look at the file. He stared at Jonathan's picture as if he was trying to make sense of everything that was going on. It was true that he had seen and unsuccessfully chased Jonathan Cross last night. However, it was also true that Detective Mercer was a good cop and new information had been introduced to him, thanks to the ranting of an angry mother. Mrs. Cross had presented some questions that would make any good cop rethink some things about this case. Detective Mercer was more than a good cop; he was *the* cop, a true master of catching the bad guy. For a man like Sebastian Mercer, it was highly unlikely he would leave a case like this alone, especially since the prime suspect had just mysteriously reappeared in the city.

CHAPTER 22

AN ACT OF WAR

The day was bright and beautiful, the wind was blowing such a peaceful breeze that it almost seemed to dance in the air. Surely, a day like this was nothing short of the divine craftsmanship of the almighty GOD. Yes indeed, a day like this was something to behold, something to stop and stare at, something to take in for a moment while escaping the normal rush of life. It was a day of days but it was also an opportunity. An opportunity for a man to prove something to himself. It was another chance to spare the city of the burden of an unnecessarily high body count if a certain Don was to come knocking on the city's door. It was a day for Rico Coloso to put a stop to the era of Kane Edwards, it was a chance for one of the knights to kill the dragon. A day like this was as good a day as any, for the simple fact that it was here and now, the present. No more delay or negotiating; there was only Rico and Marco with black hockey masks, two automatic assault rifles that were equipped with silencers, a matching pair of bullet proof vests, and two extra handguns for backup.

All of this heavy artillery was parked on the curb across the street from the Mayor's estate. It seemed that Mayor Edwards opted not to take the obvious downgrade publicly known as "The Manor" that was paid for by the city and located on the other side of town. It was clear that Kane still enjoyed his luxurious lifestyle and not even his duties as Mayor would come between that. This didn't seem to be a problem for Rico because he was going to put an abrupt end to everything in Kane's life, including his life itself. This was a brazen move made by Rico and Marco alone, without the knowledge of the other half of the group. Apparently, Marco had done some reconnaissance work and found out the Mayor was going to do a few pop-ups today to some of the underprivileged schools for some good old-fashioned charity work. If everything went correctly, Kane wouldn't make it anywhere near the schools but the morgue instead.

Rico was playing with a lighter in his hand while he watched the entrance to Kane's neighborhood.

"Man, what's taking your highness so long, doesn't he know he has an appointment with death?" asked Rico, his voice sounding agitated and anxious in the same breath.

Marco was sitting in the driver's seat as he looked over and said, "If you knew you had an appointment with death, would you rush to get there on time?" Rico continued to play with his lighter.

"I suppose you've gotta good point there Marco," he said.

"But still, I'm ready to put an end to this before something worse jumps off. I told you what the old man said and I can't have him getting involved. If he shows up, he'll think I wasn't able to handle this by myself and I can't have that. If I want to move up in the ranks, then this needs to be done by my hand and not his," Rico explained, the anxiety and agitation still having their way with his vocal cords.

It was then, that the prized moment of the day decided to present itself. Two black SUV's were pulling out of the entrance of Kane's neighborhood.

"Alright, it's showtime!" shouted Rico, with pure excitement grabbing his voice.

Marco quickly started the car and pulled off from the curb and sped up enough to get in front of the two cars before they got to the light up ahead.

"Alright remember the plan," instructed Rico as he held the assault rifle in his lap, while Marco's rifle rested on top of his lap as well. It was ironic that they decided to put silencers on the rifles. Perhaps it was a smart move due to the fact that they were about to make a lot of *noise*. The light up ahead turned red, which was perfect for the deadly duo. Rico rolled down his window and looked at the cars behind him as they pulled up. Marco put the car in park as Rico simultaneously said, "This is it." They simultaneously put on their masks, preparing for war.

In that moment, time became like a thick molasses type of consistency, as it seemed to move slower. Rico took a few deep breaths as if he were about to jump off a cliff and then he moved. Both he and Macro swung the doors open violently as they stepped out of the car with their assault rifles in hand while wearing their bulletproof vests. They moved quickly along side of their car as they aimed their weapons at the front windshield of each car. Rico aimed at the windshield of the first vehicle, while Marco aimed directly at the windshield of the second.

The moment grew quiet as time moved slower. Neither one of them said a word to the other as they both pulled the trigger and let their guns do all the talking. Then suddenly without warning, time picked up its pace and returned to its regular speed of movement. The bullets flew out of their guns at a very rapid rate of succession, while quickly and accurately hitting their target. However, something happened that wasn't planned. The windshields didn't shatter into a million pieces while revealing the driver's dead body, leaving the vehicle at a stand-still like expected. The bullets bounced off what was obviously bullet proof windows.

It was then when Rico hollered, "They're armored; aim for the tires!!"

However, this was an unexpected annoyance that Marco had a ruthless remedy for as he approached the vehicles with tactile aggression. Marco shot the tires out quickly on the car he was aiming for. His bold yet militant move caused all of the passengers, who were Mayor Kane's armed security, to hop out of the car. However Marco finished their efforts before they got started by following up with headshots, one for each man. The security obviously thought it was wise to exit the vehicle, but it proved to be nothing more than fatal ignorance. Marco proved himself to be death on two legs as he had just disabled an armored car and killed all of its occupants within sixty seconds.

A few feet away, a slightly different story was taking place. Rico appeared to be pinned down and taking heavy fire as he took cover behind his own car that wasn't armored. Rico's SUV was taking too many hits as several of the windows had been shot out and the car stood there riddled with countless bullet holes. However, Marco was coming up the rear, preparing to put a violent end to the assault on Rico. Again, Marco took aim with marksmen-like precision, as he held an unlucky target in his sights. The sight being the back of one of the bodyguard's head. Marco pulled the trigger without remorse as yet another man's life ended violently. Marco didn't even stand still long enough to watch the man's body hit the unforgiving pavement. He continued to move as the unstoppable killing machine that he was. The total body count was now six, with five of those bodies belonging to Marco. Rico claimed one so far. That left two men still standing, although it was highly unlikely that they would still be standing for much longer. The two men were closing in on Rico, while Marco was closing in on them. The two bodyguards were steadily moving closer to the front of the truck where Rico was hiding. The bodyguard on the left proved to be nothing more than Marco's next victim as Marco shot the man from close range, through the back of the head. The bodyguard on the right saw the fate of his brother in arms from the other side of the car through the shot out passenger side window. This caused him to turn and try to shoot at Marco through one of the busted windows. However, the man wasn't counting on Rico coming around the corner and unleashing a fatal stream of bullets into the unsuspecting man's body.

With the sound of the last lifeless body making a solid thud on the concrete, there was an eerie silence that swept through the streets. It was as if the grim reaper had just shown up and all living mortals had to be eternally silenced by falling dead in his presence. There was no time for standing still because they had just committed murder in broad daylight. Rico looked up and caught a glimpse of people running in terror alongside the sidewalks while people screamed. Rico watched for a moment as people reacted to the horror that had just unfolded in their eyes. There were some people on their phones screaming for the police, while cars were coming to a screeching halt, no doubt from the drivers who witnessed the carnage that lay ahead. Marco was a man of few words but had something to say for the occasion.

"We need to move now," he said.

"Where the hell is he? Where is Kane?!" Rico asked, the rage in his voice rising with every second. He's supposed to be here….he's supposed to be dead!"

While Rico was letting out his anger, a third black SUV, like the ones that they had just attacked, came out of the Mayor's neighborhood. The car sprang forth ferociously out of the neighborhood as it sped off into the distance. The sight of the identical and speeding SUV gave way to the fact that Mayor Edwards was inside *that* vehicle instead.

"It's him!" shouted Rico as he fully sprinted toward one of the other SUVs, ran and jumped on the hood, and stepped up on the roof. There Rico stood, on top of the car looking like some sort of evil monument. He opened fire at the speeding vehicle as it raced down the street in the opposite direction. His anger and bullets came to no avail as the car faded into the streets and out of Rico's sight as it took a sharp right turn at the corner onto another street.

"Rico, we have to go!" shouted Marco, his voice was strong and heavy as it carried itself in the air.

Rico looked back at Marco as he heard the faint sound of police sirens approaching in the background. Rico jumped down from the roof of the car with his rifle still in hand. They decided to take one of the armored cars since, there vehicle had been all but destroyed. Marco quickly took the license plate off of their original so the car couldn't be traced back to them. He threw the original license plate in the armored car they were stealing. Although two of the tires had been shot out, they were more than likely run flats, which meant they could at least make the drive back to the Penthouse. They quickly hopped in the car while Marco immediately punched his foot on the gas and sped off without hesitation, leaving behind the gruesome bloodbath of bodies laid out in the street, all due to a plan gone horribly wrong. It was a bold move, but Rico came up short today, while at the same time escalating the level of warfare. There were now dead bodies involved, something Jonathan expressed earlier that he didn't want. However, it was too late to turn back the clock, and what just happened could not be undone. There was an unspoken truth that stayed behind studying the corpses of the dead men that were sprawled across the street. That truth was simple and that truth was this: there would be consequences to what Rico and Marco had just done. Surely this truth would come swiftly, while riding the winds of revenge because the dragon had just been attacked, the war had begun and there was no turning back.

CHAPTER 23

BLOOD OF THE DRAGON

Across town there was a different pace being taken, away from the acts of war that Rico and Marco had just committed. It was actually around the same time that those two renegades pulled their brazen stunt that Jonathan was taking a mental breather. Now this breather that Jonathan called himself taking was at the expense of some common sense. Jonathan also decided to make his own ill-advised and brazen move by taking a stroll down the street in broad daylight. Nevermind the fact that he had been discovered the other day by a police officer that chased him through the streets and could've shot him. Perhaps, it was the warrior within that held a strong rushing wind of defiance in its very breath, that caused Jonathan not to care if he was caught. Either way it was a risky move, but that didn't seem to bother him at the moment while he walked down the street. With each step he could hear the sounds of the city speaking in his ears; the cars, the people, even some of the birds flying overhead. He could hear the life going on around him, he could hear the very breath of the city, a sound that he enjoyed.

In a way that sound was relaxing to Jonathan, a testament to the unorthodox relationship he held with the city. One minute it was trial by fire and the next the city would offer a helping hand and a shoulder to lean on. Jonathan was grateful for the complex duality that existed in the city, in a way it mimicked the complexities of life. One minute he was down and the next he was up, although the moment he currently found himself in was neutral. Or at least it was until Jonathan felt the uneasy presence of a watchful eye. His steps slowed down in their stride before he stopped completely on the sidewalk near the curb. Jonathan's head was up and looking straight ahead, then he turned to his left and saw a black town car parked next to him on the street. The passenger side window was rolled down; for some odd reason Jonathan felt he needed to look inside the car. It was then he saw a familiar face: Adrian.

"Get in," said Adrian, the raspiness of his voice carried itself to Jonathan's ears.

It was odd, because even though one of the last times Jonathan and Adrian saw each other they were trading punches, a part of Jonathan was happy to see him. This was probably due to the fact that Jonathan still believed that he could get through to Adrian to convince him to help them. Now that Adrian had just shown up and in a peaceful manner, this further floored Jonathan's belief in the matter. Jonathan nodded his head and reached for the car handle. He then hesitated and stuck his head inside the car quickly and looked to see if anyone was in the back. Jonathan's naivety had dropped several levels due to his time in the city, he wasn't about to be caught off guard so easily.

"You're fine kid, I just wanna talk," said Adrian.

Jonathan looked at him, opened the door and got in the car. Jonathan continued to stare at Adrian as he pulled the passenger side door shut. Adrian pulled off without saying a word, there was a familiar silence that emerged again between the two of them. It crept in and presented itself as if it had never left in the first place; perhaps it didn't. After all, Jonathan was never really completely comfortable about being around Adrian in the past. Though this time was slightly different, there was no fear floating around within Jonathan. He knew that he could handle himself, if anything were to arise.

"You're different," said Adrian as he looked straight ahead, keeping both hands gripped firmly on the steering wheel. "You've gotten close in a way that, other people haven't," Adrian said, all while Jonathan was looking directly at him. "I've never seen him behave the way he does around you... we can use that."

Jonathan's face communicated before his mouth through his facial expressions. "Wait, there's a *we* now?" asked Jonathan. It's not that he wasn't grateful for those beloved words to come out of Adrian's mouth, he just had to be sure that Adrian meant what he was saying. Adrian paused before responding to Jonathan's question.

"I...can help you stop him," he said.

It was in that moment Jonathan saw a glimpse of a possible future, a future that had his life restored. He imagined the freedom to hold his head high again in public, without having to look over his shoulder to see who was coming for him. Could it be, that at last Jonathan was closing in on his freedom? Was it really possible that he was going to win this time? To be honest, it shouldn't have been that big of a surprise because after all, Jonathan didn't come this far to lose. He was going to bring down the beast and now it appeared Jonathan had convinced the beast's blood to turn on it, which was in the plan for a while now.

"I need you to testify that he killed his parents and that he set me and Rachel up," said Jonathan, the excitement in his voice now making a steady rise.

Adrian looked at Jonathan for a brief moment, "It's not going to be that easy; he has some of the police in his pocket. We have to have hard evidence on him first; something that couldn't just be swept under the rug. Something that wouldn't be dismissed as rumor or accusation. I've seen him elude justice time and time again, we have to do this right. We have to catch him in the act," instructed Adrian.

"How?" asked Jonathan.

Adrian continued to look straight ahead, while driving through the city streets. "A moment will present itself, it always does when it comes to him. You look prepared. Stay that way and I'll contact you when I have something," said Adrian.

Before Jonathan responded he felt the car slow down, he then looked out the window and saw that he was at the building where he was currently living with the rest of the group. It was no surprise to Jonathan that Adrian knew where he lived, because Jonathan knew Kane had his address. Adrian parked alongside the curb and didn't say anything else; Jonathan knew this was his cue to get out. The sun greeted his skin with a warm intensity when he got out of the car, along with the sight of something odd. Jonathan closed the door behind him and saw the car pull off out of the corner of his eye. However, he was currently looking at a blacked out SUV that had two tires shot out of it pulled into the side street where the gated entrance was. He knew that only Rico and the rest of the group had access to that entrance. Jonathan made his way down to the entrance, carefully walking behind the car from a distance. He knew something was up but he had no idea that Rico and Marco were driving one of the armored cars that they stole from their earlier attack on the Mayor. Jonathan made his way down to the entrance, all the while wondering what was going on, but little did he know that something irreversible took place today, something that could prove to be fatal for him and everyone else involved.

CHAPTER 24

FEAR AND THE UNTHINKABLE OPTION

It was a solid strike and it helped that Jonathan knew when to plant his feet when using certain punches. An uppercut was definitely one of those punches where he needed to plant his feet. He could feel the energy surge through his right leg as it gained momentum pulsing inside his right arm and making its way to his fist. That energy mixed with a wave of heated rage, met its neatly groomed target: Rico's chin. Jonathan heard the slight sound of Rico's teeth knocking together as Rico stumbled back from the grueling blow. Rico would have fallen to the ground if it wasn't for Marco catching him in mid air as he fell back.

"What the hell were you thinking?!!" hollered Jonathan as he glared at Rico with vengeful eyes. It was then, during his blind fit of aggression, frustration, and anger he felt Rachel's hand as she tried to calm the sea of his emotions. To be fair, his anger was well warranted, he had just found out of Rico's evil deeds that left eight men dead. That was a body count that was eight over the amount of people that Jonathan wanted. He never wanted it to come to bloodshed because that would have taken things to a whole other level, a level of mortality that didn't need to be reached, although now it was beyond that.

"You idiot, do you have any idea what the hell you just did?!?" hollered Jonathan, his inner anger having its outward release for all to witness.

Rachel was now directly in front of him, still attempting to calm him down. "Jonathan, just breathe," said Rachel. "You're right. He's an idiot; so don't be like him."

"Rachel, he's got blood on his hands, which means it could spill over to our hands as far as the police are concerned!" said Jonathan, his voice still sharp from his aggression. "Men are dead!" The harshness of his words were taking a life of their own.

"I know, but let's not act like we didn't know the potential risk," said Rachel.

It was in that moment, that Rico decided to speak up: "Yeah exactly," while rubbing the bottom of his chin.

Rachel and Jonathan spoke in unison: "Shut up!!" they shouted.

Jonathan quickly returned his attention to Rachel, "You know as well as I do, there is no way in hell he's gonna let this go without retaliating," he said. "Any element of surprise in attacking him that we would've had, is now completely out the window."

While he looked in Rachel's eyes, he could see her frustration making its way to the rest of her face. Jonathan knew that this wasn't just bad; it was absolutely horrible. He knew that Kane was going to come knocking and it would only be a matter of time before the dragon came in spewing its life-destroying fire upon them. Jonathan knew that he had to act, but at the same time he had no idea of what he should do. Jonathan watched Marco forcibly walk Rico to the kitchen and while he poured himself a drink, Jonathan thought about Adrian. What would this mean for their recent agreement? Would this somehow alter the terms? Would Adrian tolerate a failed attempt on his brother's life, even though he was planning to betray him anyway?

These were a multitude of questions that were simultaneously presenting themselves in Jonathan's mind. Questions that would need to be answered preferably sooner than later; things were now officially out of hand in Jonathan's mind. Jonathan knew enough to know he wasn't going to find the answers in his current environment.

"Look I need to get some air. I can't stay in here, not right now and not with him," said Jonathan as he nodded in Rico's direction.

"Well look, I don't think you getting some fresh air is a bad idea," replied Rachel.

Jonathan ran his hand along the back of his head as he headed out the door. Time acted as a blur. Jonathan couldn't recall how long he was outside as he looked at the sun fading into the the darkness. Night was now approaching and with it brought about a certain level of fear. The fear of fading options, fear of running out of strategies to take down Kane. At this point, Adrian seemed like he was out of arm's reach. Jonathan didn't know if he could call him now. Besides if he did, Jonathan knew Adrian wouldn't be able to answer. There was no doubt that Kane was on high alert right now, thanks to the failed attempt on his life. For the first time upon his return to the city, he felt that uncomfortable and familiar feeling of fear creeping its deceitful way into his mind. While Jonathan found himself out and about, he knew he was in a potentially vulnerable position. Night crept its way over the city and there was no way of knowing if Kane sent some of his henchman to finish what Rico started. The city never really slept, so there were people that were still out and about. Jonathan could feel the danger in the air, wrapping itself in the night's breeze, disguising its true intentions. It was hard for him to get his mind off the fact that there were dead men involved now; an unwanted body trail. A trail that would lead straight to the illustrious penthouse that the four of them were all currently occupying. Perhaps it was the apparent lack of options that lead to this one particular thought. A thought, that until tonight, Jonathan would have never allowed to even come in his mind. However, things had obviously changed and not for the better, but there was only one option and it was as about as crazy as the stunt Rico pulled. The only difference was that there would be no body count, but it would involve doing the unthinkable: going to the police. The more this renegade thought galloped through Jonathan's mind, the more it made sense. He knew he didn't want Rachel or himself to have to pay for Rico's stupidity; after all they weren't killers. It was a long shot, but what if Jonathan was able to convince the police that he was innocent and could prove it? Jonathan had found himself yet again in a desperate situation and he knew that it would call for desperate measures.

CHAPTER 25

FIRE AND ICE

His feet were currently moving as fast as his thoughts; he kept a sharp eye out while he moved quickly through the night. It wasn't long until Jonathan reached his desired destination; a place he never thought he would voluntarily go: a police station. There Jonathan stood silently at the bottom of the stairs at the Silver Edge's 45th police precinct. This move was beyond bold, it was more so bordering on insanity. Jonathan's mind attempted to reason with its current thought of taking a chance to talk to the police. For all he knew, one of Kane's men could be on the payroll in this precinct and blow Jonathan's brains out as soon as they got him alone somewhere. Not to mention the obvious hurdle of him being a wanted man and they could simply arrest him and he'd spend the rest of his life in jail. However, it was that *one* thought; that thought that made Jonathan walk all the way to this police station. The thought that gave him enough courage to try such a crazy move, the thought that he could convince someone that he was telling the truth.

Jonathan stood there for a moment in the quietness of the night, while the quietness surrounded his body like a calm sea that gently sways back and forth, subject to the breeze of the wind. He looked to his left and then to his right, continuing to watch himself to make sure he wasn't being followed. Although, if Kane Edwards was having someone followed, that person wouldn't know until it was too late. This was something that Jonathan was completely aware of, so he also knew that there wasn't much point in looking too hard, nevertheless he still looked. He took a deep breath physically and mentally as he prepared to walk up the steps and into the station. He thought about how this could possibly be his last moment as a free man, but the glimmer of hope seemed to outweigh the opposing dark possibility. Jonathan started to make his way up the stairs while clenching his fist and focusing on the moment at hand. His heartbeat was surprisingly steady as he made his ascension. When he got to the front door he placed his hand on the door handle and held it there for a second. Another moment of reflection perhaps, although the moment passed as Jonathan opened the door. There was suddenly a warmth that came over his body, the inside of the building was nice and toasty. Perhaps the air conditioner didn't work so well or maybe they just liked it warm in the building; either way it was surpassingly pleasant to Jonathan.

Immediately, Jonathan noticed the police officer behind the front desk; since he was on the first floor there didn't seem to be any other officers around. They were probably all upstairs; this wasn't something that Jonathan was too upset about. In fact, it ultimately helped him keep his cool. From where Jonathan was standing the officer seemed friendly; he made eye contact with Jonathan and greeted him.

"Good evening sir," said the officer, his voice was unexpectedly polite for this time of night. "How can I help you?"

Jonathan replied by saying, "I'm here to see if I can talk to someone."

"Ok, what do you need?" asked the officer.

It was in that moment, while Jonathan was walking closer to the front desk, that he noticed something move out of the corner of his eye. The movement was accompanied by a sound, then a loud chime, like an elevator. Jonathan looked over to see that it actually was the elevator. He didn't even notice the elevator until now, he stopped as he watched the doors open. There was a man that walked out. Jonathan recognized the man although he didn't know the man's name, he knew his face, it was the same face that pulled a gun on him that night outside of the pizzeria. The same face that chased him through the city streets. The face belonged to Detective Mercer. Jonathan noticed Mercer before Mercer noticed him. However, it didn't take long for Mercer to lift his head from looking at his phone. When Detective Mercer looked up, his eyes immediately met Jonathan's, and upon doing so he too stopped abruptly in his tracks. There was an awkward silence that ironically entered the room with a thunderous force.

Detective Mercer dropped his phone and screamed, "Hands on your head!"

Jonathan put his hands up while watching Detective Mercer sprint at him with full force, coupled with an intense aggression. Mercer violently slammed Jonathan up against the wall. He turned Jonathan around and placed his forearm sharply in Jonathan's back while he handcuffed him. Jonathan's mind tried to go to a kinder moment in his life while he felt himself being handled with rough force. He thought of his peaceful time in Winterville and how he would love to be back there right now. He thought about when he was little, and the feeling of cold mud between his toes when he would play outside after a rainy day. The escapism into safer thoughts must have worked because the next thing Jonathan knew he was in a white room. It was as if he blacked out and had suddenly woken up to find himself in a foreign environment. It took a moment for Jonathan to realize that he was in a seated position as he snapped back into the present reality. He felt the constriction of tight handcuffs digging into his wrist while his arms were behind his back. It wasn't the most comfortable position to be in, but Jonathan wasn't going to let his discomfort manifest on his face.

He knew it was a risk for him to come waltzing into a police station. Therefore, he wasn't going to act too surprised in the presence of expected opposition; especially, since the opposition was currently seated directly across the cold steel table that stood in front of Jonathan. Jonathan looked directly at Detective Mercer and found himself studying his eyes. He saw an unfriendly combination of fire and ice; a burning passion and a cold indifference occupying the same space. Jonathan couldn't read Detective Mercer's mind but his eyes gave a hint at the kind of man Jonathan was about to encounter. If he had to take an educated guess, the burning passion that he saw in Detective Mercer's eyes was probably a passion for justice. He was probably a man who wanted to see any wrong doing be brought to justice, which obviously fit with his profession. The cold indifference that Jonathan noticed seemed to float around in the back of Detective Mercer's eyes, like a thick icy cloud that resembled fog. This was probably the indifference he felt toward the harsh fate that was bestowed on any criminal that crossed his path. Now that Jonathan found himself in Mercer's path, he knew he would have to convince Mercer that he was innocent. Jonathan tried to make himself slightly more comfortable, as he adjusted himself in his seat.

"Uncomfortable? I bet it's not as uncomfortable, as Percy Roman felt when you shot him several times over eight months ago," asserted Detective Mercer, as he tossed pictures of Percy's bullet wounds from Jonathan's case file. "Oh and allow me to introduce myself, I'm Detective Sebastian Mercer and you're Jonathan Cross." said Mercer in a very condescending tone.

Jonathan slightly frowned as he looked at the pictures of Percy's wounds. Thoughts from that day flooded his mind in random order. He thought of the feeling he felt when Percy almost punched the life out of him. Then he thought about the fact that he never knew Percy's last name was "Roman."

"That was self-defense," said Jonathan.

Detective Mercer leaned in as he responded. "Oh so you admit that you shot Percy Roman?"

"Yes, but if you look closer in that file you have over there, you'll see that there were signs of forced entry to my condo. Courtesy of the 6'4" silverback that tore the door off the hinges," said Jonathan as he nodded at Percy's picture lying on the table. Jonathan knew he didn't want to waste too much time talking about this, he needed to get to the point before his time ran out. "Look, I came here to talk. With an obvious risk on my end."

"Oh, you're beyond risk at this point son, you're going to jail," stated Detective Mercer. "I figured I'd pull you in here to see what you had to say before I throw you behind bars."

Jonathan took a deep breath. "What if I told you that the Mayor isn't as crispy clean as he pretends to be?" asked Jonathan, as he studied Detective Mercer's eyes looking for any glimmer of hope.

Detective Mercer didn't budge but he did speak; "Oh really, how so?" he asked.

"For starters, he sent good ol' Percy over to kill me," said Jonathan.

Detective Mercer laughed before responding, "And why is that?"

"Because I've seen his true face and his evil hand," answered Jonathan. "He blackmailed Mayor Caesar into not running again, had some guys nearly beat me to death in a parking lot and illegally obtained some zoning permits for one of his buildings."

"And that was just while I worked for him, along with a host of other illegal things I'm sure he's done in his life. Like framing me and Rachel Monroe for attempted murder. Think about it: some small town kid from Winterville embezzled a million dollars from his boss's company," said Jonathan, with an agitation of his current circumstance now starting to show in his voice.

Detective Mercer paused for a moment, not incredibly long but long enough for Jonathan to gain a sense of hope. Jonathan saw the thought swirl around on Detective Mercer's face as it began to ooze into his eyes. Perhaps Detective Mercer already had suspicions about his lovable Mayor that were below the surface. Perhaps Jonathan capitalized on those suspicions, or at least that's what he hoped for. He needed someone to give him a chance to prove himself and give the truth a chance to be told. While Jonathan sat there trying to think of something that would push Detective Mercer a step further, he thought of a another bombshell.

"Kane's killed people," stated Jonathan. He could tell that Detective Mercer rolled his tongue on the inside of his mouth on top of his front teeth, as it showed through his skin.

"He killed who?" asked Detective Mercer, as his face contorted into a serious stare, piercing inside Jonathan's skull. Jonathan hadn't seen that type of soul gazing since his protege days with Kane. It was a stare that he was familiar with, one that he knew all too well. He knew what the detective was trying to do, he was scanning for the truth. A truth that could be seen from the eyes and heard from the lips.

"He killed his own parents when he was younger, and his assistant Adrian can verify that," said Jonathan. He didn't want to mention that Adrian was really his younger brother Carl; he thought that truth might sound too outlandish. Jonathan wasn't trying to push his luck, he just needed enough to walk out of the station. "If you give me 24 hours, I can prove everything I just told you but you have to give me 24 hours. If I don't have hard-core proof in 24 hours, you can throw me in jail."

"You know…either you believe your own lies, to the point where you think they're true; or…" said Detective Mercer.

"Or what?" interrupted Jonathan, feeling that he may have gotten the opportunity he was hoping for.

"Or maybe there's some truth to your story," answered Detective Mercer.

"I can normally tell when someone's lying to me…but you're…mildly convincing; I'll give you that much." Detective Mercer leaned back in his chair and propped his hands behind his head. He then looked up at the ceiling and glanced at the door before leaning back toward the table. "You're in luck…I'm intrigued enough to give you the 24 hours. Let's just say that I haven't always been the biggest fan of Kane Edwards. And if you're telling me that you can prove that he's the scumbag that I always suspected he was…I'll take that chance. But let me say this: if you're lying to me, I promise you, I will rain down on you like the plagues of Egypt son, and best believe you'll never see the light of day again," affirmed Detective Mercer, his tone both blunt and powerful.

Jonathan breathed a sigh of relief. "I understand," he said, not wanting to let too much emotion show.

"Luckily that idiot at the front desk didn't recognize you and the Captain doesn't know you're here. So I won't have to explain to anyone why I let you go," said Detective Mercer, as he uncuffed Jonathan. Detective Mercer then gave Jonathan his card. "Call me when you have something, or else I'll come looking," he said.

"I will," answered Jonathan.

The walk out of the station was satisfying as well as extremely exhilarating with each passing step that Jonathan took. He could taste the freedom that presented itself in the ray of hope that was found in that interrogation room with Detective Mercer. A hand of grace had been extended to Jonathan and he wasn't going to waste it. Now was the time to strike! He had no other alternative and he would need Adrian to get the job done. While Jonathan walked out of the police station and stepped out into the night's air, he knew he had his work cut out for him. However, he had been trained for these type of stressful moments, he had been trained for war. In that moment, Jonathan saw something across the street moving in the shadows. The mystery figure suddenly stopped and stood tall like some monstrous giant. Jonathan recognized the metaphorical giant, it represented his immediate future as it held two options in its hand. The two choices were hard in nature yet simplistic in outcome, and Jonathan knew one of the outcomes would come to pass. In the next 24 hours, either Kane Edwards would fall or Jonathan would lose everything.

CHAPTER 26

TAXI

The night was still young yet old enough for Jonathan to want to go home and get some rest. It seemed that his recent conversation with the police had given him an added sense of confidence. Due to that, he didn't carry any more fear of being identified by anyone, which meant he would catch a cab back home instead of walking. When one finally arrived, Jonathan hopped in the backseat while admiring the iconic yellow paint job that defined the atheistic for all taxicabs. However, Jonathan noticed that this taxi had been freshly painted; perhaps a representation of the driver's standard of service. Jonathan closed the door behind him as he gently sat in the soft yet thick black leather seats. The comfort of the seats supported his back with ease as he sat down. Along with the unexpected level of comfort, Jonathan also noticed that the taxi also carried a pleasant aroma, that smelled like freshly washed clothes. He then looked up and noticed that there was an air freshener hanging from the rearview mirror that read *Fresh Linen.* Jonathan also noticed the man's driver license posted on the top of the dashboard. The license was laminated and propped up in a black case that clearly displayed the license to all customers. The name on the license read *Daniel Williams*; it was then that the man turned around and greeted Jonathan. He was an older man; old enough to be Jonathan's grandfather.

"How you doing tonight young man?" Mr. Williams asked.

"I'm doing well Mr. Williams," answered Jonathan, his voice sounding monotone, attempting to give no indication that he was in fact doing well.

"Well, you're observant and polite, most people don't notice my ID card," said Mr. Williams.

"How are you?" asked Jonathan, trying to mask his problems by taking the focus off of him.

"Oh, I'm well, thank you for asking," Mr. Williams responded. "So where to young man?"

"You know the building called *Nine* off of 89th street?" asked Jonathan, not remembering the full address of the Penthouse.

The man shook his head in agreement and answered, "Say no more."

Jonathan could feel the car pull off from the curb, it was good for him to take this moment for himself. Jonathan held Detective Mercer's card in his hand, staring at it as he ran his thumb across the card. He knew that even though he had convinced the detective to let him go, he still had to deliver Kane. This was a level of pressure that Jonathan hoped would never visit his doorstep again in life; yet there it was. A mounting level of pressure demanding that Jonathan deliver on his promise while threatening his life all in the same breath.

"Hey, uh…I don't mean to pry. But are you alright young man?" asked Mr. Williams.

Jonathan looked up and noticed a genuinely concerned look plastered across the man's face. Perhaps Jonathan was yet again in the presence of a good man. If that was true, Jonathan would take full advantage of the opportunity.

"What makes you ask?" Jonathan inquired.

"Well, it's just that I know a heavy burden when I see one," answered Mr. Williams.

Jonathan hesitated before answering but he figured he could still talk to get some advice without sharing details. "You ever made a mistake and then have a lot to lose if you don't find a solution?" asked Jonathan. He waited patiently for the man to respond, watching him closely, desperate for some wisdom.

"Oh yeah, let me tell you something young man; mistakes are a part of life" said Mr.

Williams. "You're made of flesh and blood and there is no guarantee for a completely mistake-free life. I've learned that everyone makes mistakes but everyone doesn't face them. Now the facing part, can be different in different situations. You may face it by accepting that you can't change it and learn to deal with the outcome. Or you can face it by correcting the mistake, if it's possible for you to do so. But you have to be looking at the mistake to face it, you can never face it when you run from it and your back is turned. My father used to tell me that a turned back can't face a problem, son. So the best thing you can do for yourself or those you feel have been affected by your mistake, is to face it and deal with it young man. When you face it, you conquer it, when you conquer it, you can move on." Mr. Williams' words were heavy with time-earned wisdom as he spoke.

Jonathan could feel the weight of the words that had just been spoken to him. He knew what he had to do, and what that meant; he'd have to face Kane to conquer him. It was a simple yet powerful truth and one that couldn't be avoided. Jonathan sat there and let what the man said sink in and resonate. It was then that Jonathan looked up and saw that they had arrived back at the Penthouse. Jonathan reached in his pocket to pay the fare but Mr. Williams refused it.

"You keep it son," said Mr. Williams.

"Thank you," said Jonathan. Jonathan then opened the door but paused before stepping out, "You know my Father's name was Daniel," he added as he pointed toward Mr. Williams' license.

"Oh is that right?" asked Mr. Williams with a smile on his face.

"Yes sir, he was a good man, like you," said Jonathan.

Mr. Williams continued to smile as he said, "Thank you. Oh and young man, make sure you take care of yourself out here."

"Yes sir," replied Jonathan, as he nodded his head and stepped out of the taxi.

The night's cool air brushed against Jonathan's face as he stood there watching Mr. Williams drive off. Jonathan was thankful for the lesson given in that moment. He then looked up at the moon as it stood perfectly still in the night's sky. He knew that he had to face Kane, and that was *exactly* what he was going to do.

CHAPTER 27

CHASING KANE

The rich experiences of the night came with their own weight and were slightly wearing on Jonathan. He was starting to get tired and could use the warm embrace of the woman he loved. He made his way inside the building with his mind chattering away, and his thoughts showed no signs of slowing down. With each physical step, he continued to think about his next step with Kane. He knew that they all were going to have to stand united against Kane, even though Jonathan was still furious with Rico and his unruly body count. Jonathan walked to the side entrance and noticed that the garage door to the parking lot was open. He paused for a moment, thinking to himself that it was odd the door would just be open like that. There was another thought that came swooping down in his mind like an eagle diving mid-air to catch its prey below. Perhaps something was wrong. Jonathan couldn't quite put his finger on it but there was something in the air that suggested something happened before he got there. He had enough experience with violence to know when it had been somewhere and he had a gut feeling that it had been in the building.

Without warning he began to run, making his way to the elevator so he could get upstairs. On his way to the elevator, he would have to pass the security control room; this is where Marco liked to spend a lot of his time when he wasn't busy killing people. While Jonathan was running, his eyes saw something sticking out of the control room doorway. He saw two feet on the ground, they were moving slowly. Jonathan immediately stopped running and put his shoulder up against the wall where the door was, and slowly moved forward. He wasn't sure what he was about to find inside the control room, but he was ready for whatever lay ahead. He paused for a moment, then moved with lightning speed as he came off the wall and stood in the doorway to see what was going on. It was then that he saw Marco crawling on the ground, slowly bringing himself to his feet. There were a few droplets of blood on the floor, dripping from Marco's lip as he turned to see Jonathan.

"I'm fine, they went upstairs," said Marco.

Instinctively, Jonathan immediately hollered "RACHEL!!!" he screamed so loud that the air from his lungs exhaled with full force. Jonathan darted toward the elevator; again with lightning speed; there was a strong amount of adrenaline pumping through his body in that moment. Naturally, it seemed that his body was shooting all that adrenaline directly to his legs, so that he could accomplish his goal as fast as he could. Unfortunately, his mind was also moving as fast as his legs, if not faster. The thoughts that came rushing in, were the possibilities of what could've happened to Rachel. Honestly there were too many to process and none of them were good. Jonathan waited for the elevator doors to open after he slammed his hand on the call button. In that moment, they couldn't move fast enough. "Come on!" he hollered as he punched the elevator doors. Then as if the elevator doors were responding to his physical threats, they opened.

Jonathan quickly hopped inside the elevator as he said Rachel's name aloud once again, while praying she was safe. Jonathan had to endure what felt like an eternity as he had to wait for the elevator to reach the penthouse level. When he finally arrived, he dashed out of the elevator like a racehorse fresh out of the gate. He saw a sign that sent another unpleasant memory flooding his mind; the penthouse door had been broken into. Jonathan recognized the handy work since he had seen it before up close and personal; Percy had been here. It was like a bad case of Deja Vu wrapped in a nightmare. Jonathan knew what happened without speaking to anyone. He knew the type of man Kane was and there was no way he could allow an open attack on him to go unpunished.

"Rachel!" screamed Jonathan as he made a mad dash to the penthouse door. When he arrived inside he saw what he expected to see, the place had been torn apart. Furniture was ripped and overturned. There was shattered glass all over the floor, not to mention the door was in the middle of the living room. However, there was one thing that was still intact, or at least not completely roughed up: Rico. Jonathan watched Rico pace back and forth, his nose bleeding badly as the blood covered his mouth and made its way down to the floor by dripping from his chin.

"Rico! Where is she?!" demanded Jonathan, his eyes starting to well up with tears for his beloved, as he feared the worst. His voice shook, losing its strength and bravado that it once held a few seconds ago. "Where?" Jonathan asked again, with tears now strolling down his face.

Rico turned to face Jonathan while Jonathan walked slowly toward him.

"You were right; they took her," said Rico, with remorse and a huge amount of humility laid on top of his voice. "I'm…I'm sorry." Rico looked at Jonathan with childlike eyes, knowing he had done something wrong to cause all of this. Without hesitation Jonathan added to Rico's sorrow as he punched him in the face as hard as he could. Rico fell to his knees from the hit and coughed violently as if he was beginning to choke on his own blood.

"I *told* you not to underestimate him!" shouted Jonathan; his agony now overriding his rage as it resonated in his tone.

Jonathan watched Rico choke on the ground as he delivered yet another blow, kicking Rico in the stomach. Jonathan tried not to let his emotions completely overtake him as he thought about what Kane would do to the woman he loved. It was then, that he heard the sound of a cell phone ringing. Perhaps it was the dramatic moment that Jonathan was currently experiencing that caused the sound of the ring to cut through the air the way it did. It was almost as if the phone demanded to be answered by the way it rang. Jonathan took his attention off of Rico and looked for the phone. He moved quickly to see where it was; he then looked at the torn and tattered couch and saw a cellphone that he didn't recognize lying there peacefully. Jonathan darted toward the phone, stepping on glass and hopping over the overturned coffee table as well as the door frame that was now in the middle of the living room. He picked up the phone as fast as he could.

"Rachel!" Jonathan instinctually hollered. A voice then came on the phone that sounded nothing like Rachel's and brought upon an intense level of fear that Jonathan was not counting on.

"Not quite," said the voice, Jonathan knew this voice and who it belonged to. Which is why he felt his heart rate rise with rapid speed, he knew the voice's owner was capable of unspeakable evil. It was the voice of an angry dragon, a provoked beast…it was the voice of Kane Edwards.

"Listen to me, I had nothing to do with what happened today and neither did she!" said Jonathan as he began to plead with Kane while physically falling to his knees in the process.

Kane spoke over Jonathan's plea for mercy, "I have something that belongs to you," he said.

"Please…please don't hurt her…I'm begging you…please don't do this!" Jonathan cried out. "She didn't do anything, she didn't kill any of those men!"

Kane appeared deaf to the pleas of a desperate man. "And you have something that belongs to me. You want what you want; and I want what *I* want. Bring it to me, and she'll be spared," said Kane.

Jonathan paused for a moment, not fully understanding what Kane was referring to when he said Jonathan had something he wanted.

"I don't understand," replied Jonathan, his tone of voice now a mixture of sorrow and confusion. "Please, I'll do anything to protect her but

I don't know what you're talking about. What do I have that you want?"

Then suddenly there was a deep silence that came over the phone before Kane responded. Jonathan waited desperately to hear what this prized possession was, that Kane accused him of having.

"Oh, that's simple Jonathan. Your life. I repay blood with blood," said Kane "You killed some of my men and I now require your life as payment for hers," instructed Kane. "Your foolish actions have forced my hand. I attempted to accept you back into the fold and even offered you grace. Yet you returned my kindness with bullets. It's been made clear to me Jonathan that I can no longer help you, which means I have no further use for you. This in turn, ultimately means that you are dead to me. Both metaphorically and soon-to-be literally." Kane's words were harsh and unforgiving like a violent storm.

Then without warning, Kane hung up the phone and left Jonathan to his own terror, stuck in his current reality. There were no instructions given as to when or where Kane wanted to meet, leaving Jonathan completely in the dark. Even worse, Jonathan had no idea where Rachel was or how she was doing. For all he knew, she could've been tied up somewhere being tortured for things she didn't do. The thought alone of Rachel being in the unforgiving hands of a madman, hurt Jonathan to his core. It was the dealings of a nasty double-sided coin as it flipped mid-air in Jonathan's life. The coin itself represented responsibility; on one side Kane was mistaken about Jonathan being responsible for killing his men. However, on the tails side of it Jonathan *did* feel responsible for Rachel. He knew that if it wasn't for him, Rachel would have never been involved in all of this. He convinced her to trust him and this is where it got her; taken hostage by a ruthless psychopath. If that wasn't enough to plague his thoughts, Jonathan also knew that he had to keep his end of the bargain with Detective Mercer. He had twenty-four hours to get evidence on Kane or else the detective would come looking for him. However, this was no longer his top priority; getting Rachel back was now his main focus, everything else would have to wait.

It was in that moment when Jonathan stood to his feet, as the warrior within refused to quit but instead rose to the occasion. Now wasn't the time to panic or to cry, for Rachel's sake as well as his own. Jonathan had to be strong. He could feel the strength and courage he needed, taking over his total being and calming the uncertainty in the sea of his thoughts. This was not his first fight with Kane and he knew well before he stepped foot back into Edge City, that he had to be ready for anything. The fact that Rachel had been kidnapped due to the selfish actions of another man, was a prime example of *anything.* Suddenly Jonathan heard the sound of movement; it broke his current train of thought as he looked over and saw the cause of his recent pain: Rico. He watched as Rico rose to his feet, worn down and bloody. The thought of taking Rico's life came into Jonathan's mind as he stared at him. Then without warning, another thought took precedence, which kept Jonathan's wrath at bay. It was true that Rico was the cause of the problem that stood before Jonathan, yet Rico could also prove to be the solution.

While Jonathan continued to stare at Rico, he decided to focus on his origins instead of the dark cloud of shame that hovered over him. In that moment, Jonathan realized that he had been going about hunting this dragon the wrong way. Perhaps using a sword and shield to bring down this beast was the wrong approach; maybe what he needed was another dragon. In truth, there was another. One that lay dormant and undisturbed over in Harbor Stone City: Rico's Father Nero. A man of old, who could match Kane thought for thought and blow for blow. Yes, the truth stood before Jonathan's eyes as clear as day; he would enlist the help of Nero Coloso to stop Kane once and for all. With this new revelation unfolding before him, Jonathan now understood why he couldn't stop Kane before and what it would take to finally defeat him. He needed someone like Kane to defeat Kane. It would take a ruthless man to stop a ruthless man. A dragon to kill a dragon; indeed, it would take a Kingpin to stop a Kingpin.

www.ingramcontent.com/pod-product-compliance
Lightning Source LLC
Chambersburg PA
CBHW060544310726
48982CB00009B/1373/J

* 9 7 8 0 9 9 6 2 3 9 4 3 1 *